"Are you all right?"

Greg could only imagine what must be going through Jenny's mind—if she was even able to think at all. She looked shell-shocked.

Jenny gave her head a slow, negative shake.

"I didn't think you were."

He murmured the words. He'd never seen anyone look as lost and alone as she did at that moment. Or, if he had, he'd never allowed the depth of that awful helplessness to register. It wasn't as if he allowed it now. It simply happened as he knelt there, touching her.

Something twisted inside him. Something that made him feel what she felt, and left him feeling as vulnerable as she looked in the moments before he scrambled for the protective detachment that came so automatically with everyone else....

Dear Reader,

Celebrate those April showers this month by curling up inside with a good book—and we at Silhouette Special Edition are happy to start you off with *What's Cooking?* by Sherryl Woods, the next in her series THE ROSE COTTAGE SISTERS. When a playboy photographer is determined to seduce a beautiful food critic fed up with men who won't commit...things *really* start to heat up! In Judy Duarte's *Their Unexpected Family,* next in our MONTANA MAVERICKS: GOLD RUSH GROOMS continuity, a very pregnant—not to mention, single—small-town waitress and a globe-trotting reporter find themselves drawn to each other despite their obvious differences. Stella Bagwell concludes THE FORTUNES OF TEXAS: REUNION with *In a Texas Minute.* A woman who has finally found the baby of her dreams to adopt lacks the one element that can make it happen—a husband—or *does* she? She's suddenly looking at her handsome "best friend" in a new light. Christine Flynn begins her new GOING HOME miniseries—which centers around a small Vermont town—with *Trading Secrets,* in which a down-but-not-out native repairs to her hometown to get over her heartbreak...and falls smack into the arms of the town's handsome new doctor. *Least Likely Wedding?* by Patricia McLinn, the first in her SOMETHING OLD, SOMETHING NEW... series, features a lovely filmmaker whose "groom" on celluloid is all too eager to assume the role in real life. And in *The Million Dollar Cowboy* by Judith Lyons, a woman who's fallen hard for a cowboy has to convince him to take a chance on love.

So don't let those April showers get you down! May is just around the corner—and with it, six fabulous new reads, all from Silhouette Special Edition.

Happy reading!

Gail Chasan
Senior Editor

Please address questions and book requests to:
Silhouette Reader Service
U.S.: 3010 Walden Ave., P.O. Box 1325, Buffalo, NY 14269
Canadian: P.O. Box 609, Fort Erie, Ont. L2A 5X3

TRADING SECRETS

CHRISTINE FLYNN

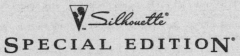

Published by Silhouette Books

America's Publisher of Contemporary Romance

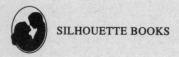 **SILHOUETTE BOOKS**

ISBN 0-373-24678-1

TRADING SECRETS

Copyright © 2005 by Christine Flynn

This edition published by arrangement with Harlequin Books S.A.

® and TM are trademarks of Harlequin Books S.A., used under license.
Trademarks indicated with ® are registered in the United States Patent
and Trademark Office, the Canadian Trade Marks Office and in other
countries.

Visit Silhouette Books at www.eHarlequin.com

Printed in U.S.A.

Books by Christine Flynn

CHRISTINE FLYNN

admits to being interested in just about everything, which is why she considers herself fortunate to have turned her interest in writing into a career. She feels that a writer gets to explore it all and, to her, exploring relationships—especially the intense, bittersweet or even lighthearted relationships between men and women—is fascinating.

Chapter One

Once a person hit bottom, the only way to go was up.

Not sure if she felt encouraged or depressed by that thought, Jenny Baker absently rubbed beside the sore abrasion on her forehead and unpacked another dish from the cardboard box. The house she would now call home was practically falling down around her. Paint peeled from the cabinets. A crack in the window over the chipped porcelain sink distorted the rain-grayed view of a weed-choked garden. But at least she had a roof over her head.

A pot on the floor caught drips from the ceiling.

Even the weather had turned on her.

Mid-August in northern Vermont was usually warm and sunny, a lovely respite between the harsh winters and the brilliance of the autumn to come. This far north the leaves were always the first to change, and that change would soon begin. In a few weeks, lush green would turn to shades of crimson and burnished gold. The leaf-peepers would arrive in droves. The loons and crows would fly south. But, for now, late summer reigned.

Jenny had always loved Vermont this time of year. The velvet green of the meadows, the farms and the rolling hills, the way the birch and maple leaves shimmered in the sunlight. It had all been exactly as she'd remembered, too, as she'd left the interstate for the slower, winding drive deeper into the country, heading toward Maple Mountain and home.

Unfortunately, the little black cloud that had hovered over her life for the past month had apparently followed her from Boston. Within an hour of prying off boards from a few downstairs windows and unloading her car—the latter of which had taken less than fifteen minutes now that her possessions had been reduced to little more than her luggage and four cardboard boxes— clouds had rolled in, dusk had descended and a summer thunderstorm had put a major damper on her new beginning.

Despite the rain, the optimist in her struggled to surface. Bemoaning her fate wouldn't change it, so she focused on the good news—which was that the two oil lamps she'd found in the pantry provided plenty of light to see.

The not-so-encouraging part was that the storm had nothing to do with the lack of electricity. She wouldn't have power even after the clouds passed. The house had sat vacant for years.

One of the lamps glowed from a beige Formica countertop. The other cast its circle of light from the pot-bellied stove that provided heat during the long, snow-bound winters. Not wanting to think about winter any more than she did the rain, Jenny set her bright-red cereal bowls on a fresh sheet of shelf liner and ignored the rhythmic plink of water into the pot. She had bigger problems than no electricity, no phone and a roof that leaked.

Until a little after ten o'clock that morning, she had lived in a charming brownstone in a trendy little neighborhood in Boston. She'd been within walking distance of a fabulous Italian deli, chic restaurants and great bars she and her girlfriends sometimes frequented during happy hour so they could fill up on free appetizers for dinner. She'd become acquainted with the woman at the corner news kiosk where she'd bought the newspaper for an elderly neighbor who sometimes didn't feel like navigating her stairs. She'd come to know the guy who worked the flower cart during the summer and who slipped a few extra tulips into the bouquets she occasionally bought, just because he liked her smile.

She'd had good neighbors. She'd had a good life.

Until a month ago, she'd even had a good job.

Armed with her associate's degree and the same dogged determination that had gotten her out of Maple Mountain, she'd worked her way up from the general secretarial pool of a major brokerage house to administrative assistant to a senior vice president. The man had depended on her for everything from keeping him supplied with antacids to handling the confidential correspondence, paperwork and computer accounts of clients with more money than some small third-world countries. Her job had been exciting, interesting and filled with all the opportunities Maple Mountain had lacked.

She had also been dating an up-and-coming broker with a brilliant future who had started hinting heavily at marriage and babies.

She reached into the box, her stomach knotting as she unwrapped a bowl.

She had honestly believed that Brent Collier cared about her. She had wanted to marry him, to have his children, to do his laundry—or, at least, send it out—and to live the rest of her life growing old with him.

But Brent had turned out to be the world's biggest louse. And she, the biggest fool. He'd used her, used her feelings for him and ruined every ounce of credibility she'd had. Because she'd believed in him, because she'd *trusted* him, she'd been arrested, fired from the brokerage, questioned, her home searched, her possessions confiscated and her reputation ruined. Now her only prospect for employment was at the diner where, years ago, she'd worked her way through community college.

Taking a deep breath, she set the bowl in place, reached for another. It was still tourist season in the section of Vermont known as the Northern Kingdom, and the little town and surrounding villages would only get busier when the leaves changed. Because of that, there was at least a chance that the local diner could use another waitress. She was in debt up to the scrape on her forehead to the attorney who'd kept her out of jail. She still had a year's worth of car payments to make. She had a roof to repair.

She was trying to imagine how she could possibly afford the latter when a sharp bang on the door sent her heart to her throat and the bowl in her hand to floor.

Chips of red ceramic flew in an arc across scarred beige linoleum.

"I know someone's in there. I can see light. Open up, will you?" The deep, distinctly male voice faltered. "I need some help."

Jenny didn't budge. She'd already had one unpleasant encounter with a strange male today and she wasn't at all interested in pushing her lousy luck with another. Her nearest neighbor was half a mile away.

The door rattled with another heavy bang. "Come on. Please? I'm hurt."

Short of telling her the house was on fire and seeing sparks herself, she couldn't have imagined anything he could have said that would change her mind about moving. Saying he was hurt did it, though. Even then, it wasn't the claim that had her hand sliding slowly from her throat. It was the plea in his voice and the strain behind it.

Her heart pounding, she slipped through the dim and empty living room and peeked through the oval of etched glass on the front door.

The window needed cleaning. Between its film of dust and frosted etching, she could only see a blur of the dark-haired man on the other side. What she could see looked tall, broad-shouldered and built. From the way he held his left arm, she also suspected that he hadn't knocked on the door. He'd kicked it. He looked as if he was about to do it again, when he saw her and took a step back.

Apparently sensing the door wouldn't open until he was farther from it, he took another step and backed up as far as the sagging porch railing.

She'd used the lug-nut wrench for her tire jack to pry the boards from the kitchen windows. It still lay where she'd left it three feet away.

With her fingers wrapped around the long piece of metal, she cautiously eased open the door.

Thunder rumbled, rattling the panes of the old house as she peeked around the door frame. It was barely seven o'clock, but the rain robbed the evening of much of its light. Still, she could see easily enough as her glance skimmed his broad brow and lean, even features.

Her first impression was that he would be quite attractive— if not for his grimace. Her second was that he was drenched. The rain had plastered his dark hair to his head. Wet chambray molded his broad shoulders. Wet khaki clung to powerful thighs.

Her glance jerked to the arm he held close to his body.

Because of the distance he'd put between them, but mostly because he looked hurt, she eased the door farther open. The groan of arthritic hinges joined the savage beat of the rain.

He eyed what she held. "My car skidded off the road. About a quarter of a mile that way." Pulling his glance from her weapon, he started to nod behind him. Wincing instead, he tightened his grip on his arm. "I've dislocated my shoulder. Any chance you can help me with it?"

Jenny watched the stranger's forehead pinch. There had been a time when she would have aided him without question. But four years of living in the city and the events of the past month, had done a number on the naiveté she'd once possessed. For all she knew now, the guy was totally faking and once inside would do her all manner of bodily harm.

"Is there anyone else in the car?"

He shook his head. "I'm alone."

"Where did you say you wrecked it?"

"By Widow Maker curve. That's why they call it that. Look—"

"Which side?"

Swallowing hard, he sagged against the post. "West."

His lips went pale. Having only recently become a cynic, Jenny felt her caution slip along with the wrench. Metal clattered against the hardwood floor. She doubted that even the most talented con could change color on command.

Praying he wouldn't pass out, she stepped onto the porch, reaching toward him. "Hang on. Just lean there a minute. Okay?" He was big. Far bigger than she could handle alone. "Just let me get my purse and my keys."

"You don't need your keys. I just need you to help me."

"That's what I'm doing," she explained, wondering if he'd hit his head on something and his logic was impaired. She couldn't drive without keys. "I'm going to take you to the doctor."

"I *am* the doctor."

Jenny had already spun on her heel. She spun right back, eyes narrowed. "I happen to know the doctor here," she informed him, her doubts surfacing all over again. "Doc Wilson is barely taller than I am and happens to be as old as dirt."

"I know he's old. That's why he retired. I took over his practice two years ago."

"Then I'll take you to his assistant."

"Bess is at a potluck in West Pond."

Jenny's doubt slipped again. He knew Bess.

"Look," he said, before she could come up with anything else, "I know you don't know me. I don't know who you are, either. Or what you're doing here. But I promise I'm not going to cause you any trouble. My name is Greg Reid. I live in the house at the end of Main, a couple of blocks from the clinic. Check my driver's license if you want. It's in my wallet in my back pocket," he told her, more color draining. "I'd get it myself but I can't let go of my arm."

She thought she detected desperation in the deep tones of his voice. Mostly what she heard was pain. The fact that he seemed to be doing his best to fight both replaced her skepticism with a sharp tug of guilt.

She was having one of the more rotten days of her life. But he didn't seem to be having such a good one, either. All the man wanted was help.

It seemed wiser to abandon caution than to stick her hand in his back pocket. "I'm sorry," she said, apologizing for his pain and her paranoia. "But there has to be somewhere else we can take you." There was a hospital, but it was almost an hour and a half away. Skepticism turned to worry. Now that she was really looking at it, the angle of his shoulder looked strangely squared-off. "I have no idea what to do for you."

"I'll tell you what to do. It's not that complicated." His assurance came as lightning flashed. "Just let me sit down. Okay?"

Greg desperately needed to sit. Mostly because he wasn't sure how much longer he could stand. Pain, searing and sharp radiated over his collarbone and chest, across his back, down his arm. He could feel sweat breaking out on his upper lip and the thought of letting go of his arm nearly made him nauseous. But at least the exasperatingly skeptical young woman uneasily stepping back to allow him inside looked capable of helping him out. He hadn't been sure who he would find inside the old abandoned Baker place when he'd noticed the car and the faint glow of light from the window. As badly as he hurt and as hard as it was raining, he hadn't cared so long as whoever it was could help.

His reluctant rescuer closed the door behind her as she followed him into the nearly dark and empty room. Light spilled from a doorway to his left.

"In here," she said, moving past him. "There's a stool by the sink."

He followed her into the empty kitchen. As he did, a shard of bright red ceramic flew across the floor. Her foot had caught it in her haste to move one of the two oil lamps closer to the sink.

There didn't appear to be any furniture in the house. The only place to sit was the stool she had mentioned.

In agony, he watched her lift a cardboard box off it, then shove back the bangs of her boyishly short, sable-colored hair. She was young and pretty, and had he not been so preoccupied with the ripping sensations in his muscles, he might have paid more than passing notice to the lovely blue of her eyes. But she could have looked like a beagle and been built like a trucker for all he cared just then. All that mattered to him when he sank onto the wooden stool was the intelligence in those eyes. That and the fact that he was finally sitting down.

The base of the metal lamp clunked against the counter when Jenny moved it closer.

He looked even worse to her in the light. The moisture slicking his face was more than the rain that dripped from the ends of his hair and ran in rivulets down his neck. It was sweat. Fine beads of it lined his upper lip.

With his eyes closed, he shivered.

Growing more worried by the second, she touched her hand to his uninjured arm. Beneath the wet fabric, his hard muscles felt like stone.

"Hang on," she said, letting her hand stay on his arm long enough to make sure he wasn't going to fall off the stool. "I'll get you a towel."

She didn't know if he was just cold, or if shivering was a sign of shock. But the thought that he could get worse than he already was had her silently swearing to herself. The book she might have looked up _shock_ in was still impounded.

"Can you take off your shirt?" she asked, reminding herself that she could just ask him what the symptoms were. He was the doctor. "It's drenched."

"I don't want to let go of my arm."

She took that to mean he'd need help.

Two more boxes sat in the corner where she'd swept the floor and piled her blankets and comforter. Ripping open the nearest one, she dug under her sheets and pulled out a butter-yellow bath towel.

Hurrying back, she saw that he'd leaned forward to brace the elbow of his injured arm against his thigh. With his free hand, he fumbled with the first button of his shirt.

His awkward position and the wet fabric made the task harder than it needed to be.

She dropped the towel on the box she'd been unpacking. "Hold your arm. I'll do this."

His quiet "Thanks," sounded terribly strained.

That strain and the intensity of his discomfort kept her from dwelling too much on how awkward she felt unbuttoning his shirt. Because he wore it with its long sleeves rolled up to just below his elbows, she didn't have to mess with buttons at his wrists. Once she reached his belt buckle, however, she did have to tug it from his pants.

He didn't seem to care that a woman he didn't even know had her hands inches from his zipper as she tugged the dry shirttail from the front, or her arms around his waist as she tugged from the back. In turn, she tried not to care about the way her nerves had tightened. He smelled of spicy soap, fresh air and something distinctly, decidedly male. As close as she stood to him, she could feel the heat of his big body radiating toward her, and the brush of his inner thighs against the outsides of her legs.

One of the droplets clinging to his hair broke free, sluiced down the side of his face and clung to the sharp line of his jaw.

Resisting the urge to wipe it away, she glanced back to his shoulder.

"You're going to have to let go again."

It seemed that he complied before he could let himself think too much about the pain involved. Biting down on a groan, he let her peel the wet fabric off his right side, then promptly grabbed his arm again the second she'd pulled it off his left.

The wet denim hit the counter with a soft plop, then slid to the floor.

Jenny barely noticed.

In the golden glow of the lamps, the sculpted muscles of his shoulders, arms and chest rippled with lean and latent power. The men at the club where she'd once been a trial member worked hours a week to look so carved and cut. There was no gym or health club in Maple Mountain, though. Never had been. Never would be. But it wasn't his impressive and rather intimidating body that had the bulk of her attention as she reached toward the towel. It was the bruising that had already started to spread over his chest, the baseball sized lump beneath his collar bone and the way the edge of his left shoulder seemed to be missing.

"I don't need that now." He blew out a breath. "Let's just get this over with."

The towel landed back on the box. "What do you want me to do?"

"Put your hand over the head of the humerus."

Seeing what she was dealing with made her even more apprehensive. "You're going to have to speak civilian."

"The round thing under my collar bone."

With caution clawing at her every nerve, she stepped back into the space between his legs and did as he asked.

He sucked in a sharp breath at the contact.

"That's it."

"Oh, geez."

His reddened skin somehow felt cool beneath her hand but hot beneath her fingers. Bone protruded against her palm. Honed muscles knotted around it. Feeling them twitch and tighten as his body's nerves objected violently to the damage, she jerked her glance to his face once more.

With his eyes closed, his lashes formed sooty crescents beneath the dark slashes of his eyebrows. The skin stretched taut over his cheekbones looked as pale as his beautifully carved mouth. His lips parted as he blew a slow breath.

Exhaling with him, she watched him open his eyes.

For the first time she noticed his eyes were gray, the silver gray of old pewter. Mostly she noticed the sheer stoicism that kept him from caving in to the pain and hitting the floor.

"Now what?" she asked, mentally bracing herself for whatever came next.

"The muscles have started to spasm, so you're going to have to use some muscle yourself. Take my arm and when I let go, pull while you push the head over and down. I'll brace myself against you."

Glancing from the rigid muscles of his jaw and chest, she uneasily curled her fingers above his elbow. His big body stiffened the instant he removed the support of his own hand, but she was more aware of how her own body went still as that hand anchored at her waist.

With his strong fingers curved at her side and digging into her back, her voice sounded pitifully thin. "Like this?"

Teeth clinched, he muttered a terse, "Go."

Shaking inside, feeling his muscles quivering, Jenny pulled on his arm. Its heaviness caught her totally off guard. Tightening her grip, she pushed on bone.

He grunted a breath. "Harder."

There was no doubt in her mind that she was hurting him. His damp skin became even slicker, his breathing more harsh. Fighting the frantic urge to stop, she felt the bone slip.

He bit off another, "Harder."

"I'm pushing as hard as I can."

With the muscles constricted around it, the bone wouldn't move far enough.

He grabbed for his arm again, told her to stop. As he did, Jenny jerked back to see his features twist while he cradled his elbow.

"I was afraid that wouldn't work."

Disbelief shot through her distress. "Then why did we do it?"

"Because it's the easiest method of reduction. When it works," he qualified, frightfully pale beneath his five-o'clock shadow. He took a few deep breaths, rocked a little.

They'd only made it worse.

"Oh, man," he groaned.

"Oh, geez," she repeated and put her hand on his shoulder to calm his motion.

Jenny had never regarded herself as particularly squeamish. She had never fainted at the sight of blood, and she could handle everything but eating gross insects or animal parts on survivor shows. She was learning in a hurry, though, that she apparently didn't have a terribly high tolerance for other people's distress. Either that or her basic sense of empathy was working overtime now that her reservations about him had taken a hike. Doing her best to shake off the uneasiness she felt herself at the misaligned body part, she wiped away a drip running from the hair at his temple to his jaw.

"Do you have anything for pain?" Another drip ran down the other side. She caught that, too. "In your little black bag or something? Is it in your car?"

"I don't have mine with me."

"Country doctors always carry little black bags."

"Only when they're making house calls. That's not what I was doing. Come on. Let's just do this."

He shifted, the intensity of his discomfort making his voice tight enough to snap rubber bands. "We need more leverage. You're going to have to take my arm and pull it down and out to the side." He glanced at the sink beside him. "I'll pull one way while you pull the other. The head of the bone should slip back into the socket." He swallowed. Hard. "Take my elbow in one hand and my wrist in the other. Once you start to pull, don't stop until I tell you to. Okay?"

It was most definitely not okay. "I'll only hurt you again."

"No," he insisted, grabbing her arm as she started to back away. This time, it was she who winced.

Apparently thinking he'd grabbed her too hard, he immediately let go.

"You're helping," he insisted. "We'll try again. The longer this goes, the worse the spasms are going to get."

The plea in his voice underscored the need to hurry. But it was the way he'd said "we" that kept her right where she was. He couldn't do this alone. And without her, he would only get worse.

"Okay," she conceded, rubbing where he'd grasped. "But try something you know will work this time."

"This will."

At his assurance she opened her mouth, closed it again. Since he had far more at stake than she did, she decided not to push for a promise—and worriedly waited for him let go of his arm again.

Letting go was clearly something he didn't want to do. Grimacing along with him when he finally did, Jenny curled her fingers around the top of his corded forearm and grasped the hard bones of his wrist with the other. His breathing sounded more rapid to her in the moments before he hooked his free arm over the edge of the sink.

Breathing rapidly herself, she asked, "On three?" and watched him give a sharp nod.

Desperately hoping he knew what he had her doing, she counted to their mark. When she hit it and pulled, the sound he made was half growl, half groan and had her heart slamming against her breast bone. A sick sensation gripped her stomach. But she could feel the bone in his arm moving, and even though that made her a little sick, too, that movement was exactly what they were after.

Sweat gleamed on his face.

Jenny could feel perspiration dampening her skin, too.

His breathing became more labored. With his jaw clenched, air hissed between his teeth. "Rotate it down."

Thunder cracked overhead. The drip of rain into the pot picked up its cadence. Jenny barely noticed the crunch of ceramic beneath her shoe as she shifted her stance to carefully increase her leverage. She was too busying praying he wouldn't crumple when, hearing a sickening pop, she felt the bone lock into place.

For an instant she didn't move. She wasn't sure she even breathed. She wasn't sure Greg was breathing, either.

"Can I let go?" she ventured, afraid to believe the maneuver had worked.

He said nothing. With his eyes closed, he sat dragging in long drafts of air, looking too weak or too spent to move.

With as much care as she could manage, she slowly eased the pressure of her grip.

The lump wasn't there. Reaching toward him, she placed her palm where the head of the bone had been. The muscles beneath her hand still felt horribly knotted, and she didn't doubt for a moment that he still hurt. Yet, she could tell from the way the tension drained from his face that the worst of the pain was gone.

Close enough to feel the heat of his thighs once more, she helped him lean from the sink to straighten on the stool. He'd barely reached upright when his whole body sagged, and his dark head fell to her shoulder.

His relief was so profound that she felt it to the very center of her soul. Her own relief joined it as she cupped her hand to the back of his head. She didn't question what she did. She didn't even think about it. She simply held him close and let the sensation of reprieve wash over them both.

She'd had no idea what she would have done had the second attempt not worked. He could have argued all he wanted, but she doubted she could have watched him go through that agony again. She was not a strong person. She could fake it when she had to, but she'd pretty much used up her supply of sheer nerve for the day. The best she could probably have done was haul him into town and get someone, anyone, else to help them. Or left him while she'd raced off in search of help herself.

She tightened her hold, stroked her fingers through his wet hair. The man was stoic to a fault, and probably stubborn to the core. He would have fought her every step of the way.

He was getting her wet. She could feel the dampness of his pants seep into the sides of her jeans. Though she could feel his heat through the arms of her thin pink sweatshirt, she could also feel the gooseflesh on his broad back.

She'd wrapped both arms around him. Thinking to keep him warm, she drew him closer.

Realizing what she was doing, she felt herself go still.

A fine tension entered her body. Greg became aware of it at nearly the same instant the unfamiliar peace that had filled him began to fade. For a few surreal moments he'd had the sensation of being cared for, of being…comforted. He freely offered his support to others, but the quiet reassurance he felt in this woman's touch, in her arms, was something he'd never before experienced himself. Not as a child. Not as an adult. Not even with the woman he'd been with for the past two years.

He lifted his head. Now that the pain that had taken precedence had reduced itself to a dull, throbbing ache, he was conscious of his lovely angel of mercy's clean, powdery scent, the gentleness of her touch, the nearness of her body.

With his head still inches from hers, he was also aware of the curve of her throat, the feminine line of her jaw and her lush, unadorned mouth.

Her breath caressed his skin as it slowly shuddered out. Feeling its warmth, the sensations that had touched something starving in his soul gave way to an unmistakable pull low in his groin.

Caution colored her delicate features as she lifted her hand to the side of his face and brushed off the moisture still dripping from his hair. With a faint smile, she eased her hand away.

Stepping back, she picked up the towel she'd brought him earlier and draped it over his shoulders. "You're better."

"Much." He cupped his throbbing shoulder with his hand, felt the alignment of joint and bone. He couldn't tell if he'd torn anything major, or if his shoulder and arm were just going to be the color of an eggplant for the next few weeks. All he cared about just then was that the searing pain was gone. "Thank you."

With another small smile, she picked up the edge of the towel, wiped it over one side of his hair and took another step back. "You could use another one of these."

"What I could use is something to make a sling. Or I could use this for one," he suggested, speaking of the towel she'd draped over him. "Do you have something to fasten it with?"

He'd seemed big to her before. Now, with his feet planted wide as he sat watching her, his six-pack of abdominal muscle clearly visible between the sides of the towel and with the need for urgency gone, he totally dominated the small, dilapidated space.

Not sure if she felt susceptible or simply aware, anxious to shake the unnerving feelings, she turned to the box she'd opened earlier.

"How did you wreck your car?"

"I was trying to avoid a deer. The road was slick and I lost control."

"Did you hit it?"

"Missed the deer. Hit a tree."

She picked up another towel for him to dry off with and held up a safety pin.

"That'll work," he told her.

Only moments ago she had cradled his head while she'd quietly stroked his hair. Now there was no mistaking the faint wariness in her delicate features as she stepped in front of him once more.

He'd tucked the middle of the rectangular terry cloth under his arm and pulled one end over his shoulder. Apparently realizing what he had in mind, she caught the other end to draw to the other side and, while he held his arm, pinned the sling into place behind his neck.

"Thanks," he said again, conscious of how quickly she stepped away. Glad to have use of his other arm, he took the hand towel she'd dropped on his thigh and wiped it over his face. She was disturbed by him. That was as apparent as the uneasy smile in her eyes.

They were even, he supposed. He was disturbed by her effect on him, too. He was also more than a little curious about who she was.

If she knew old Doc Wilson, she had to be a local. Yet, he knew he had never seen her before. He would have remembered her eyes. They were the crystalline blue of a summer sky, clear, vibrant. And troubled.

He looked from where she now bent to pick up what looked like bits of broken pottery to the cardboard boxes. One sat on the counter. Dishes matching the crimson red of the shards filled part of the cabinet above it. Another box sat empty, presumably relieved of the cleaning supplies and pots and bright-red canisters piled on the old electric range.

"Moving in?"

"Trying to."

"That's interesting," he observed mildly. "I hadn't heard anything about this place being rented or sold." He knew he would have, too. Word would have hit the clinic or Dora's Diner within minutes of papers being signed. "The way people talk around here, something like this doesn't usually slip by."

Without glancing up, she rose with several pieces of bowl in her hand and dumped them into the empty box.

In the far corner of the room, near the space a table and chairs should have occupied, bedding the color of spring grass and sunshine was laid out by four pieces of luggage.

"I imagine word would have leaked out by way of the power or phone company, too. My office manager has a cousin who works for one of the utility companies over in St. Johnsbury. I'm pretty sure someone would have mentioned utilities being hooked up out here."

He clearly knew they hadn't been. He just as clearly thought she was a squatter.

"I haven't had a chance to have the electricity turned on." Utility companies tended to want their customers to have jobs. And even if she did get work at the diner, it would be a while before she could afford a phone. "I just got here this afternoon. And I'm not renting or buying," she explained, trying not to feel defeated by what she'd been reduced to doing. "This house belongs to my family. My name's Jenny. Jenny Baker."

He'd wiped the spare towel over his head, leaving his hair ruffled as it probably was after he'd dried from his shower. His focus never left her face as he set the towel on the counter and raked his fingers through his hair.

Without the pain clouding his eyes, his level gaze seemed harder to hold. From the way he watched her, she couldn't tell if he believed her or not.

She'd had to prove herself entirely too often lately.

"This place has been vacant since Grandma died three years ago." A squatter wouldn't know that. "The real estate market has been so bad since the quarry had all those layoffs that Mom hasn't been able to sell it. She was barely able to sell the house I grew up in after dad died last year."

With no other relatives in Maple Mountain, her mom had moved to Maine to live with Jenny's sister, Michelle, and Michelle's growing family. Jenny might have mentioned that, too, had Greg not been frowning at her.

"What?" she asked, thinking he could at least have the decency to believe her after causing her to break her bowl.

Greg rose from the stool. With his arm supported by the makeshift sling, he took a step toward her. The light from the oil lamps cast everything in a pale-golden glow. That soft light also had a certain concealing effect. Not only did it take the worst of the dinginess from the derelict-looking room, it helped mask the faint bruising that bloomed along her jaw and the raw scrape beneath her thick bangs.

It was the glimpse of the scrape that had caught his attention when she spoke. Until then, he'd only noticed the discoloration along her jaw when she'd turned her head.

She'd winced when he'd grabbed her arm a while ago.

"I hurt you." He spoke the conclusion quietly as he glanced

at the sleeve of her sweatshirt. Wondering if there were more bruises he couldn't see, his physician's training and experience kicked in. "When I grabbed your arm," he explained, since she suddenly looked puzzled, "I hurt you, didn't I?"

"No. No," she quickly repeated. The discomfort had been nothing compared to his. "You didn't do anything."

"Let me see your arm."

"That's not necessary."

She'd suspected he was stubborn. She knew it for a fact when he reached over and tugged up her loose sleeve himself.

Three long bruises slashed her forearm.

Jenny stared down at them. "Oh," she murmured. A few hours ago, they were merely stripes of pale pink.

"Bad relationship?" he asked.

"Bad luck," she returned, pulling down her sleeve. "I'm not camping out in an abandoned house to escape an abusive boyfriend, if that's what you're thinking." She didn't care to mention that a relationship was responsible for that bad luck to begin with. If she'd never met Brent, she wouldn't have lost everything and been forced to move. "I was mugged this morning."

Greg was clearly an intelligent man. He was also, apparently, a hard sell.

"It's true!" she insisted, seeing his doubt, hating the awful helpless feeling that came with not being believed. "I moved from Boston this morning. This guy was hiding behind the bushes near my apartment while I was loading up my car. When I crossed from my stoop to my car with my last box, he shoved me down and tried to grab my purse. I'd had a really bad week. A really bad month, actually," she qualified, her hands now on her hips, "and I wasn't about to let some greasy little jerk in a hooded sweatshirt take what little cash I have, my credit cards and my car keys."

"So you hung on to your purse," he concluded flatly.

"You bet I did. That's when he grabbed my arm to make me let go. But that wasn't going to happen," she assured him. "When he started dragging me, I wrapped myself around a parking meter and kicked him in his crotch. The last I saw of him, he was limping down the hill holding himself."

Greg lifted his chin, slowly nodded. Hitting a sidewalk would explain the scrape on her forehead. The force of being grabbed explained the fingerprints on her arm. The bruising on her jaw could have been caused by colliding with the metal pole of the parking meter, the ground or even the guy's hand.

His glance moved from her boyishly short, sassy hair to her running shoes. He figured she was somewhere around five feet four inches, 120 pounds, tops. Considering that there didn't appear to be a whole lot to her curvy little body musclewise, he didn't know whether to admire her gutsy tenacity or think her utterly foolish. He'd known gang-types to maim or kill for pocket change. Having worked his residency in an inner-city hospital, he'd treated their victims often enough.

"Did the police catch the guy?"

Her glance shied from his. "I didn't want to deal with the police."

"You didn't file a report? Give them a description?"

"Of what? An average-size, twenty-something Hispanic, Puerto Rican, black, Haitian, Mediterranean or very tanned white male in baggy black pants and a gray sweatshirt with the hood tied so all that showed was eyes?"

"What color were they?"

"Brown."

"There had to be something distinguishing about him."

"If there was, I was too busy hanging on to my purse to notice it. I've had enough of detectives to last me a lifetime. The last thing I wanted to do was put myself in the position of having to answer to them again."

Sudden discomfort had her glancing down at a broken nail. "So that's what happened to my arm," she concluded, looking back up. "How's yours? You're bruised up way worse than I am. Do you want me to drive you over to the hospital in St. Johnsbury or should I take you home?"

It was as clear as the blue of her eyes that she had said more than she'd intended when she'd mentioned detectives. It was also apparent that she felt a little uneasy with him now that she had.

His shoulder throbbed. His arm ached like the devil. The discomfort alone should have been enough to distract him. But it was the thought of how he'd felt when she'd held him, those few moments of odd and compelling peace, that made him decide to make it easy on them both.

He could use an X-ray, but the drive to St. Johnsbury was miserable on a rainy night, and Bess would be available eventually. His house was only a couple miles away.

He opted for home, and watched her give him a relieved little nod before she walked over to blow out one of the lamps and, now that dusk had given way to dark, carry the other with them to the front door before she blew out that one, too.

Chapter Two

The wipers of Jenny's sporty four-year-old sedan whipped across the windshield, their beat as steady as the drum of rain on the roof and the road in front of her. Though she kept her focus on what she could see in the beam of her headlights, her awareness was on the man occupying her passenger seat.

She really wished she hadn't said what she had about the detectives.

"You said you live in the last house on Main," she reminded him, desperately trying to think of how to fix her little faux paux. "Do you mean Doc Wilson's old house?"

"That's the one. He and his wife retired to Florida."

"Doc Wilson's wife always wanted to live in Florida," she mused. "I just hadn't realized they'd gone."

She glanced over, found him watching her, glanced back.

"By the way, I'm sorry I doubted you back there. About being the doctor, I mean. Since my mom moved, I don't hear much of anything about Maple Mountain."

"Forget it." Absently rubbing his shoulder, he distractedly added, "I just appreciate the help."

She lifted her chin, kept her eyes straight ahead.

In the rain and dark, she couldn't tell if anything had changed along the narrow two-lane road into town. She doubted anything had. Little had changed in the twenty-two years she'd lived there before moving on herself. So it wasn't likely that much had changed in the four years she'd been gone. Teenagers probably still stole their first kisses under the old covered bridge. The old men who gathered to play checkers at the general store, probably still discussed the weather and farm reports with the same laconic zeal they always had, and regarded anything invented after 1950 as newfangled. The good-hearted-but-opinionated church ladies probably still baked pies for every function. Every season and major holiday was celebrated with a festival or a parade on the town's four-block-long main street. And with the way the locals loved to talk, something the disturbing man beside her had noted himself, there was rarely such a thing as a secret.

The uneasiness she felt turned to dread.

There was so much about all that had happened to her that she didn't want anyone here to know. And Dr. Greg Reid already knew part of it.

Her tires hummed on wet pavement as she passed the white scrollwork sign that let visitors know they'd arrived—Welcome To Maple Mountain, Population 704.

"You should come by the clinic in the morning and let Bess check you over."

He had a delicious voice. Deep, rich, like honey laced with smoke and brandy. Without pain tightening it, it also held authority, and thoughtfulness.

"Why?"

"Since you didn't want to deal with the police, I assume you didn't bother going to a hospital, either."

She gripped the wheel a little tighter, forced herself to smile. "All I have are bruises."

"Your pupils looked fine, but I should have taken a look at your forehead."

He'd checked her pupils? "It's just a scrape. Nothing a little makeup won't cover." Fervently wanting to forget that morning's incident, wishing he would, too, she cut a quick glance toward him. "You're the one who needs to be checked over. You could have broken something. Or maybe you hit your head and didn't even realize it."

His only concern had been his arm. Considering the pain he'd been in, and the intense and rather intimate relief they'd shared once his body parts had been aligned, she hadn't thought to be concerned about anything else herself.

She turned her attention to the street, mostly so she wouldn't hit the truck parked in front of the general store, partly because thinking about how he'd sagged against her did strange things to the pit of her stomach.

"Are you sure you don't want me to take you to St. Johnsbury?"

"Positive. I'll leave a message for Bess to stop by when she gets in."

"But what if she's late? If you did hit your head, you shouldn't be by yourself. Is there anyone home to take care of you?"

"I live alone, but I'm fine. Honest."

She sighed. "Are you right-handed or left?"

"Right."

It was his left arm he was holding, even with the sling. "At least you can undress yourself," she concluded, "but I'm still worried about your head."

She was worried about him.

"You don't need to be," Greg assured her, unwillingly touched that she was. "I only hurt my shoulder. You're the one who hit her head."

She went quiet at that.

The storm and the dark had cleared the street of summer tourists. Cars lined the block in front of Dora's Diner and the video-and-bookstore seemed to be doing a fair business. Something appeared to be going on at the community church, too. The square white building was surrounded by vehicles, and its simple spire was lit and gleaming like the blade of a sword. But the end of the street was nearly deserted as they left Maple Mountain's not-so-booming commercial district and passed two blocks of tidy little homes.

Greg's was the last house on the right before the road through town disappeared into a forest of birch, maple and evergreen trees. It was a comfortable old place with a porch that wrapped around three sides and, as far as Greg was concerned, more rooms than a bachelor needed. But use of it had come with his contract with the community, and he could walk to the clinic. Because of its size he'd also been able to convert the pantry into a darkroom so he had something to do during the long winter nights.

He should have left the porch light on, he thought. Without it, with the rain, he couldn't even see his front steps.

Jenny Baker seemed to notice that, too. In the green glow of the dashboard lights, he saw her hesitate only a moment before she reached to turn off the engine of her cramped little car. "Stay put for a minute. I'll get the door and get you inside."

"You've done enough. Thank you," he quickly added, softening his abruptness. "But I can take it from here."

Cold, wet, and with the steady ache reminding him that his arm had been literally ripped from its socket, getting inside was exactly what Greg wanted to do. He wanted a hot shower. He wanted to get ice packs on his shoulder before the swelling got worse than it was.

He had no intention, however, of further imposing on the intriguing and rather mysterious woman now turning toward him. He didn't want to be intrigued by her. He didn't want to think about what he'd felt when she'd held him. He didn't want her on his mind at all. There were questions about her that begged to be answered, but he didn't want to be that interested.

"Are you sure?" she asked, the concern he'd heard in her voice now evident in her face.

"Positive. Thanks."

Jenny opened her mouth, closed it again. He wasn't simply being stubborn. He didn't want her help anymore. And if didn't want it, she wasn't about to impose it on him.

She couldn't, however, let him go without clearing up one little detail.

He'd already turned to open his door.

"Wait," she said, splaying her fingers over his thigh to stop him. Drawing back her hand when his glance shot toward it, she curled her fingers into her palm.

"I need to ask you not to say anything about that remark I made. The one about having dealt enough with detectives.

"As long as you've lived in Maple Mountain," she continued, not sure which made her more uncomfortable, him or her circumstances, "you have to know that people love to talk…and I'd really rather that didn't get around. That oath you took says you're not supposed to repeat what you hear, anyway."

"That oath?"

"The Hippocratic one. You're supposed to keep what people tell you confidential."

Greg wasn't quite sure what he heard in the quiet tones of her voice, desperation or defensiveness. Either way, he couldn't deny his quick curiosity why either would be there.

"My silence is only required of doctor-patient relationships." He tipped his head, studied the plea in her lovely features. "In this case, I was the patient."

"Please…"

"Are you here because you're in trouble with the law?"

"No. No," she repeated, more grateful than he could imagine that she no longer had to deal with people with badges who refused to believe a word she said. "I was completely cleared. So, please, just keep what I said to yourself. Okay?"

Completely cleared of what? he was about to ask when a blinding white light cut him off.

A vehicle came to a stop behind them. The dual beams of its

headlights filled the car, causing Jenny to flinch as the light reflected off the rearview mirror.

The solid slam of a door preceded the appearance of another beam from a flashlight a moment before a black gloved fist tapped on the window on the driver's side.

Jenny rolled the window down. Rain pounding, she saw Deputy Joe Sheldon lean down to see who was inside.

Clear plastic covered the local ex-football hero's State Trooper-style hat. A yellow raincoat hid his uniform. In between, sharp eyes darted from her to Greg and back again.

Sharpness turned to recognition.

"Jenny Baker," he said, speaking in the unhurried, deliberate way of a native of rural Vermont. His craggy face broke into a grin, calling attention to the hook-shaped scar at the corner of his mouth and making him look as if he might ruffle her hair the way he'd done years ago when he'd dated her older sister. "What are you doing here?"

"I'm moving back, Joe."

"You don't say." Rain dripped from the brim of his hat. "Didn't think you'd be one of the ones to do that. Huh," he grunted. "Then, that must be your stuff I saw in your grandma's place. Thought we had ourselves a squatter." Satisfied with his conclusion, he leaned lower so he could look past her. "Say, Doc. I saw your Tahoe in the ditch out by Widow Maker." He took in the towel, the way it was pinned at his shoulder and the wet shirt lying in his lap. "You okay?"

"I am now. Thanks, Joe."

"Gave me a scare there, Doc. Looked all over the place for you when I saw you weren't in your car. Thought you might have taken shelter at the old Baker place," he told him, explaining how he'd come across Jenny's few remaining possessions. "Just came by here to see if you'd made it back."

His glance narrowed on the makeshift sling. "Need any help getting inside?"

Jenny looked toward Greg. He didn't want her help, but there was no need for him to refuse Joe's.

"You might get his front door for him," Jenny suggested.

"Not a problem," the deputy replied and headed around to pull open the car door for him, too.

Jenny was worried.

Greg hadn't said that he would keep quiet. After he'd accepted Joe's offer to help him into his house, he hadn't said anything to her, except to thank her again for everything she'd done.

He'd been profuse with his thanks. What she'd wanted was his promise.

As she walked the block from the diner to the clinic the next morning, under skies of blessedly brilliant blue, she still didn't know which bothered her more. That he hadn't promised, or that he had so obviously preferred someone else's help over hers after what she'd been through with him.

To be fair, she supposed she couldn't blame him for not wanting anything else to do with her. All he really knew about her was where she currently lived, that she'd recently been involved with detectives and that she was a tad desperate to keep him quiet about that.

A knot of quiet anxiety had taken up permanent residence in her stomach. With her hand over it, she smoothed the front of the cocoa-colored blouse tucked into her beige slacks and climbed the four steps leading into the white clapboard building that had housed Maple Mountain's only clinic for over a hundred years. She had come home to start over. No matter what Dr. Greg Reid's impression of her, she didn't want him making that start any harder than it was already.

The screen door opened with a squeak a moment before a bell over the white wooden door gave a faint tinkle.

Six dark wood chairs lined one wall of the tidy, pale-green reception room. Only one was occupied. A teenage mother—one of the McGraw girls from the looks of her flaming-red hair—

sat with a listless toddler, soothing the child with pictures from an office copy of *Parenting* magazine.

"Hi," said Jenny on her way to the reception window.

The girl smiled and went back to pointing at pictures.

From inside the front office, a very pregnant brunette in a light-blue scrub smock and ponytail turned to see who had just come in.

"May I help you?" she asked, an instant before her eyes widened. "Jenny Baker!"

Pressing her hand to the small of her back, thirty-something Rhonda Pembroke turned to get a better look at the girl she hadn't seen in four years. "Bess told me this morning that you were back. And Lois Neely was in here not two hours ago sayin' you've moved into your grandma's old place."

Word had definitely preceded her—which meant at least one of the two men she'd encountered during her first hours home had wasted no time spreading it. Jenny's money was on Joe as the culprit. Lois worked as dispatcher at the sheriff's office, and Joe's name had come up when Jenny had been met with virtually the same greeting at the diner an hour ago.

"Are you really going to restore your grandma's house?"

Jenny's smile faltered. She had no idea who had assumed such a thing, though she could see where someone might take it for granted. No one in her right mind would live there without redoing the place. Restoration, however, would cost a fortune she would never have.

"It certainly needs work," she replied, deliberately hedging as she nodded toward the woman's girth. "How are you and your family doing? Is this your third?"

"Fourth. I had a little girl while you were gone. But you didn't come by to hear about me," she insisted. "Who are you here to see? The doctor?" Her glance made a quick sweep of the bruises barely visible beneath the makeup on Jenny's jaw. "Or Bess?"

Jenny felt herself hesitate. Being Greg's receptionist and office manager, Rhonda would know that he'd been hurt. He might even have told her that she'd helped him, and the woman simply assumed that she was there to see how he was doing. Which she was. Partly.

It was whatever else he might have said that worried her.

"The doctor," she replied. "Is he available?"

"He's with a patient. But give me a minute." Turning from the desk below the wide window, she dropped her hand from her back. "I'll tell him you're here."

A large bulletin board hung by the door that separated the waiting area from the exam rooms. Wanting to take her mind off her growing uneasiness, Jenny glanced over a poster for a senior citizens' exercise classes at the local community center. She had no idea why the local seniors needed a formal exercise routine. Most of those she'd known growing up got plenty of exercise working their gardens and gathering berries in the woods in the summer and shoveling snow and snowshoeing in the winter. The people in the North Woods seemed to be of hardier stock than those she'd encountered in the city.

She was wondering if she could pick up a few extra dollars this winter shoveling snow for those who weren't so hardy when the door suddenly opened.

There was a little more white in Bess Amherst's tight crop of salt-and-pepper curls than Jenny had remembered, and the crow's feet around her narrowed hazel eyes seemed to have fanned a little farther toward her temples, but she hadn't otherwise changed since Jenny had last seen her. The midfifties, suffer-no-whiners nurse practitioner still wore her reading glasses on a silver chain around her neck, still preferred pastel plaid shirts and elastic-waist pants to the nurse's scrub uniform Dr. Wilson had never been able to get her to wear, and still wore white athletic shoes—which more or less matched her short lab jacket.

Stylish, she wasn't.

Interested, she always was.

Jenny had known Bess since she was a child.

"You're too thin," the woman immediately pronounced, hands on her hips. "I don't know why you girls go off to the city and come back looking like waifs. Everybody's always bragging about what great restaurants they have in Boston, but seems to me you girls never eat in 'em. And your hair." Had it not been for the twinkle in her eyes, Bess might have looked as disapproving as she sounded. "How big-city you look with it all short and wispy like that." She shook her head as she stepped forward, shoes squeaking. "Let me see that forehead of yours."

Before Jenny could even say hello herself, Bess nudged back the sweep of her dark bangs. She smelled faintly of anti-bacterial soap, rubbing alcohol and—vanilla. "The doctor said he didn't get a chance to look at that," she said, frowning, as she concentrated on the two-inch sidewalk burn above Jenny's right eye. "What have you put on it?"

"Nothing. I just dabbed at it with soap and water."

"Well, you need to keep your hair away from it. And it needs ointment. Come on back and I'll get you some. And don't go putting any makeup on it. Not until it heals. It doesn't look like it'll scar now, but it will if you get it infected."

Her shoes gave another chirp as she turned. After waiting for Jenny to pass, she closed the door behind her and glanced down the wide hallway to where Rhonda headed toward them, her hand at her back.

"How's her head?" Rhonda asked.

"Just an abrasion. I'm going to give her some salve to put on it."

"I told Dr. Reid you're here," she said to Jenny. Her voice dropped to nearly a whisper as she moved past. "And I don't blame you for wanting to come home."

Bess turned into a white room lined with black counters and lab equipment and pointed Jenny to a chrome-legged stool. A faint frown pinched her mouth. "She must have overheard the doctor tell me he wanted me to check on you. He felt bad that he wasn't thinking clearly enough to check you himself."

"He wanted you to check on me?"

"That's the kind of man he is. If he thinks a person needs help, he sees that she gets it." Her shrug looked vaguely preoccupied as she pulled open one of the dozens of drawers and motioned again for Jenny to sit. "Considering the pain he had to be in, I'm surprised he was thinking at all. Good that you were there for him."

Taking out what she was after, she closed the drawer, collected a small packet, a gauze pad and paper tape and walked to where Jenny stood by the stool. Since Jenny hadn't sat, she proceeded to work on her where she stood. "Hold your bangs back."

"Bess, you don't have to—"

"Yes, I do," she said, and pushed them back herself to dab at the scrape with the orange-brown pad from the packet.

Jenny didn't know what was on it, only that it smelled awful and stung like the devil.

"It's just too bad it took something like this to bring you to your senses and move back to where it's safe. You're lucky that hoodlum didn't have something worse on his mind."

Paper crackled as she opened a gauze pad. Removing the lid from a little silver tube, she looped a coil of ointment onto the pad and moved Jenny's finger to hold it in place when she positioned it above her eye.

As desperately as Jenny wanted to leave the events of the past month behind, it seemed easiest to let the women assume she had come home only because she hadn't felt secure where she'd been. The older residents of Maple Mountain had always regarded cities as dens of iniquity that lured and swallowed up their young people. Having one of their own back, battered and bruised, undoubtedly vindicated the attitude.

All Jenny cared about was that Greg apparently hadn't mentioned her comment about having been cleared by the detectives. If he had, the outspoken nurse practitioner would have already demanded to know what he'd been talking about. Bess had been good friends with her mother.

"Keep this covered." Deftly applying strips of tape, Bess secured the pad in place. With that done, she handed her the silver tube, a handful of gauze pads and the tape roll. "Use the salve twice a day." The woman's friendly scolding suddenly softened. "Welcome home, Jenny."

Bess often had the manner of a field marshal, but Jenny knew there wasn't a more sincere soul on the planet than the woman now patting her on the shoulder.

Jenny smiled back, accepting the welcome with guilty grace.

"Thank you," she murmured, torn between the comfort of a friendly and familiar face and feeling like a total fraud. "And thank you for all this," she said, hoping she wouldn't appear terribly ungrateful as she held out her filled hands. "But I really don't think I need it." She couldn't afford it even if she did. She had exactly $46.08 to last until she got her first paycheck—which, if she'd calculated correctly, would be less than two hundred dollars before taxes. "Can you just bill me for taking care of my head?"

"You do need that," Bess informed her. Taking what Jenny held, she stuffed it into the small purse hanging by a thin strap from Jenny's shoulder. "I know you didn't come for an examination. Rhonda said you're here to see the doctor. I imagine you're wanting to know if he's all right after helping him out last night. But that," she said, pointing at Jenny's forehead, "is a nasty scrape and it needs to heal properly. And don't you worry about a bill," she admonished. "All I did was slap a bandage on you. That antibiotic is a sample. No charge. Now, come on. You can wait for Dr. Reid in his office."

Bess obviously knew all about the help Jenny had given her boss. Because she did know about it, and because Jenny asked if he would be all right, the briskly efficient woman confided that she had X-rayed and wrapped his shoulder herself last evening and that he would be just fine in a couple of weeks. She offered nothing else, though, before she ushered Jenny into the office near the end of the hall, told her the doctor wouldn't be long and closed the door behind her.

Jenny stared at the carved panel of dark wood. She hoped desperately that she'd done the right thing coming here.

Wishing the nerves in her stomach would stop jumping, something she'd been wishing now for weeks, she slowly faced the neat and comfortable space. Across from her, the sunshine spilling through the slatted wooden window blinds cut a pattern of shadow and light over a maple pedestal table and four bow back chairs. A coffee mug sat on the table near stacks of open medical books. At the other end of the room, a large maple desk sat in front of a wall of bookcases and a hanging fern.

Between the warm woods, the colorful braided rug beneath the table and the old furniture, the room looked much as it always had. Quaint and rather charming in a reassuring, old-fashioned sort of way. It was only the laptop computer on the table by the books, the dish of peppermint candies on the painfully tidy desk and the wall of photos and certificates that gave any hint of the new doctor's personality. If she were pressed for a quick assessment, she would say that the new doctor was far neater than the old one had been. More open to technology. And that he apparently possessed a sweet tooth.

That small weakness would have made her smile had she not felt so anxious. Too restless to stand still, wondering how long she would be left to pace, she moved toward the desk with its single file neatly centered on the blotter and pens standing upright like good little soldiers in their holder. As she did, she absently pushed back her bangs, and promptly bumped into the bandage Bess had more or less slapped onto her forehead.

With everything else she'd had on her mind, the abrasion and her bruises truly had been of the least consequence. In no time the soreness would go away. The scrape and bruises would heal. The other damage done to her life felt infinitely more immediate and would take far longer to remedy.

She couldn't believe Greg had actually asked Bess to check on her. With her faith in the human species, men in particular, sorely shaken, she'd almost forgotten that every man wasn't out just for himself.

That's just the kind of man he is. If someone needs help, he sees that he gets it.

She let her hand fall. It had seemed so much easier to ignore what had happened to her yesterday morning without the chunk of white gauze that undoubtedly made the little injury that much more noticeable. It had been as if by ignoring the abrasion and bruises, she could ignore the incident. She knew she was playing ostrich, but she simply didn't have the mental energy to deal with the assault and thwarted robbery on top of everything else. Not when she was trying so desperately to focus her energy on something—anything—positive.

Needing to focus on something positive now, she thought about Dora Schaeffer. Dora, bless her, had given her back her old part-time job at the café. She was feeling exceedingly grateful to the older woman when she turned to the wall beside her.

The ivory-colored wall was covered with a collage of photos. Many were large, matted photographs of the area's flaming fall foliage, stands of bare birch trees in pristine fields of snow, apple trees blossoming in the spring. Most were photos of the local Little League team and individual players with gap-toothed grins. Snapshots of babies, some held by their proud parents, obliterated a bulletin board. A child's handmade Valentine, its paper lace doily curling, dangled from one corner.

A black-framed diploma hung near the edge of the wall. Its placement by a state medical board certificate and a medical license seemed almost incidental, as if it were displayed only because convention or law required it.

It seemed that Gregory Matthias Reid had been awarded his medical degree from Harvard.

She was definitely impressed. A Harvard education was not only academically challenging to obtain, it cost a fortune. She knew. She'd heard brokers she'd worked with complaining about it, either because they were paying it off for themselves or their offspring.

His alma mater surprised her, too. The Harvard men she'd met wouldn't have spent more than a weekend in this remote and rural community, and then only for one of the quaint local festivals. There were no ski lodges nearby, no reliable cell phone service, no latte machines, martini bars or night life. But then the only Harvard graduates she'd known were hungry MBAs clawing their way to the top of the shark tank. Those who swore to beat the stock market undoubtedly possessed less compassion per gene than those who swore to beat injury and disease.

Shaking off her thoughts before they could move to one MBA in particular, her glance dropped to the shades of coral and orange in a small gold-framed photograph. The photo sat askew among the books and files jammed along the credenza. In it, the good doctor stood with a view of the Eiffel Tower at sunset in the distant background—and his arm around a drop-dead-gorgeous blonde.

The woman was tall, built like a model and had been blessed with long, corn-silk-colored hair that flew in the breeze. Jenny couldn't tell the color of her eyes, but her smile was wide, her teeth perfect. It wasn't the perfection, however, that had Jenny picking up the picture. It was the air of utter self-assurance the woman seemed to exude.

With her own self-confidence having disappeared along with her life as she'd known it, Jenny was wondering if she would ever feel certain about anything again when the door opened and Greg walked in.

Chapter Three

A dark-blue sling covered Greg's left arm. Much of it was hidden by the white lab coat he wore open over a forest-green golf shirt and tan khakis, but there was no hiding that he'd been injured. Even if one side of the coat hadn't been draped over his shoulder, the bruising she'd seen last night would have given him away. It had darkened to the color of a Bing cherry and now crept to almost an inch above his collar.

It was the rest of him that had the bulk of her attention, though.

Even with his arm bound in a sling, there was nothing about him that hinted at any sort of vulnerability. Nothing to indicate how dependent he had been on her less than twelve hours ago. Beneath the dark slash of his eyebrows, his gray eyes smiled at her with a quiet intensity that weighed and assessed and put strange little flutters in her stomach.

Without the pain he'd dealt with last night, he was more than an attractive man. He was a man who looked big, capable and totally in control of himself and everything around him.

That quiet power seemed to radiate toward her, drawing her in as he looked to what she held.

Aware that she'd just been caught with one of his photographs, Jenny's guilty glance fell before she smiled and turned to set the picture back in its place.

"I don't suppose she's a relative."

Seeing which picture she'd had, he hesitated. "She's...a friend."

Wondering at that slight pause, thinking maybe her innocent interest had just caught him off guard, Jenny left the photo exactly as she'd found it. Of course he had a "friend," she thought, stepping aside as he passed her to drop the file he carried onto his desk. The man was gorgeous. He was caring. He was a doctor.

Not that she was at all interested in him that way herself. As badly as she'd been burned, she had no desire whatsoever to face that particular brand of fire again. That didn't keep her from appreciating the compelling aura of quiet strength surrounding him, though, or the ease of his manner when he turned back to her.

Though his eyes remained on her face, she had the interesting feeling that he took in every inch of her body as she stood by the credenza six feet away.

"I understand you're here to check on my welfare."

She tipped her head, studying him back. "I just wanted to know how you're doing." Considering what he'd gone through— what she'd gone through with him—she'd have to be as insensitive as stone not to wonder how he was. "You were in a lot of pain last night."

"Not as much as I would have been in if you hadn't been there. Thanks again, by the way. For everything." A hint of self-reproach entered his eyes. "I probably scared the hell out of you, kicking your door like that."

"You're welcome. And you did." She shrugged, seeing no reason to deny the obvious. He'd seen the tire iron she'd prepared to defend herself with. "But I think I was more afraid that you'd pass out."

Reproach turned into a smile. "I did my best not to."

She smiled back. "You have no idea how I appreciate that."

There were slivers of silver in his eyes. She noticed them a moment before his glance dropped to the curve of her mouth. Last night, his own had been inches from hers. Too easily, she could remember the feel of his warm breath on her skin, and the quicksilver change in his eyes when she'd touched her hand to his cheek.

As his eyes lifted to meet hers now, she had the feeling he remembered those disturbing moments, too.

He also looked as if he'd rather not think about them.

Clearing his throat, he absently rubbed his shoulder as voices drifted toward them from the hall.

"So," he said, dropping his hand to push it into the pocket of his lab coat. He nodded toward the bandage beneath her bangs. "I see Bess got hold of you."

"She got me on my way in." Feeling a sudden need to move herself, thinking it best to get her business here over with, she edged toward the door and closed it with a quiet click.

"There's another reason I came by," she admitted, reclaiming her spot by the picture of his friend. His relationship with the beautiful woman in the photo was none of her business. *He* was none of her business. At least not beyond extracting one small promise. "I really did want to make sure you were okay," she hurried to explain. "And I'm really glad you are. But there's something I need from you."

Curiosity creased his brow. Or maybe it was caution. With the discomfiting feeling it was more the latter, she took a step closer, reducing the space between them so she could lower her voice even more. She didn't think Rhonda or Bess would repeat anything personal that went on in the clinic. At least, she'd never heard that they had, and people in Maple Mountain knew who they could confide in and who couldn't keep her—or his—mouth shut. But it sounded as if there were other people out there now.

"I know you omitted parts of what we talked about when you

told Bess that I was mugged. I don't mind that you told her," she hurried on, "about the mugging, I mean. And I appreciate that you wanted her to check on me. But I need to know you won't say anything about why I didn't go to the police. I want to fit back in here the way I did before I left. This is really the only place I have to go right now," she explained, the anxiety in her expression sneaking into her voice. "And I'd really hate to be the subject of speculation and gossip." She'd had more than enough of that where she'd just come from. "It's awful when you can't go anywhere without someone whispering behind your back."

Greg's glance narrowed, his sense of caution growing in direct proportion to his interest. There was an air of style and polish about the lovely young woman anxiously watching him that she could have only acquired in the city. The unhurried, thoughtful pattern of speech possessed by many of those born in the region seemed to have been consciously trained from her voice. Dressed as she had been last night in a baggy sweatshirt and jeans, he hadn't paid any attention to the layer of sophistication that set her apart from most of the area's residents. But he hadn't exactly been on top of his game last night, either.

The one thing he definitely had picked up was the feeling that she was running from something. Seeing the disquiet in her eyes, he was even more convinced of it now.

There wasn't a doubt in his mind that she was seeking escape. From what, he had no idea. He just knew that if there was anything he recognized, it was that need. Until he'd turned twenty, he'd lived with it nearly every day of his life.

Three months ago that need had returned with a vengeance.

That was when his father had died—and left him a fortune he absolutely did not want, one that his father never intended him to have, and which was exerting a certain control over his life simply because he now had to deal with the only thing his father ever truly cared about. His money.

The thoughts kicked up acid his stomach. Not a soul in Maple Mountain knew his inheritance existed. No one in Maple Mountain even knew his father had died. Or that he'd had one living for that matter. He didn't speak of his past beyond what little he could get away with, and the last thing he would have wanted were condolences from well-meaning, good-hearted people who would have made him the main topic on the local grapevine— especially if they knew about the money.

When an inheritance was involved, people tended to want to know what a person was going do with it. And when. His attorney, his father's attorney and Elizabeth Brandt, the woman he'd soon be moving in with, were certainly anxious for the information. Part of his problem was that just hearing those questions knotted his gut with reminders of why he wanted nothing to do with it at all. Every time any one of them mentioned the estate, he felt a powerful need to escape. The rest of the time, he simply felt…restless.

Except for last night. Only then, when he'd experienced the odd and compelling comfort in the arms of a woman he didn't even know, had he not been aware of the restiveness he lived with nearly every other hour of the day.

Watching that woman now, he tried to tell himself he had only imagined that peace. Endorphins had probably been released into his blood when the trauma to his body had been eased. Or release from the pain had come as such a relief that he would have felt that comfort with anyone.

Rationalization helped. It just didn't explain how the scent and feel of her had taunted every nerve in his body. Or how watching her mouth as she waited for his assurance made those nerves tighten all over again.

"I know what you mean about talk," he confided, forcing his glance up. She seemed desperate for his discretion. Quietly so, but desperate nonetheless. "And I understand how important reputations are around here. Stop worrying. Okay? I'm not going to say anything."

He wondered if she was always so easy to read. Or if the anxiety he sensed in her had simply robbed her of the ability to mask what she would prefer others didn't see. The distress in her eyes faded with undisguised relief.

The warmth of her thankful smile washed over him, soft, inviting and as gentle as spring rain. The same pull he'd felt toward her last night tugged hard in his chest. He'd barely noticed it when a tap on the door jerked his attention from the sensation, along with the curiosity about her that grew with each passing second.

The door opened. Bess's head poked around it, the silver in her tightly curled hair catching the overhead light.

"I just had the most brilliant idea." With that announcement, she left the door open and walked in, smiling at Jenny before she looked to him. "Jenny's mom and I still exchange Christmas cards," she prefaced, ignoring his blank look and Jenny's quick confusion. "She always writes one of those Christmas letters. A nice, newsy one that tells how her children and grandchildren are and how her garden was the past summer.

"In her Christmas letter last year," she continued, looking thoughtful, "she mentioned that Jenny was still at the same big brokerage she'd gone to work for when she'd moved to Boston. Salomon something."

"Salomon Bennett?" he asked, identifying the huge investment firm his more affluent acquaintances used.

"That's it." Bess gave a nod. "I remember she also mentioned that Jenny was still administrative assistant to one of the vice presidents. Since a job like that must require considerable organizational skill, and since Rhonda is going on maternity leave as soon as she goes into labor, we should hire her."

Without waiting for a response, she turned to Jenny. "Can you do accounting on a computer?"

Greg's eyebrow's merged. "Hang on, Bess. We can't just—"

"It depends on the program," Jenny cut in, uncomfortably aware that Greg wasn't nearly as enamored with the idea as Bess was. Not that she could blame him. What he knew about her hardly recommended her as an employee. "I've used several. But I just got a job. I'm starting at the diner Thursday. Dinner shift."

Greg's quick objection turned just as quickly to confusion. "Why did you take a job there?"

"Because I need it," she replied, ever so reasonably.

Tolerance laced his tone. "What I mean," he explained, "is why wait tables with your qualifications? Why not go where you can get a job that pays? You could apply at the bank or the school district over in St. Johnsbury. I know it's a drive, but you'd make three times the money there."

The man had the eyes of a hawk, the instincts of a wolf after prey. His powers of observation weren't too shabby, either. She supposed all that came in handy when trying to figuring out how to help a patient, but when a person wanted to keep certain things to herself, those abilities were downright unnerving.

Her shrug didn't feel nearly as casual as she hoped it looked. "As you said, it's a long drive, and I don't want the commute. Especially in the winter." Both he and Bess should appreciate that. Ice and blowing snow often turned the hour-plus drive into two hours or more. "I worked at the diner before I left, so it's not as if I don't have experience there, too."

She also hadn't had to supply references to get the job. References were a major problem at the moment. No company hired without references, and she couldn't give those she had. That was the main reason she'd come back to Maple Mountain.

"Aside from that," she said, more comfortable with Bess's faintly perplexed expression, "I don't have an updated résumé to give you." She smiled, hoping to end the conversation before either could ask more questions. It was obvious from Greg's frown that something wasn't adding up to him. "Thanks for thinking of me, though."

The sound Bess made was somewhere between a tsk and a snort.

"You don't need to show us a résumé. You're qualified. You have a good work ethic." Her tone turned confiding. "I know that because of how hard you worked to get your associate's degree," she told her, "and by how well you did for yourself in Boston. Even if you don't know the program we use, Rhonda can help you figure it out. You're experienced, and experienced is what we need."

Looking utterly convinced that she had just solved their staffing problem, she glanced to where Greg stood with his forehead furrowed. "It's not as if she needs character references," she insisted, clearly not understanding his hesitation. "I can vouch for her myself. So can half the town. Aside from that, we haven't had any other qualified applicants, and Rhonda is already overdue."

"And feeling every minute of it," the miserable-looking office manager announced in low tones as she walked in. "Sorry for the interruption, but Lorna Bagley just brought in her youngest with some sort of rash. I put them back in the isolation room since Bertie Buell is here for her blood pressure check. You know how Bertie is about being around anything she thinks might be contagious."

At the mention of patients, Greg turned his frown to his watch. "You take Bertie, Bess. I'll get the rash," he said to Rhonda. "Tell Lorna I'll be right there."

Grasping the opportunity for escape, undeniably grateful for it, Jenny watched Bess, thwarted and disgruntled, head for the door as she backed toward it herself.

"Thank you, Bess," she called, thinking of the bandage, the ointment, the welcome and for thinking of her for the job that, if not for Greg and his obvious reservations, she would have loved to take.

"I didn't mean to keep you so long," she said, turning back to see him move to the door himself.

He stopped an arm's length away, his hand on the edge of the door, his body towering over hers. Glancing from the swath of blue covering the middle of his impressive chest, thinking it highly unfair that she could so easily recall how hard it had felt beneath her fingers, she jerked her eyes to his.

"Take care of that shoulder," she reminded him, and slipped out with the feel of his uncertainty about her hounding every step.

* * *

The positive thing about a place as small as Maple Mountain was that neighbors always knew if a person had a problem or if they needed help. If someone hadn't been seen or heard from for a while, someone else would inevitably call or drop by just to make sure everything was all right. People watched out for each other. People cared about each other.

Jenny had missed that.

What she hadn't missed was the relative lack of privacy that came with such neighborly concern.

The people in and around Maple Mountain were a fiercely independent lot, opinionated to a fault about politics, their land and protecting it from anyone who might try to change the way of life that had worked just fine for them for however long they'd lived there. But for all that independence, they were also intensely interested in everything that went on around them. Strangers were easily identified, and a car didn't pass through town that someone along Main Street didn't note its license plate to see where it was from.

A car with plates from any state other than Vermont would elicit speculation about where its occupants were going and how long they would stay. A vehicle they recognized as belonging to their little part of the world invited solemn conjecture about its occupant's destination. Especially if they knew, or knew of, its owner.

Old Parker must be heading into St. Johnsbury for that tractor part he's needin'.

Bet Essie's on her way out to her daughter's to help with the twins.

Or observations about the vehicle itself.

Been a while since Charlie washed that truck of his.

Wonder how long it'll be before Amos's bumper falls off.

There wasn't much that slipped by the locals. Where other locals were concerned, anyway. Visitors were treated politely, especially when they came to vacation on the lake in the summer and for the festivals that fed the town's coffers. Their spending helped pay for everything from the newly paved parking lot at the community center to sports equipment for the elementary school. But only the residents warranted true interest in conversations at the diner or around the checkerboard at the general store. Especially if whatever that person was up to proved more interesting than what seemed to be going on anywhere else.

That was why Jenny wasn't surprised when, by six o'clock that evening, she'd had no fewer than four visitors, including Joe who'd stopped by with a crowbar when he'd heard that she hadn't wanted to pay ten dollars for one at the general store. He'd helped her pry off the particularly stubborn board covering the living room window and told her he'd be back tomorrow with a ladder and help her take the boards off the windows upstairs.

Carrie Higgins, who'd been Carrie Rogers when she'd hung out with Jenny's older sister and Dora's daughter, Kelsey, at the old grist mill behind the house, had stopped by to see for herself that Jenny was actually back and living in her grandma's old place. Jenny hadn't invited her in. She hadn't invited anyone in because she hadn't wanted to lie and say her furniture hadn't been delivered yet, which was the only way she could think to explain why her bed was a pile of blankets and a comforter in a corner of the kitchen.

Carrie hadn't seemed to mind the lack of an invitation. She'd just wanted to say hi and bring her a welcome-back Jell-O salad, the kind with pistachio pudding in it. So they'd stood outside under the old maple tree, Jenny holding the plastic bowl and Carrie holding her ten-month-old on her hip while her four- and six-year-olds tormented a caterpillar and promised each other they'd get together soon.

Gap-toothed Smiley Jefferson, who had the postal route and was the mayor's brother-in-law, stopped to see if she would be putting up a mailbox, since the one out by the road had fallen to wood rot years ago, or if she'd be using a box at the post office.

Sally McNeff, who now ran her aging mother's bookstore,

stopped by on her way home from work to welcome Jenny home and tell her she was so sorry she'd been mugged.

Jenny had been alone for all of fifteen minutes and was inside washing the multi-paned front window when another vehicle pulled onto the rutted driveway.

Across the narrow ribbon of road that led into town, the land rose in a long and gentle hill. Only the trees at the top were illuminated by sunlight. In another hour it would be dusk. But just then the air glowed golden. In that gentle light she watched a gray bull-nosed truck rumble toward the house. She had already cleaned the outside of the glass, and light spilled across the dusty hardwood floor, taking some of the dreariness from the room. Or maybe simply illuminating it. In the brighter light, she could more easily see how badly the ivy-print wallpaper was pealing.

The truck pulled to a stop behind her sporty black sedan. Finishing the pane she was washing, careful of the crack in it so she wouldn't wind up with a hole where the foot-wide pane had been, she tried to make out who was driving it. With the wide maple trees shading the weedy and overgrown lawn, all she could see was the pattern of light and shadow on the windshield.

Curiosity got the better of her. Leaving her task, she absently tugged her short white T-shirt over the waistband of her denim capris and moved to the open front door as the truck came to a stop. The screen door screeched in protest when she pushed it open.

Reminding herself to go through the collection of odds and ends on the back porch to see if a can of oil lurked in their midst, she sidestepped the loose board on the porch and came to a halt at the top step.

Greg climbed from behind the wheel. Before she could even begin to imagine why he was there, the slam of his door sent birds squawking as they scattered from the trees.

He had her yellow towel with him. Seeing her framed by the posts on the porch, he headed toward her, his stride relaxed and unhurried. Without the lab coat covering his golf shirt and khakis, she could see that the sling completely encased his arm, holding it nearly as close to his body as he'd held it himself last night.

She needed to forget last night. Certain parts of it, anyway.

"I hear Charlie Moorehouse loaned you his truck," she called, thinking the comment as good a way as any to keep things neighborly.

She watched him glance toward Charlie's newest acquisition. The fact that the old guy had lent the doctor his pride and joy attested to how grateful he had been to Greg for getting him through his last bout of gout.

"He's saved me a lot of hassle," he admitted, sounding grateful himself. She'd also heard that truck was an automatic. With the use of only one arm, he couldn't have driven anything else. "He dropped it off for me after he and his son towed my SUV into St. Johnsbury."

"How long before you get it back?"

"Not sure," he replied, and stopped at the foot of the steps. He hadn't come to exchange small talk. He wanted something. She could tell from the way his deceptively casual glance slid over her frame, his mouth forming an upside down *U* in the moments before he held out her neatly folded towel.

He also didn't appear totally convinced that he should be there.

"Do you have a few minutes?" he asked as she took what he offered.

"Sure." Despite a quick sense of unease, she gave a shrug. "I was just cleaning."

Behind her, the window sparkled. Above, cobwebs laced the corners of the porch roof.

"That ought to keep you busy for a while."

"Until spring, I would imagine."

The *U* gave way to a faint smile. "Then, I won't keep you long. Bess is on me to hire you," he admitted, getting straight to the point. "She said she's sure you'll have no trouble picking up medical terminology and our procedures. Since you appear to have considerable office experience, I wondered if you wanted to tell me why I shouldn't offer you the job."

The question threw her. So did the intent way he watched her as she crossed her arms over the folded yellow terry cloth and waited for her to either recover from his blunt query or invite him in and answer it.

"Because I already have one?"

Something in his eyes seemed to soften. She wasn't sure what it was. It hinted at patience, yet looked more like weariness. The draining kind of weariness that sucked the spirit from deep inside a man.

"You know that's not what I mean."

Unfortunately, she did. She also knew she had several very good reasons to ignore the quick tug of empathy she felt for what she saw. For starters, if he was tired, it was probably because he hadn't slept well with his arm throbbing or aching or whatever it was probably still doing. More important, he seemed far more perplexed by her than interested in her sympathy.

Perplexed didn't begin to describe what Greg felt when it came to the quietly pretty woman warily eyeing him from three steps away. The more he learned about her, the more bits and pieces of her past and personality he picked up, the more mysterious she seemed. And the more interested he became.

That interest bothered him. She wasn't his patient, so he couldn't excuse his curiosity about her as a way to better tend her needs. Even if she had been a patient, his interest went light-years beyond the professional. Yet he wasn't about to fully acknowledge the inexplicable pull he felt toward her. He was already involved with someone. He had been for two years. Unlike the other men in his family, he would not cheat on a woman—even if he *was* having serious second thoughts about the relationship.

A familiar tension started creeping through him. Colliding with that struggle were all the problems he'd acquired since his father died. Not a week had gone by in the past few months that the mail hadn't brought a new batch of documents, receipts and queries he didn't want to deal with. He'd gotten to where he'd hated to see Smiley coming, and had finally asked his attorney to hold on to everything until he could get to Boston to take care of whatever needed to be done. His attorney had now taken to e-mailing him, wanting to know when that would be.

He shoved down the resentment, buried it as he so often did lately. Between the estate and Elizabeth, the last thing he needed was another problem, and Jenny Baker clearly had plenty of her own, but the clinic needed a competent office manager who could double as a receptionist. That should be all he considered right now.

"Is working at the diner what you really want to do? I'm not saying there's a thing wrong with being a waitress," he explained, dead certain she was in need of help herself. "But wouldn't you rather have a job that used your skills and paid more than minimum wage and tips?"

Jenny was okay with omission. A little less comfortable with evasion. But there was no way she could look him in the eye and lie.

"I didn't think so," he said, when her only response was to glance away.

"Look." The faint breeze chased a leaf across the porch. "We need an office manager. I trust Bess's judgment, so I'm more than willing to listen to her when it comes to decisions about staffing. But you're hiding something," he told her, wondering if fear had driven her here, hoping for her sake that it hadn't. "Or running from it."

He held up his hand, cutting her off when she started to protest. "I don't like owing anyone, Jenny. And after what I put you through last night, I owe you. Something isn't right here." His glance swept her face, quietly searching. "If you're in trouble, I might be able to help."

Jenny had no idea why he didn't care to be obligated to anyone. She didn't get a chance to wonder about it, though. The thought that he wanted to help caught her as unprepared as the quick pang of need she felt to let him. She had never felt as alone as she had in the past month, as alone as she had last night curled up in the dark. Unfortunately, dealing with the mess she'd made of her life was something she would have to do on her own.

Suddenly tired herself, she sank to the top step and motioned for him to help himself to a stair. Boards groaned beneath his weight as he tugged at the knees of his khakis and sat down a yard away. With his big body taking up more than his half of the space, he planted his feet wide on the step below.

The yellow dots on his brown socks were tiny ducks. Had she not felt so miserable she would have smiled at that totally unexpected bit of whimsy. The kids in the pictures in his office would have to love a guy who wore something like that.

"Thank you," she said, genuinely moved by his offer. "But there isn't anything you can do. Except for the job," she conceded, almost afraid to think of how far a real salary could go. "The job really would make things easier."

Something like regret entered his tone. He could help, but there were strings. "I can't give you the job until I know what's going on. I have Bess and my patients to consider."

Her shoulders fell. "You don't think I was mugged," she said flatly.

"Honestly?" he asked, pinning her with his deceptively undemanding gaze. "I don't know what to think."

His bluntness she could handle. It was the way he had of looking at her, looking into her, that had her wanting to shy away. There was kindness in his darkly lashed eyes, but there was a lot of doubt and suspicion, too. "I wasn't abused and I'm not hiding from anyone," she insisted, making herself hold his glance. She was nothing if not honest. She wasn't about to have him think otherwise. "What happened yesterday morning happened just as I told you. No one is going to follow me here and cause a problem, if that's what you're worried about. I promise. Bess and your patients are safe."

The insistence faded from her voice. "I made a bad choice that led to an even worse situation. It will never, ever happen again. Can we please just let it go at that?"

The masculine lines carved in his cheeks deepened with the pinch of his mouth. Seeing nothing promising in Greg's expression, Jenny's glance finally faltered. She blinked at the board between her white canvas shoes. The blue paint that had once made the porch look so bright and cheerful had been weathered and worn to little more than flecks and streaks on the splintering wood. Waiting for Greg to make his decision, she felt like that herself, exposed and worn, and were she to dig too deep, fully capable of breaking into dozens of tiny pieces.

"What about the detectives. You said something about having been cleared, but you never said what you'd been charged with."

Her focus stayed on the boards. "I was never formally charged."

"That doesn't answer my question."

"I was never guilty, so there's no…"

"Jenny."

From the corner of her eyes, she caught the motion of his hand a moment before she felt his finger curve under her chin.

His deep voice was as gentle as the brush of his thumb along her jaw. "I keep my word," he promised. "Anything you say to me goes no further."

For a moment she said nothing. She just studied the strong lines of his face while her mind absorbed his quiet assurance and her battered heart his quiet strength. In the past month she had grown reluctant to confide anything to anyone. It had come to the point where she honestly hadn't known who she could trust anymore. Authorities who'd appeared to want only to help her had wanted only to find a way to trip her up so she would confess to a crime she had known nothing about. Friends she'd thought she could count on had turned their backs on her. She couldn't even trust her own judgment.

Yet, this man had nothing to gain from her that wouldn't help her, too.

His glance dropped to follow the motion of his thumb. As if he only now realized he was still touching her, he pulled a deep breath and eased his hand away.

It puzzled her that she hadn't questioned the contact herself. What puzzled her more was what she'd felt in his touch, the quiet assurance that by trusting him, maybe things could be all right.

"I really wasn't charged with anything. Just suspected and questioned," she told him, still hesitating to mention exactly what she'd been suspected of doing. The words embezzlement and theft could immediately shade a person's opinion. She'd learned the hard way that it was far easier to get a person to listen to her if he didn't have a lot of preconceived notions.

"There is an explanation." She hesitated. "I'm just not sure where to start."

He rested the elbow nearest her on his thigh. With his hand dangling in the wide space between his legs, he looked as if he were prepared to give her however long she needed to take.

"Start anywhere you want."

Chapter Four

The evening breeze rustled the bushes at the end of the porch and nudged at the grass and weeds stretching to the road. The quiet babble of the stream that curved the property line sounded softly in the distance. Breathing in the sweet scent of the balmy air, Jenny leaned over the towel still tucked against her and picked up a twig that had jammed itself into the crack of a step.

Start anywhere you want, Greg had said. Thinking of the dream that had led her into her little mess, the only place she could think to start was at the beginning.

"Have you ever wanted something badly?" she asked, focused on the slender twig as she slowly twirled it between her fingers. "I mean so badly that it becomes almost consuming?"

"Absolutely."

His lack of hesitation intrigued as much as it encouraged. She glanced to where he sat beside her, his broad shoulders taking up most of the space. His expression revealed nothing beyond a quiet interest.

"What was it? To become a doctor?"

"No. But we're talking about you," he reminded her. "What is it that you wanted?"

She looked back to her twig. She would have thought the desire to be a doctor would be a passion so great it would eclipse nearly everything else. It seemed it would have to be, for a person to get through all those years of study and training.

"To get out of here. You know how this place is," she said, unable to imagine what else a doctor's dream could have been. Her own had been so simple. "Once a person graduates from high school, you can either go away to college, get married or go to work for your family or someone else's. Most of the jobs that don't require a family connection or a degree are at the quarry or in the shops, and once you start either place that's where you'll be for the rest of your life." Her family hadn't had a business to run. Her dad had worked at the quarry, her mom had been a homemaker, and they hadn't been able to afford college for either her or her sister. "I'd wanted more than to get married at nineteen, the way most of my friends did. Or to work at the diner for the rest of my life wondering what I'd missed."

"That's why you worked so hard to put yourself through school."

Bess had mentioned that just that morning.

She gave a nod, still twirling the little piece of wood. "An associate's degree usually only takes two years, but it took me three because I had to work full-time. As soon as I had it, I headed for Boston. My savings had just about run out when I got a job at Salomon in staff support."

"Staff support?"

"I was a secretary," she clarified. "They don't call secretaries secretaries anymore. At least, not there.

"Anyway," she continued, now shredding away a bit of bark, "four years later, I'd worked my way up to administrative assistant to one of the company's senior VPs. Then, a month ago," she explained, going for the condensed version of her life to that point, "I found myself in the middle of a criminal investigation." A piece of the bark fluttered to the step. "My boyfriend worked at Salomon, too," she said quietly. "It seems that he had been using my computer to transfer rather large sums of other people's money into his own bank accounts."

"That's where the detectives came in," Greg concluded.

"About six of them. Part of them were at the city level. Brent had apparently taken some office equipment home with him, too, so there were theft charges against him along with the federal ones for embezzlement and I can't remember what all else."

The federal investigators had been the most frightening for her to deal with. The city police detectives had backed off on her once they'd realized only Brent had company property and how little of it there was. It had been over three weeks before the federal investigators had let her go, though, and then not until what had seemed like a dozen people had asked her the same hundred questions.

"I hadn't known anything. Nothing," she insisted. "But no one would believe me." The strain clouding her expression slipped into her voice. "I obviously hadn't even known the man I'd dated for over two years." Which was just a few months shy of how long his little scheme had been going on.

She couldn't believe how hurt, foolish and betrayed she felt. The emotions sat like a rock in her chest, making it hard to breathe at times, making every breath she took remind her of how easily she had been taken in. She'd been a kid from the backwoods, easy prey as far as a man like Brent Collier had been concerned. A trusting innocent armed with nothing more than a hunger to experience sophistication and excitement and no experience at all swimming with sharks. But what she felt more than anything else was anger at herself for the naiveté that had allowed her to be charmed by a man who'd wanted nothing but to use her.

"I'd even saved myself until I was twenty-three, waiting for the right man, and he'd just been using me in bed, too."

She gave the stripped twig a toss. It was only when Greg

reached over and handed her another one to peel that she realized she'd spoken her last thought aloud.

The admission brought color to her cheeks—and a look of sympathy from the man beside her.

He had to think her truly pathetic. Wanting badly to mask the depth of how very hurt, used and betrayed she felt, she tried to dismiss the emotional slaughter as inconsequential.

"Do you know what's the real icing on this little cake?" she asked, able to mask everything but her agitation. "The investigators confiscated most of my possessions in case they'd been purchased with any of the illegal funds. They took my furniture, the great little paintings I'd collected at art fairs, and my television. They even took my clock radio," she said, unable to imagine why they'd want something that had only cost $24.95 and would barely fetch five dollars at a flea market. "The only reason I still have my car is because I could prove I'd bought it before I'd met Brent. But you know what's even worse than that? "I can't get a job doing anything that requires references," she fumed into Greg's coaxing silence. "Even if I'd wanted my old job back," which she hadn't, considering how humiliating the whole scenario had been, "I couldn't get it. I was fired. After the dust settled and I called my boss to change my status from having been fired to having quit, he informed me that the firing stood. He said that a person with access to privileged information should be a better judge of character than I was. If I was duped once, it could happen again."

Not in this lifetime, she could have told him. But there had been no convincing way for her to defend his argument. "So now, in addition to being a lousy judge of men," she concluded, "I have no references to get an office job in Boston or anywhere else."

She couldn't even count on character references. Her social circle had also been her professional one, and the people she'd thought were her friends at work had backed way from her as if she'd just contracted Ebola.

From beside her, Greg watched her start to pick at the new

twig he'd given her. He'd halfway expected her to snap it in two when she'd mentioned her possessions having been confiscated. He'd thought she might even toss it as she had the other and start to pace when she explained what had happened to her references. Anger had clipped her tone and touched color to her cheeks. The emotion sounded more than justified, given how cavalierly her affections and reputation had been treated. But he had sensed a wealth of hurt in her, too. And that hurt robbed the energy from her agitation.

"This Brent," he said, thinking she'd been cheated there, too. Anger could be like a protective skin. Stripped of it, there was nothing left to shield the raw and hurting nerves. "What did he do when you were implicated?"

She turned her head toward him. "What do you mean?"

She'd been a babe in the woods, he thought, seeing the injury clouding her lovely blue eyes. Clearly, totally unprepared to be manipulated and exploited by the sophistication she'd so eagerly sought.

He knew all about that soulless kind of greed. He'd grown up with it.

"Did he say you were involved, or did he tell them you didn't know anything?"

Jenny went back to picking at bits of bark. Of everything the louse had done, he at least hadn't tried to drag her down with him. "He told them I was clueless." According to one of the detectives, that had been his exact word, too. Clueless.

"That didn't make them back off sooner?"

"They thought he was protecting me."

From the corner of her eye she saw Greg's mouth thin.

"So, how did he do it?"

By wining and dining me, she thought.

"I had to work late at least one night a week," she told him. "Usually, I stayed to put together folders and charts for a client presentation and set up the conference room for an early meeting. Brent would come in to wait for me before we went to dinner and he'd play solitaire on my computer. At least, that's all I'd thought he was doing."

Absently rubbing his injured shoulder, Greg gave her a considering glance.

"I can see where you felt you had nothing to suspect," he conceded. "The average person wouldn't think someone who supposedly cares is actually conning them."

He eased his hand down.

"So, you came home planning to work at the diner," he concluded, still watching her.

She blinked at his easy acceptance of how completely she'd been taken in.

"Thank you," she murmured.

"For what?"

"For not making it sound as if I lacked basic intelligence because I didn't question what Brent was doing. Everyone else insisted that I must have been at least a little suspicious of his timing. Every night I worked late, he always showed up to take me to dinner."

"What did you think of that?"

"I just thought he was being thoughtful."

Her response didn't surprise him. "And the rest of your plans?"

"My only plans now are to work. I have to pay off my attorney," she replied, mentally cringing at the size of the bill hanging over her head. Ten thousand dollars Brent had cost her. "I won't be able to save a penny before then. Dora could only hire me part-time. Dinner shift Thursday through Sunday. The diner closes at eight, so I thought after work there, I'd see if I can pick up weekend shifts out at The Dig Inn."

The Dig, as everyone knew it, was a tavern near the stone quarry twenty minutes west of Maple Mountain. The idea of working there had occurred to her on her drive home from Greg's office and seemed as good a way as any to add to her meager coffers.

"Once I'm out of debt, I'll probably leave again. With my family moved away, there really isn't anything for me here."

The energy had leaked from her tone. Feeling as if it had just seeped out of her body, too, she offered an apologetic smile.

"I'm sorry. I didn't mean to dump all of that on you."

Especially the part about having given up her prized virginity to the louse, she thought. Once she'd started, though, the pressure of all she'd held in had simply given way. The man whose presence seemed as supportive as it did compelling had allowed a crack in the dam and everything had flooded out. But then, he was a doctor. It was his job to get people to open up and tell him where it hurt.

The golden glow of early evening had left the air. With the sun no longer burnishing the tree tops on the hill, the light had turned the pale gray of dusk that muted their surroundings and had critters rustling leaves as they settled in for the evening.

In that pale light, Jenny saw a vehicle coming around the curve in the road. She'd actually heard it first and glanced up as the tan Jeep with the big push-bar in front and police lights on top sailed by on its way into town.

It was Joe. Seeing them sitting on the porch step, he stuck his arm out his open window and waved.

Jenny and Greg both waved back.

"Anyway," she murmured, thinking she should probably just shut up about her past now. "Things can only go uphill from here. I'm having better luck already."

Pure skepticism slashed Greg's brow. "How do you figure?"

"By living in my grandma's old house, I don't have to pay rent."

The way he glanced toward the house made her think he questioned her definition of *better*. "What about your family? What do they think of you living without electricity or a phone? Or decent plumbing."

"The plumbing works well enough." She could even take baths, now that she'd scrubbed out the old claw-foot tub in the bathroom. All she had to do was boil water on the woodstove, add it to the cold water she'd drawn and save out enough warm water to rinse her hair. The process had worked just fine last night. Even if it had taken forever.

"I'll get to the rest. Eventually," she qualified. "Mom's happy I'm fixing up the place." Which was something she would eventually do, too. "I didn't tell her what happened. All I said was that I was moving back because things didn't work out."

Her mom had been relieved by that. Audibly so. She had never liked the idea of Jenny living alone in the city.

"My sister and her family have problems of their own," she confided, explaining why turning to them had not been an option. Their home and their lives had been crowded even before her mom had moved in with them. "I got myself into this mess. I'll get myself out of it."

The breeze ruffled her hair as she tipped back her head and took a long deep breath.

Greg promptly dragged his glance from the curve of her dark lashes against her cheek and the soft-looking line of her throat.

He didn't know too many people who would acknowledge anything positive about her present situation. Everything she'd worked for was gone. Her sense of trust was shot. And she was alone in a house that would depress most people just to look at. After what she'd said about having to pay off her attorney, he strongly suspected she was low on funds, too. Or, at least, being very frugal with whatever she had left.

Yet, instead of sitting around feeling sorry for herself, she already had her old job back and wanted to get a part-time job to back up that one. She'd even taken a stab at brightening her surroundings. He didn't know where she'd gotten them. From alongside the house perhaps, where he'd noticed other flowers struggling to survive through the weeds. But she'd planted two bright yellow mums in old pots and set them on either side of her front door.

He wondered if she felt an affinity for the small, stunted blooms. Over the seasons, rains had beaten them down, weeds had choked them, they'd gone other times without water and the winters had frozen them. Yet, they'd managed to survive.

She was clearly a survivor herself. He didn't doubt that her plan for herself would somehow work out. He just didn't like the idea of her working out at The Dig. It could get crazy out there on Saturday nights.

The odd surge of protectiveness he felt at that thought caught him off guard. He could admit to being drawn by her refusal to be defeated. He could admire her bright optimism. He could feel a sense of relief for her that her gullibility hadn't bought her even bigger problems. But feeling protective felt a little too…personal.

He'd come to appease Bess—and his own curiosity. Since it sounded as if the worst was behind her, he needed to focus on practicalities.

He needed an office manager. She needed a better job. Knowing she had a means to fix the roof over her head would just be an added bonus.

"Okay," he said flatly. "So you weren't charged with embezzlement, theft and…"

"Collusion," she supplied, now that she'd explained.

"Of course." He gave a nod. She really had been naive, and far too trusting for her own good. Had inexperience been a crime, she'd be as guilty as sin. "So the job is yours if you want it," he continued, thinking there was still a certain quiet innocence about her. "The clinic is funded by grants as well as the community, so the pay is a lot better than you'll get at the diner. You won't have to spend your weekends in a smoky tavern, either."

Or make that drive late at night and come back to this place, he thought, only to cut off the concern in his thoughts. He'd heard of people who'd moved into similar structural nightmares simply for the experience of renovating them. Though part of him insisted she needed a keeper, a more self-protective part insisted that she would be fine.

"Being office manager of the clinic will also give you something to put on your résumé for when you do leave again."

Some of the constant anxiety haunting Jenny eased. She desperately needed the redeeming reference the job would bring. She wanted badly to pay off her attorney so she wouldn't have that monthly reminder of how gullible she'd been. Yet at that moment what felt even more important than the opportunity Greg offered was that he believed her.

"Thank you." She practically sighed the word. "I'd love the job."

The tiny lines fanning from the corners of his eyes deepened with his smile "Good."

She smiled back, feeling better than she'd felt in a month.

What Greg felt wasn't so easy to define. Caught by the light in her eyes, he was aware of its warmth easing through him. He liked her smile. He liked that he'd been able to cause it.

"So," he said, reluctant to move.

"So," she murmured back, tempted to hug him.

He needed to go. With her so close, looking so grateful, the temptation to touch her grew with each breath he drew. All he had to do was reach over and he could nudge back her hair just to see if those shining wisps felt as soft as they looked. He knew her skin felt like velvet. Her hands, anyway. He remembered the feel of them on his bare chest, his back, and the softness of her palm against his cheek.

He knew the slenderness of her waist.

The thought that he could probably span it with both hands occurred to him even as he jerked his thoughts from that unwanted place. Reaching for his sore arm as he leaned forward, he rose with a surge of lean muscle and turned to face her.

She had just started to stand herself when he held out his hand.

Setting aside the towel he'd returned, she slipped her slender fingers over his broad palm.

"I'll see you in the morning," he said, pulling her up. "You'll need to pick up all you can from Rhonda before she goes. Bess knows her stuff when it comes to medicine, but her eyes glaze over at insurance forms and computers."

His glance fell to their hands. Slowly, consciously, he pulled his back and pushed it into the pocket of his pants.

His heat still burned her palm when she curled her fingers over it. "What time?"

"Rhonda gets there at eight-thirty."

She said she would be there. A heartbeat later his glance skimmed her face, a muscle in his jaw jerked, and he told her he'd see her then.

It seemed he still didn't quite know what to make of her. At least, that was the impression Jenny had in the moments before he headed for his truck and pulled out of the drive. But she didn't worry about it. She was too busy feeling grateful and relieved that she wouldn't have to work at The Dig. As the last of the day's remaining light waned and she turned to face her cheerless house, she wondered, though, if she should have mentioned that she had no intention of giving up her job at the diner.

"I swear that man is getting more uptight by the minute."

At Bess's muttering, Jenny looked up from where Rhonda had spread grant forms over the worktable between the computer desk and the wall of filing cabinets. She had spent the morning being familiarized with no fewer than a dozen different insurance forms, Medicare forms, state assistance forms and forms to request more forms. They hadn't gotten around to the online forms yet, but Rhonda had insisted that the grant forms were more important.

"Andy Kohl?" Jenny asked, thinking Bess must be referring to the patient who'd just left. She didn't know much about the youngest of the Kohl brothers, other than that he worked as a mechanic at the quarry where he'd just put a nasty slice in his index finger.

"I mean Dr. Reid. He just left for lunch," she muttered.

Jenny had no idea what Bess was talking about. She'd seen Greg less than five minutes ago and he'd seemed the same to her as he had all morning. The same as since she'd met him.

"Maybe his shoulder is bothering him," she suggested, thinking that could easily be the reason for the faint edge she sometimes sensed in him herself.

"It's not just his shoulder. He's been like this for weeks. I think the only time he relaxes anymore is when he's coaching T-ball or playing checkers with Amos."

Jenny had no trouble at all picturing him coaching little kids. A guy who wore duck socks would do that sort of thing. She just couldn't quite picture him sitting around a checkerboard the way the cantankerous old men did at the general store. "He plays checkers?"

"Not really," Rhonda confided, her voice low despite the fact that the three of them were the only ones there at the moment. "He and Amos just call it that. Everybody knows he's really teaching Amos to read."

"He's been going to his house every Tuesday night for the past six months." Light bounced off her reading glasses as Bess lifted them from where they dangled on their neck chain. Slipping them on, she sat down at the desk with her chart and picked up a pen. "Amos was never able to help his kids with their reading or their homework. He wants to be able to read to his grandchildren.

"I gave Andy Kohl a tetanus shot," she continued, segueing easily from Greg's not-so-secret kindness. "The doctor put in eight stitches and wants him back in a week. Andy was in too much of a hurry to get back to work to make an appointment now. So, Jenny, you might want to call his wife in a couple of days if he hasn't called himself to set up an appointment."

After adding those notes to the file, she tossed it on top of two others in the in-box and swiveled in her chair. "How are we doing with the grant renewal?"

"I was just starting to explain what all we need to apply for it." Rhonda lumbered toward the computer. Grabbing the back of the chair in front of it, she turned with all the grace her beach-ball belly would allow and lowered herself into it. "A lot of what you'll need is right here," she said, her fingers flying over the keyboard. "Budget. Expenses by quarter. A summary of scope of treatment. Population demographics. The deadline for this is the fifteenth of next month, but we want it in early. We just got another doctor through the Rural Health Corp and all we need for the contract with him to be final is to prove we can maintain our funding to pay him and keep the clinic running."

"It's not easy getting a doctor here," Bess explained at Jenny's quick frown of incomprehension. "Most of them are already in an established practice. The ones coming out of school want to stay near cities. Dr. Wilson stayed on way past the time he should have been practicing, and I can't practice unless I'm working for a physician. We were starting to panic around here before we finally got Dr. Reid a couple of years ago. I know he talked up the place to Dr…. What's his name again, Rhonda?'

"Cochran."

"Dr. Cochran," Bess continued. "He must have, to get the guy to take the job so quickly. He's sort of a quiet man. Young wife. Two children. Dr. Cochran, I mean."

An impending sense of disappointment battled Jenny's incomprehension. "I don't understand. Why are you getting another doctor?"

"Because Dr. Reid is leaving in four months," replied Rhonda.

"Three months and twenty-seven days," Bess corrected, looking none too pleased by that.

"I thought he'd taken over the practice."

"He did. But his contract is expiring." The older woman held up her hands as if to ask what a person could do. "He came to us through the same program we're getting the new one through. It helps doctors pay off their medical school loans in return for service in medically underserved parts of the country. He's leaving the middle of December to return to Cambridge." A frown deepened the wrinkles in her forehead. "He's joining the family clinic where his girlfriend practices."

"She's a pediatrician," Rhonda dutifully supplied, printing out the file she'd pulled up. "Doctor Elizabeth Brandt. We've only seen her once, but she seems all right…for a city woman."

Considering how most locals truly felt about people from the city, with their often self-important ways and their tendency to regard those in Maple Mountain as "quaint," Rhonda's comment was practically praise.

Bess wasn't quite so forthcoming. The woman who had helped deliver most of the population under the age of twenty-five said only, "She's pleasant enough, I suppose."

Pushing her ponytail back over her shoulder, Rhonda waited by the ancient printer. A geriatric tortoise moved faster than the page inching its way toward the tray.

"Do you think that's what's wrong with him lately?" she ventured. "That he just has a lot on his mind with moving and all? He gets a lot of those big envelopes from that law office," she mentioned, crossing her arms high over the bulge beneath her scrub smock. Her prepregnancy work uniforms were folded in a sack under the desk for Jenny to borrow. Jenny would swim in the bottoms, but she could wear the scrub jackets over her slacks and tops until she could order her own. "I bet he's working out details of his new partnership. He has a lot to tie up here, too.

"On top of that," Rhonda continued, all but tapping her foot at the lumbering printer, "he's probably getting anxious to spend more time with his girlfriend. I don't think he sees her but once a month, and lack of sex does tend to make a man cranky."

At Rhonda's unexpected conclusion, Jenny stifled a startled smile.

Bess gave her co-worker a look of benign reproach. She looked as if she might well agree. She just didn't think the conversation appropriate. At least not on their new co-worker's first day on the job.

"The doctor's love life is his business, Rhonda. But you're probably right about the rest of it. I hadn't given any thought to what might be on his mind the past few months. I don't tend to think about much beyond what needs to be done around here and at home."

What needed to be done at the moment was for her to gather the files she would need for her rural rounds that afternoon. Several of the patients the clinic served in the villages and communities around Maple Mountain were elderly and housebound and needed ongoing care, along with a little socializing to make sure their basic needs were being met. Bess's day for those rounds was Tuesday. The doctor, as Bess always referred to Greg, had rural rounds on Thursday—which was important for Jenny to know so she wouldn't schedule clinic appointments for him then. On Friday the clinic closed at two.

Jenny did her best to pay attention, to absorb all she could as quickly as possible from the two women inundating her with information—especially since Rhonda was staying through her lunch hour when she looked like what she really needed was to put up her swelling feet and rest. Or, better still, have her baby. She had confided to Jenny that she'd only planned to take six weeks off, had wanted six months, but now that Jenny was there, would love to stay home for a year.

Jenny had assured her that a year would be no problem. Yet, beneath her relief over having a year's worth of full-time employment, her growing list of questions about procedures and her politely masked dismay at the office's antiquated equipment, she felt strangely let down.

Logically she knew that the concern Greg had shown for her when he'd thought she might be in trouble didn't mean anything special to him. After all, helping people was what he did. Bess had even said so. But it had meant a lot to her. The way he'd put her at ease right off this morning had meant a lot to her, too. She'd been in the break room where Rhonda had been showing her where to find coffee supplies when he'd come in and asked her to please always make the first pot extra strong.

"Think double espresso," he'd said, smiling as if he knew she would be familiar with what the traditionalists in Maple Mountain either hadn't heard of, or called coffee "with muscles." He'd then added that it was in everyone's best interests that he be conscious and coherent when the first patient arrived.

She wasn't surprised that he was leaving. As little as she'd thought there was for her in Maple Mountain, she was sure that a man of his education and experience would find far less. He'd gone to Harvard. He'd been to Paris. His significant other was a Cambridge pediatrician. From what Bess had said, it sounded as if he might even be from Cambridge himself. Of course he'd go back.

It never occurred to her to question her conclusion. Within two days, however, she began to question Rhonda's diagnosis about the restiveness she was beginning to see in him herself.

The clinic stayed comfortably busy. Since school would start in a few weeks, a steady stream of five- to seventeen-year-olds showed up for immunizations, which Bess took, and athletic exams, which Greg did. The schedule was full of more of the same for the rest of the week and most of the next. In between were the occasional tourist complaints of mosquito bites, stomach upsets, a couple of bad sunburns and an allergic reaction to the berries someone had gathered out by the old grist mill.

As busy as she was herself, she saw little of Greg other than to hand him his next patient's file, and the only time she saw him alone was if he happened to be in his office when she took in his mail or picked up the dictation tapes from his out-box. His only comments to her were "Thanks" and to ask how the training was coming. She told him that if Rhonda's baby could hang on for another day or two, she'd be fine. The archaic systems were slow but basic.

He told her she could use his laptop computer if it would help.

If he was interested in anything else about her, he gave no indication at all. He was clearly preoccupied with his patients, which she would expect any good doctor to be. At least, that was what she chalked his preoccupation up to until the next morning when she walked in with his next patient's chart and found him standing at his desk.

He was staring at his laptop opened to e-mail. His jaw seemed to be locked tight enough to shatter his teeth before he disgustedly closed whatever he'd been reading and looked up.

Suddenly cautious, she set the file on his desk. "Toby Mc-Neff is in exam room two. Do you want me to tell him you'll be a few minutes?"

"No. No," he repeated, visibly dismissing whatever it was that had so agitated his thoughts. Ignoring the question in her eyes, he took a deep breath and reached for the file. "He's waited all summer to see if his knee has healed enough to play football. There's no need to make him wait any longer."

The same tension she'd seen in him that morning resurrected itself a few hours later when she walked in with the day's mail. She'd stacked the tests results and correspondence she'd clipped to the appropriate files atop a thick manila envelope from the Boston law firm of Brawly, Cohen and Schmidt. Because of what Rhonda had concluded, Jenny thought the bulkier piece of mail might have something to do with his new partnership, so she'd turned it to make the return address label visible in his in-box.

The moment he noticed it, a muscle in his jaw jerked. After letting his jaw work for a moment, he visibly checked his odd reaction, thanked her and dropped the envelope, unopened, into his bottom desk drawer.

She had no chance then to wonder what was going on with him. The phone, which had been busy all day, started ringing out front. Since Rhonda was in the bathroom again, Jenny had to hurry to answer it.

She had plenty of time to speculate that evening, though, as she scrubbed the walls and cabinets in her kitchen while the woodstove overheated the room and took its time heating the water for her bath. She'd been a morning shower person, but the ability to adapt had become a necessity.

She knew good stress from bad stress. She knew that even good stress could make a person feel pressured and snappish. But good stress was underlayered with anticipation and a certain eagerness.

There was no anticipation in Greg.

She didn't know what he'd been like before she'd met him, but she now understood what Bess had meant about him getting more uptight every day. She didn't doubt for a moment that something was disturbing him. But she'd be willing to bet the only possessions she had left, that it was something more deep-seated than missing his girlfriend or lack of sex.

Her last thought brought a too-vivid mental image of his rock-hard chest. He had a beautiful body. A very compelling, very male and amazingly powerful body. A woman would feel very protected in such strong arms.

There were some things she really wished she didn't know about him.

With a sigh, she dropped her brush into the bucket of water and disinfectant. Turning her back to the cabinet she'd just washed, she sagged against the wall and slowly slid to the floor. She had to wash the cabinets before she could paint them, but before she could finish washing them she needed sleep. As she had for weeks, she felt tired to the bone and wished for nothing more than for her mind to go blank.

She glanced around the room, taking in her little makeshift bed in the corner and the boxes that served as her dresser. She didn't want to think about all she had to do to make the place livable. She didn't want to think about a man she had no business feeling so drawn to. More than anything else just then, she didn't want to think about how disappointed she felt knowing he was leaving.

She thought about all of it, anyway. Alone, she had only her thoughts for company. It was easier to distract herself during the day when there were others around.

It was easiest of all at the diner. Working there after finishing at the clinic the next afternoon, she just hadn't considered that Greg would be there, too.

Chapter Five

Dora's Diner occupied an old dormered house on Main street a block up from the clinic. Dora Schaeffer, a widow for nearly twenty years, had converted the downstairs into a welcoming space of maple tables and chairs and shelves displaying local artists' pottery. At the back of the wainscoted room, a display case of cookies and the best pies in town angled the long counter where Greg often had coffee and Dora's incredible pancakes on weekend mornings. The place could comfortably seat twenty, often held thirty and was the best place around for coffee and conversation.

The din of conversation greeted Greg even before he pulled open the green screen door, pushed open the blue door behind it and breathed in the smell of good old-fashioned home cooking. It was home cooking as far as people in the area were concerned, anyway. Where he'd grown up, meals prepared by his father's chef had come in courses on imported china or were served to him in the kitchen with the staff.

He didn't feel much like visiting tonight. His shoulder still ached. He'd just spent ten hours making a hundred-mile round of house calls which would have been far easier had he not had his arm in a sling. He still had dictation on those rounds to do tonight. And he was starving. But cooking for himself was a task that bordered between awkward and downright dangerous with the use of only one hand.

He figured he'd get takeout from Dora and eat at home while he went through the day's files. At least, that was his plan as he nodded to the couple nodding at him from the middle of the room and lifted his hand to the half-dozen other people he recognized. Most of the diners tonight seemed to be strangers escaping the city for a long weekend and eating at the only place in town that served something other than hamburgers.

Dora waved at him through the service window over the counter. She wore her silver-streaked blond braids the same way she had for years, woven into a tight figure eight at the back of her head. Her cheeks were rosy from heat. Her green eyes sparkled with good humor, and her ample body spoke of a certain appreciation of her own cooking.

It was Jenny who held most of his attention, however.

She had her focus on the two heaped plates she carried to a table by the counter. The last time he'd seen her, a blue scrub smock had mercifully camouflaged the soft curves of her breasts, her small waist, the gentle roundness of her hips. Now, she wore a white apron over a white blouse and black skirt that accentuated everything soft and feminine about her. The skirt was plain, knee-length and very similar to the ones Lorna Bagley and her sister wore when they worked for Doris, only the style did a whole lot more for her legs than the style did for the Bagley girls. Maybe it was because he could see how shapely they were. Or, maybe, he thought, as his glance skimmed her slender frame, he just seemed to notice more about her than he should.

Thinking about her body never seemed wise to him. Thinking about it while surrounded by people who might wonder why he was watching her so closely didn't seem terribly smart, either.

He hadn't expected to see her working there.

Charlie Moorehouse turned from the table beside where he'd stopped. "Say, Doc. How's the truck runnin'?"

"It's doing just great, Charlie. I couldn't have made rounds today without it. Thanks again."

The older man gave a thoughtful nod. "You let me know if it gives you any trouble. Hear?" His silver hair had spiked up in back when he'd pulled off his cap. The spike swayed as he nodded again. "I know it's darn near new, but they don't make things the way they used to."

As far as Charlie and his cronies were concerned, there hadn't been a decent car made since 1955. His white-haired wife adjusted her bifocals as she smiled in benign agreement.

"I'll do that." The table for two behind Charlie and his wife was vacant. Deciding he could order takeout just as easily from there, he pulled out the chair, more conscious than he wanted to be of the woman setting down plates in front of a couple he didn't recognize.

"How's the tree thinning going out at the Larkin place?" he asked Charlie.

"'Bout done," the older man replied. "Say," he said again.

He poked his fork toward Jenny as she looked up to see who had just come in. The moment she saw him, she hesitated and smiled.

"Jenny over there. Didn't I hear she's workin' for you?"

Over the clatter of silverware and muffled conversations, Jenny heard the retired maple farmer's friendly question. She just didn't hear Greg's response as she turned her attention back to her customers and asked if she could get them anything else. She hadn't yet mentioned to Greg that she intended to keep her job there. She had meant to. There just hadn't been time the past couple of days. There hadn't been time that morning, either. He'd been in the clinic only long enough to collect the files and supplies he needed for the rural rounds that had taken him all day.

Taking a second job had been grounds for dismissal at the brokerage. The huge company wanted nothing less than 110 percent of their employees' loyalty, and outside employment was regarded as squandering energy the company could use. When Greg had offered her the position at the clinic, he'd made a point of mentioning that by taking it, she wouldn't have to work at The Dig or the diner.

He hadn't given her the sense that he employed the Machiavellian method of business management, but she didn't know him all that well, either. Even if he hadn't held her best employment prospects in his very capable hands, he knew far too much about her to not have him on her good side.

Pulling an order pad from the pocket of her apron, she skimmed a smile past her old third-grade teacher and headed toward her new boss.

"How did your rounds go?" she asked, stopping beside to his table.

She'd taken to wearing a much smaller bandage than the one Bess had first applied. The edge of white was barely visible beneath her cap of shining dark hair, and the little bruises along her jaw were hardly noticeable at all under the makeup she'd dabbed over them. He noticed both, anyway. Mostly he noticed her expression.

It looked a little uneasy.

"Good," he replied, more aware of that uncertainty than the restlessness that had accompanied him inside. "How were things at the clinic?"

"Good," she echoed. "Rhonda and Bess both thought it was kind of quiet."

"Rhonda still hasn't gone into labor?"

"She hadn't as of five o'clock."

"So, what time did you start here?"

He'd asked merely out of curiosity. Yet, the way her glance quickly faltered made her look even more uncertain.

"Five-fifteen," she quietly said, lining up the salt-and-pepper shakers with the napkin holder on the table. With her back to the rest of the room, she caught his eye, her expression part plea, part promise as her voice dropped. "I can do both jobs," she all but whispered. "Honest."

Greg felt himself frown. It seemed she was afraid he would disagree. It seemed equally clear that she felt concerned about saying anything that might draw attention. *Can we talk later?* she seemed to silently beg.

He truly hadn't expected to see her there, but that didn't mean he was surprised by what she was doing. The sooner she could pay off the debt to her lawyer, the sooner she could put the past behind her. The diner just wasn't the place to tell her that no one knew better than he did how the need to be free of an obligation could weigh on a person.

All she'd been through was wearing on her, too. He could see it. The faint circles beneath her eyes were new.

There was no need to talk later. He could put her mind at ease now.

"I take it the house needs more work than you thought?" he asked. He knew from Bess that Jenny was scrubbing walls in the evenings. He also knew her house was the perfect reason for everyone else to think she'd taken the extra job. Anyone who'd seen the place would know fixing it would cost a fortune.

Caution slipped into her eyes. "Much more."

"Are you going to replace those steps?"

"I'm...as soon as I can."

"What about that sagging roof?"

"Definitely. At least the sagging part," she amended, caution giving way to relief. He was not only telling her he had no objection to what she was doing, he was providing the perfect excuse for her to be moonlighting. "But first I need the wiring checked so I can get the power on."

Charlie wiped his mouth with his napkin as he leaned his head toward her. "Talk to Amos Calder's boy about that," he suggested. "He's an electrician by trade. He's over in West Pond."

"Or, Edna Farber's son-in-law," his wife piped in ever so helpfully. "He's looking to buy him a new tractor."

"Old one blew pulling out a stump," Charlie explained.

"He can use the work," Mrs. Moorehouse continued. "Best get on it soon, though, dear. It's only a month now before the rains set in. Month after that, could be snow."

Charlie seemed to think the Calder boy, who was actually a man of forty, would be the better choice. He told Jenny that, too, before he returned to his plate of fried chicken with Jenny thanking him for his advice.

In Maple Mountain, there was no such thing as a private conversation in public. Not when the people around knew you and felt they could help.

The phenomenon had seemed terribly intrusive to Greg when he'd first arrived. But then, when he'd first arrived, everything about this town had been foreign. With their set ways and reluctance to change, the people had seemed as different to him as he was to them and it had been a while before they'd figured each other out.

He hadn't been accepted easily. Especially by the older folk like Charlie. Charlie hadn't trusted anything about him, including his "newfangled" methods of treatment. At least, not until his last bout of gout had driven him to desperation and Charlie discovered that the new doc's methods had cut the time of the flare-up in half. The fact that Greg had incorporated some of Dr. Wilson's older methods to ease Charlie's mind had helped, too— and surprised the heck out of Greg when he'd discovered that the combination worked even better than the modern way alone.

He sat back in his chair, looked up at the fragile lines of Jenny's face. Now he accepted friendly interference as nothing but the sign of a caring neighbor. "I'd listen to Charlie," he admitted. "He's never steered me wrong."

Silverware clanked against a plate as a toddler decided to turn the dishware into a drum. His young mother snatched the spoon away while his dad handed the child his milk to thwart an outburst.

At the table ahead of them, two older men were discussing the pros and cons of running lines to tanks to collect maple sap for syrup and the old-fashioned method of hanging buckets from taps.

"So." Pulling his glance from the vee of creamy skin exposed by her blouse, Greg glanced at the chalkboard by the kitchen where the daily menu was written. As long as he was sitting there, he might as well stay and eat. "What do you recommend tonight?"

The grateful smile in her eyes made its way to her mouth. She recommended the meat loaf, since the chicken and dumplings were gone. He would have asked her recommendation for dessert, too, just to keep her there a moment longer, but the toddler decided that pouring his milk on the floor made rather interesting patterns when it splashed.

Within seconds of the mom's horrified gasp, Jenny promised she'd get his dinner right to him, tossed a sympathetic glance at the mom and grabbed the spare napkin from his table to wipe up the mess on the floor.

Chair legs scraped as a party of four rose to leave.

Jenny thanked them for coming and cleared away their dessert plates on her way to the kitchen.

Nothing about her gave the impression that she was hustling. She moved with an almost gracious ease that made those around her as comfortable as she made his patients in the office. But then, he told himself, she knew many of these people, just as she'd known nearly everyone who'd come to clinic the past few days. It was only natural that her manner around them would seem so effortless.

He didn't question why it seemed necessary to excuse anything he found special about her. He just told himself that what she did away from the clinic really was none of his concern. She did need to get out of debt. And heaven knew she could use electricity and a roof that didn't leak. As long as her evening job didn't interfere with her day job, she was free to do whatever she wanted.

The side benefit to him was that he'd feel a lot better about where she was living once she had power and a decent roof over her head.

The gratitude Jenny felt toward Greg was growing to embarrassing proportions. Afraid she might be making too much of what he'd so thoughtfully done for her last night, she didn't know if she should thank him for being so understanding about the second job or just let it go. There was no time to indulge the minor dilemma when she arrived at the office the next morning, though. Rhonda had finally gone into labor.

Many of the babies born in and around Maple Mountain were delivered at home, or in the single hospital-like room in the back of the clinic. Women with expected complications were sent to the hospital in St. Johnsbury at the first sign of labor, provided it wasn't the dead of winter and the roads weren't closed.

Fortunately, over the years such crises had been rare. The women in the north country were healthy stock. So were their offspring.

Rhonda was no exception. She would have her baby at home, in the sleigh bed she'd inherited from her maternal grandmother just as she'd had her others. She had called in before nine to put Bess on alert, since Bess doubled as a midwife. Between panting breaths she'd also reminded Jenny to order more toner for the copy machine so it could be on the Thursday UPS truck. As small and rural as they were, they only received deliveries every other day.

Jenny had promised that she would, told her to call if she needed *anything,* wished her good luck and prayed for a little luck herself.

Jenny couldn't remember who had mentioned the phenomenon, Rhonda or Bess. But illness and accidents tended to come in waves for the clinic. During the lulls it wasn't unusual to have no patients at all. If someone came in, it was just to say hello because they were passing by.

Today wasn't one of those days. Seven back-to-school appointments were scheduled along with two follow-up appointments. Joanna McNeff, Sally's mom, was in for blood tests. She was next after a three-year-old who'd awakened with a fever and a sore throat who already in with Greg. Bess, on standby for Rhonda, had started the first of the immunizations so that left Jenny to make sure everything out front ran smoothly.

She suffered only minor glitches until Bess left at four because Rhonda's pains were two minutes apart and the dispatcher from the sheriff's office called to say that Joe had just called in.

"Hey, Jenny. Heard you were back," came Lois Neely's laconic greeting. "Listen, there's a bad accident at the quarry. A couple of kids were at the swimming hole diving off the cliff. Joe said they're not locals," she relayed, since everyone's first concern would be who had been hurt. "Said he didn't recognize either of 'em. The one boy dove in after his friend and pulled him out, but the first one's not conscious. Sounds like he's broken himself some bones, too. The one who did the rescuing hit his arm on the way down and is bleeding all over the place. He managed to get to the road, and flagged down a couple from North Stratford. They called Joe."

Jenny's first thought was that Lois needed to hang up and call 911. Her second thought was that Lois was the local equivalent of emergency response, and it was now apparently up to Jenny to get the victims help.

No one had explained this part of the job. "I'll call for an ambulance," she said, hurriedly searching the lists and sticky notes of phone numbers taped to the shelf above the desk.

"I already did that," came the amazingly calm reply. "It'll be an hour and half before they can get there. Joe needs the doc."

Of course he did, she thought. "I'll tell him. They're at the quarry swimming hole?"

"Down by where they closed off the road so the kids wouldn't go down it."

"Got it," she replied, and hung up to hear two sets of footsteps in the hallway. One heavy and even, the other muffled and clipped.

"Set Mrs. Buell for a follow up next week, will you, Jenny?" Greg asked when he appeared at the front office doorway. "She'll need instructions for a fasting-blood sugar test, too."

His eyes met hers. An instant later his eyebrows merged.

Bertie was frowning at her, too. But the head of the community women's league always looked as if she'd been sucking the fruit for the lemon pies she took to every function.

"I'm sorry," Jenny said, aware that her expression must have caused theirs. Worry was something she never could hide well. "There's been an accident," she said to Greg. "Joe needs you as soon as you can get there."

Bertie's narrow features pinched. "Who's been hurt?"

Jenny told them both they weren't locals, her attention on Greg as she then told him everything the dispatcher had relayed to her.

His glance cut to the waiting room. His last two appointments of the day were coloring on the little table in the corner.

"Tell their moms you'll call tomorrow and reschedule. "I'll get what we'll need while you explain that we have an emergency. You'll have to help me with the backboard," he told her, patting Bertie on her thin arm as if to apologize for cutting her short. "We'll leave as soon you lock up."

"We?" Jenny called, as he disappeared.

"I've only got one hand," he called back. "Bess isn't here. You're going to have to be my other."

The road to the quarry was narrow, winding and for much of the way had no shoulder. In winter the road could be positively treacherous. In summer, the drive was lovely, if not slow.

It took twenty minutes to get to the turnoff that led to the swimming hole. It took a few more to bounce down the abandoned road of crushed gray granite.

This end of the quarry hadn't been mined since the eighties and the trees and vegetation had grown back along the top. Below, the gaping hole had filled with snow melt and rainwater.

The appeal for the kids was in the near wall where staggered blocks of uncut granite allowed perches of various heights for the brave and the brainless to plunge into that cold, crystalline pool.

Every year, a new barrier or barricade went up.

Every year, kids managed to find a way over or around it.

"Hey, Doc! Over here!"

Joe's voice rang out from below them, echoing off the stone walls as Greg grabbed his bag. Snatching up a paper sack he had filled with supplies, Jenny scrambled after him, heading to where Joe had stepped from behind a boulder.

"Man, am I glad to see you." Looking apprehensive, the beefy deputy sheriff motioned to the two boys on the ground.

Both looked to be somewhere around seventeen. Both had the olive-green wool blankets Joe had taken from his Jeep draped over them. The blond one propped against the boulder held a blood soaked T-shirt to his arm and looked scared to death. Seeing the one lying a yard from his soaked athletic shoes, Jenny could understand why.

The only color about the youth was his pale red eyebrows and the mat of red hair sticking to his head. His lips and skin were as pale as milk. It was the unnatural angle of his legs that had her going still, though. There was no question that they were broken.

Greg had already crouched beside the boy's head. His fingers moved deftly to the side of his neck before he lifted one eyelid with his thumb. He'd just checked the other when he pulled back the blanket.

His remarkably unreadable expression didn't change by so much as a blink as he noted the awkward position of the legs, quickly probed the boy's belly, then looked to the young man watching anxiously from the rock.

"Did he go in head first, or feet?"

"Feet."

"Did you see him hit the water?"

The boy gave a quick nod. "He looked fine going in." He swallowed. "He just didn't come up right away. When he did, he was floating."

"How about you? What hurts?"

"Just my arm."

"Joe," Greg said, his tone amazingly calm. "We're going to need the backboard from the truck. Jenny, I need you over here. Kneel at the top of his head." He looked back to the boy sitting as still as the stone holding him up. "What's your name?"

"Brady."

"And your friend?"

"Jake." His voice cracked. "Is he going to be all right?"

"Well, Brady," he said, reaching into the bag of supplies Jenny set beside him. "Your friend is lucky to be alive right now. It's good you were a strong enough swimmer to get him out."

Jenny saw Greg's lips tighten as he turned his full attention to the lean young body before him. It seemed that he wasn't a man to give false hope. Or, to beat a person when he was down. What the kids had done was foolish. But Brady was clearly afraid his friend was going to die. Short of being able to assure him that he wouldn't, Greg had focused on the only positive aspect he could find.

His deep voice dropped as, wincing, he wedged the cervical collar under his sling and opened it with his free hand. "I need for you to grasp his head in your hands so we can get this on him. Gently," he emphasized, catching her glance to make sure she understood. "I'm going to keep my hand on the back of his neck so I can feel what's going on. If I tell you to stop, stop right then and just hold it where it is. Okay?"

She didn't want to do this. It wasn't that she didn't want to help. She just didn't want to do further damage. The boy's neck could be broken. "Greg, I'm not trained—"

"We can't wait for more help. If this kid's going to make it, we have to meet the ambulance. You did great helping me before. Don't let me down now."

Don't let him down.

"You can do this, Jenny."

Dear heaven, she thought. She had no confidence for risks anymore. No desire at all to venture beyond her comfort zone. But as she looked from the conviction, or maybe it was determination, in his eyes, she figured she didn't have to have any. She'd just borrow the confidence he seemed to have in her.

Without another word, she positioned her hands on either side of the young man's smooth face. His skin felt cold against her palms.

She was just as conscious of the warmth of Greg's hand on hers when he positioned her fingers under the boy's jaw and checked his neck.

Jenny didn't release her breath until the boy's neck and head were supported by the wide, stiff collar. Even then, there was no time to feel relief. She acted as Greg's other hand, following his quick and clipped directions so he could start an IV in the boy's arm. She held vials of drugs so he could fill the syringes, then held the IV port steady so he could administer the life-preserving medications.

Hearing Joe return with the board, still working on his patient, Greg asked the deputy to radio the ambulance, find out where they were on their route and tell the driver they would be meeting him. Enlisting Brady, he had him hold the IV bag high above his friend's arm, then motioned her with him to where he checked over the boy's legs.

Greg's expression was grim. One of young Jake's knees jutted at an odd angle. Midway down the other calf, broken bone protruded. Mercifully, it hadn't broken the skin enough for bleeding to be profuse, but the bleeding Greg worried about was on the inside. The kid had hit rocks beneath the surface of the water.

With Jenny kneeling across from him, Greg carefully eased the first leg straight.

"Breathe, Jenny," he said, fearing she was holding her breath again. "I can't afford to have you pass out on me."

"I'm just afraid it hurts him."

As intently as Greg was concentrating on his patient, her quiet response caught him off guard. He was accustomed to maintaining professional distance in such situations. In a crisis, it was imperative that the ability to assess and act not be impaired by emotion. That didn't mean he was insensitive to suffering. He just didn't allow himself to consider what could cloud his judgment.

The woman who gamely responded to his every request didn't have his professional detachment to fall back on. There was no guile about her as she held his eyes. Nothing but the unmasked concern he'd seen when she had helped him. She had been afraid of hurting him, too.

Even after having her heart handed to her on a platter, her sense of compassion and empathy remained untouched.

The thought tugged hard. The soft curve of her mouth beckoned.

The need to detach had never seemed so necessary.

"He can't feel anything," he quietly assured her, and jerked his glance to his patient.

The concentration that so impressed Jenny looked more like dispassion to her in the trying minutes that followed. She managed to help Greg apply an inflatable splint to one leg, stabilize the other and with Joe's help, ease the backboard under their young victim. With the safety straps fastened over the boy's body to hold him in place and his friend Brady carrying the IV bag high, she, Greg and Joe carried the still unconscious boy to the back of Charlie's truck.

Brady needed about a dozen stitches himself, but the worst of his bleeding had been staunched with gauze pads Joe had secured with an elastic bandage. After Greg climbed into the back of the truck bed with his patient and took the IV bag to hold himself, Brady climbed into the Jeep with Joe.

Joe led, siren blaring. Jenny followed, driving the truck.

With the siren clearing the way, they made it to and through Maple Mountain in fifteen minutes. They met the ambulance forty minutes later, a mile from the highway cutoff. In the time it took to open the boxy white vehicle's back doors and carry the most injured victim from the truck while Greg related his treatments and suspicions to the paramedics, both boys were transferred.

The back doors of the ambulance had barely closed before Joe slapped Greg on his uninjured shoulder, gave Jenny a nod and said he was going back to write up his incident report. He'd see them back in town.

Jenny hadn't moved from where she'd stopped at the back of the truck. With the emergency suddenly over, she listened to the ambulance siren fade in the distance. Joe's Jeep had disappeared in the opposite direction when she watched Greg plow his fingers through his hair and walk toward her.

He had thrown off his lab coat on the way out the clinic door. The collar of his chambray shirt lay open against the darker blue sling.

Remembering how he had used the hand and arm of his injured side, thinking of how he'd grimaced with the movements, she nodded toward him. "How is your shoulder?"

He looked as if he hadn't give it a single thought. "Doing fine," he replied, stopping in front of her. A smile sneaked into his eyes. "You did good, Jenny."

The narrow road was deserted except for the two of them—and the hundred or so dairy cows in the meadows on either side. Thinking how lovely the quiet suddenly was, she tipped her head, gave a small shrug. "I just did what you told me to do."

"Don't do that."

"Do what?"

"Short-change yourself," he muttered not caring at all for the way she tended to minimize her efforts. "I couldn't have done that without you."

"Well, I don't know how you do it all." Grasping the tailgate with both hands, she lifted it up. Metal creaked in the bucolic stillness. "Stay so calm like that, I mean. In a crisis, my first re-action is to fall apart."

"It might be your first reaction, but it's not what you do. You did fine out there. And you didn't fall apart when I showed up at your door," he reminded her. "I have the feeling you didn't fall apart with all you went through in Boston, either."

Her glance moved to his. He towered beside her, lifting the gate with her, his expression as matter-of-fact as his tone.

He was right. She hadn't. She'd just gone numb.

"I mean inside," she explained, wondering if that's what he did, too. Numbed himself. They gave the tailgate a shove, metal clanking as it locked into place. "I don't know how you stay so calm inside."

A hint of defeat underscored her tone. Hearing it, Greg let his glance skim her profile. He already suspected that she wasn't doing as well as she was letting on to every one else. But, then, no one else knew what she'd gone through. Out-wardly, she seemed fine. At least she did when there were peo-ple around to see. There were times, though, when she'd thought no one was watching that he'd caught a certain weari-ness about her.

He caught a hint of it now.

"Calm is a relative term." In an emergency, with adrenaline pumping, his mind going a mile a minute, he felt anything but peaceful. "It's more of a detachment that comes with the profes-sion." Greg suspected that ability had come easier to him than to most people. Detaching himself had been what he'd done most of his life. It had been how he'd survived.

He didn't feel that sense of disconnection just then, though. Not with her looking at him so puzzled and the silk of her short hair blowing in wisps around her head.

"How? Is there a course in medical school? Composure 101 or something?"

"It's more seat-of-the pants than that. After a few months in an inner city E.R. you learn to separate the injury from the person. If you don't, you jeopardize patients because emotion can interfere with the ability to make decisions."

She seemed to deliberate that as she considered him. As she did, he found himself studying her back. He couldn't believe how she'd distracted him as he'd worked on his patient, how totally she distracted him now.

She still wore the blue scrub smock that hid her slender shape from him. But he had no trouble visualizing her curvy little body, the length of her legs. Everything from the blue of her eyes to the freckle on her left ankle had burned itself into his brain.

What he wanted to do to everything in between hit with force of a sledgehammer.

She had way of looking at him that did nothing to shake that betraying, dismaying desire. She seemed to trust nearly everything he said or did. He doubted she would even move from him now if he were to reach for her. She might seem bewildered or surprised, but he knew she wouldn't move.

All he had to do to test his theory was slip his hand along the side of her face and tip her head to his. In a matter of seconds, he would know for certain if her lips were as soft as they looked. He would know her taste. He would know if she felt the same heat he dutifully denied nearly every time they smiled at each other.

The tension flowing through him felt infinitely different from what he normally battled. Reining it in along with his thoughts, he stepped back before he could kiss his common sense goodbye.

The last thing he needed was to lose the ease they had with each other. He knew how badly Brent had burned her. He knew she was aware of Elizabeth and his plans to move on. Crossing the line with her would do nothing for their working relationship, or help rebuild her badly battered sense of trust in herself or other men.

He held out his hand, motioned with his fingers for the keys.

"I'll drive." If he was occupied with driving, he'd keep his hands where they belonged. Where they did not belong was anywhere on Jenny Baker. There wasn't a doubt in his mind that touching her would only complicate the growing uncertainty he felt about Elizabeth and his relationship with her. Elizabeth was a good, beautiful and intelligent woman. Everything a man should want in a partner. Business and otherwise. She deserved his loyalty.

Jenny's expression went suddenly cautious as she handed him the keys.

"Are you okay?" she asked, apparently concerned with the way his jaw had locked.

"Yeah. Fine." Keys jangled as he found the one for the ignition. "How about you? Are you ready?"

He'd withdrawn from her. Jenny had no idea why, but she felt it as surely as she had the hard bump of her heart against her ribs when his glance had settled on her mouth.

Truck doors slammed. Seat belts snapped into place. The engine roared to life. But the silence between them as he pulled onto the tree-lined road and headed for Maple Mountain felt as awkward to her as it had in the moments after they'd worked together on his shoulder.

Loathe to let that silence lengthen, she glanced toward Greg's preoccupied profile.

"Bess said no other doctor had been willing to come here," she confided quietly. "But I'm glad you did. Those boys were lucky you were there for them." She looked down at her slacks, brushed slowly at the dirt clinging to her knees. "The whole town is lucky to have you."

It's just too bad you have to leave, she thought, but couldn't bring herself to say it.

Greg looked to where she picked at a small tear below her knee. The sincerity in her tone added a dose of guilt to his mental tug of war. He knew she felt grateful to him. He could see it sometimes in her eyes. But he didn't want her gratitude. And he definitely didn't want her to have any illusions about him.

"I don't deserve anyone's thanks, Jenny." His reasons for being there were far from altruistic. Pure necessity had led him to Maple Mountain. "Just between you and me, I hadn't cared where I went as long as my medical school loans got paid. Maple Mountain had simply been first on the list."

His indifference caught Jenny by surprise. As involved as he had become in the town, as accepted as he had become, she would have thought for certain that he had deliberately sought out the very sense of community he'd found there.

"You might have started out not caring," she allowed, though she didn't believe that, either, "but I don't believe for a minute that you don't care about the people here. I've seen you with your patients. I know what you do for Amos Calder. You even made sure another doctor was lined up so you don't leave everyone stranded when you go."

She'd seen a copy of a letter in Rhonda's Rural Health Corps file. The one where he'd extolled the virtues of the town and its people to Dr. Cochran and offered to help any way he could to get the man to come to Maple Mountain.

"Someone who didn't care wouldn't get so edgy when he has to deal with something about his departure, either." She smoothed the little rip, carefully so as not to tear it farther. "I imagine you're excited about all your plans for when you leave here," she murmured, thinking of how eager she'd been herself those four long years ago, "but I can tell that part of you doesn't really want to go."

For a moment, Greg said nothing. Of all he'd had on his mind, he truly hadn't considered how he would feel leaving the little town behind. With the mental upheaval of the past few months, his only thoughts about moving had concerned his reluctance to deal with his father's estate and a growing fear that mixing his professional and personal life with Elizabeth was a mistake.

Those were the reasons he felt so restive all the time. Leaving had little to do with it. And she'd missed by a mile on the excitement part.

"How can you tell?"

Beneath pale blue cotton, her shoulder lifted in a faint shrug. "You get kind of...tense...whenever something comes up about going."

He wasn't at all accustomed to a woman being so sensitive to him.

"I just want to make sure my patients are taken care of," he insisted, feeling the exact tension she'd just referred to. He was going to Cambridge in a week. He couldn't avoid it any longer. "I just don't like loose ends."

He leaned forward, reached toward the radio. "Which do you want to listen to? Music or the farm reports?"

Jenny glanced from his strong profile. She didn't know which bothered her more just then; the sense that she might have overstepped herself, the indifference he professed, or that she had just caused the very edginess she'd mentioned. All she knew for certain as she quietly told him he could choose and that edge began to fade was that when it came to changing the subject, the man was anything but subtle.

Chapter Six

Visitors filled the diner over the weekend, crowding out the locals who preferred to stay home, anyway, when there were so many outsiders around. Jenny worked both days, saw Greg only briefly when he came in for breakfast, stopped for a quick visit with Rhonda to greet precious, little Amy Lynn Pembroke and spent her evenings nailing down loose porch boards and peeling off wallpaper.

She dutifully ignored the tiredness nagging her, along with the faint queasiness she sometimes felt from lack of sleep. She knew from the sleepless nights she'd spent when she'd first been implicated in Brent's scheme that emotions and fatigue could make a person feel rotten. She just hated that her attempts to work off the feelings of betrayal haunting her weren't working as well as she'd hope. Staying busy was the only defense she had.

Fortunately, keeping occupied wasn't a problem. The weekend flew by. So did the following week. It helped enormously that she began to settle into a routine. What helped most, though she would have admitted it to no one, was being with Greg. When she was around him, she was more aware of his tension than her own, more easily distracted from the ball of anxiety in her stomach that had yet to go away.

He wasn't an easy man to understand, but he was easy to work with, patient with her questions and, as she had learned at the quarry, quick to praise. By tacit agreement, neither spoke of anything personal. Yet, in many ways he was also becoming a friend.

Every evening before she closed the clinic, he poked his head around the front office doorway and told her not to work too late, or that he'd see her later at the diner. Every morning he asked, over the coffee she made extra strong, how she was progressing on the house.

He seemed genuinely pleased for her when she learned two days after meeting with the electrician that she wouldn't have to spend a penny for new wiring. The old wiring was actually in good shape, since some had been replaced by Mrs. Baker. Because no repairs were needed, she could have electricity by the end of the week. Knowing how much debt she had, Greg was also totally sympathetic when she found out how much a new roof would cost.

She liked his interest, liked the little rituals. They gave a sense of normalcy and routine to her life, and heaven knew she craved both.

She missed his little habits when they were gone, too. At least, she told herself that was what she missed—and not Greg himself—when she went four days without seeing him at all.

Greg had his usual rounds on Thursday, then took Friday off to spend a long weekend in Cambridge. It had been on the tip of Jenny's tongue to ask if he was going to see his friend. But she'd bitten back the question because the answer had seemed obvious. What hadn't seemed so apparent was why she'd felt so little enthusiasm when she told him she hoped he had a nice time.

* * *

Jenny heard Greg before she saw him when he walked in the back door of the clinic Monday morning. Afraid that it really had been him she'd missed and not just their little routines, she made herself stay by her desk.

"I smell coffee," he announced, his footsteps heavy in the hall. "Thank you, Jenny."

"You're welcome," she called back, only now letting herself head for the hallway.

She barely caught a glimpse of his yellow oxford shirt and tan slacks as he disappeared into the break room. Beyond the impressive width of his shoulders, what registered most was that the sling was gone.

"Good morning," she heard him say to Bess.

"Morning, yourself, Doctor." Standing by the coffeemaker, Bess handed him a white ceramic mug and went back to adding milk from the little refrigerator to her coffee. "How was your weekend?"

The phenomenon was interesting, Jenny thought. Greg had glanced toward her as she'd walked in, his easy smile meeting her own. At Bess's question, the light in his eyes died like a candle flame snuffed by the wind.

He turned to the coffeepot, picked it up.

"It was fine." His enthusiasm clearly dead, he splashed coffee into his mug. "How was yours?" he asked, trying to resurrect it again as he slid the pot back into place. "Did you get your tomatoes canned?"

"Squash. It was squash this weekend. I left a loaf of zucchini bread on your desk for you."

A hint of curiosity emerged. "With or without that white frosting?"

"With."

"You spoil me, Bess."

"Can't say anyone ever accused me of that before."

Jenny thought he'd tease Bess a little. Maybe tell her he

promised he wouldn't say anything to anyone and spoil her reputation.

All he said was, "Thanks, anyway."

He glanced toward Jenny. Because he had done it every other morning, she expected him to ask how her house was coming along. At the very least she thought he might inquire about the power, since he knew it was to have been turned on last Friday.

She was ready to tell him about the paint she had picked up Saturday morning in St. Johnsbury and to tell him that the best part about having electricity was having running hot water. It had taken forever for the rusty old water heater to heat and Bud Calder had told her she'd probably have to replace it before too long, but she was now living as one of the civilized.

Greg said nothing. His features a study in stone, he walked right past her with his mug trailing steam and headed for his office.

Bess leaned an ample hip against the counter. Her voice lowered along with her brow. "Wonder what that was all about."

"Me, too," Jenny all but whispered back. It was as clear as a specimen slide that Greg hadn't cared to share anything about his weekend. It had also been as obvious as the cords in his neck that something about his weekend had not gone well.

"Trouble in paradise?" Bess ventured.

Jenny hadn't a clue.

He was seeing the last patient of the day, however, when she got one.

Bess had taken the files and supplies she would need for her rounds the next day and gone home at four. With no other patients expected, Jenny was finishing the billing so she could stay and finally complete the grant application when the tinkle of the bell over the front door drew her glance to the reception window.

She had never met the stunning blonde entering the waiting area. Yet she knew even as she took in the woman's tailored gray pantsuit and the stylish, casual upsweep of her gleaming hair that she was the woman in the photograph in Greg's office.

"Hi," his *friend* said, her voice as cultured as the pearls in her ears. She didn't bother with a smile. She simply gave Jenny a glance that immediately dismissed her as nothing more than office help and stopped at the window. "I'm Dr. Brandt. Is Dr. Reid in?"

"He's with a patient."

"Oh, don't interrupt him," she said, as if she thought Jenny might actually do that on her account. "I'll just wait in his office."

Jenny wasn't sure what the protocol was here. The woman clearly had a personal relationship with Greg. But his office was his private space.

Surprised by the surge of hesitation she felt, determined to believe it nothing more than professional protectiveness, Jenny did as she would have done at the brokerage. Her boss there would have had her head if she'd let anyone he wasn't expecting into his office alone without his permission.

Not sure Greg wasn't expecting her, she forced some of the starch from her spine.

"If you'll wait here for a moment?" she asked and turned before the woman could open her beautiful gloss-shined mouth.

She rapped her knuckles softly on the exam room door. "Doctor?" she quietly called and opened the door far enough to see that the privacy curtain had already been pulled away.

Seven-year-old Josh Hill sat on the exam table, vigorously rubbing his arm where Greg had just vaccinated him. The Hills ran a dairy farm in North Stratford thirty miles away. His mom stood beside the little boy stroking his hair and telling him how brave he'd been.

"Dr. Brandt is here to see you," she said, her tone all business. "Shall I have her wait in your office?"

His brow slammed low. "She's here?"

He hadn't expected her. No question.

"In the waiting room."

"My office is fine," he said, regrouping. "It'll be a few minutes though."

She gave a nod and left him to finish his appointment. Moments later she opened the door to the waiting room.

Elizabeth stood in the middle of the well-used and uninspired space, her arms tightly crossed and her expression mildly preoccupied. Or maybe mildly annoyed. Jenny knew that Rhonda thought the woman "all right" and that Bess had called her "pleasant enough," but Jenny's impression wasn't so favorable. Dr. Elizabeth Brandt looked to her as if she were none to pleased to be in her present surroundings. She also gave Jenny the feeling that she didn't care to so much as touch anything in the place.

"If you'll follow me?" Jenny asked.

Elizabeth turned on her pretty-but-practical pumps.

"Please. Don't let me keep you from what you're doing. I know where it is."

She swept past with a faint air of impatience, her surprisingly soft and decidedly expensive scent drifting behind her like the wake of a steamer.

Jenny headed back to her desk. She had more than enough to do for the next couple of hours, more than enough to keep herself occupied and her mind off the man and his girlfriend down the hall. Whatever was going on was none of her business, anyway.

With that pointed reminder, she stuffed the bills into their envelopes, ran them through the postage meter and answered a call to reschedule an appointment. She gave Josh Hill an extra lollipop for being so stoic when he and his mom left and pulled the files for tomorrow's appointments. She even maintained her usual casual professionalism when Greg came in, dropped Marty's file on her desk and headed back out without a word.

She heard him head back down the hall, his footsteps hesitating halfway before he continued on and she heard his door close.

Jenny forced her attention to the computer. Eavesdropping was not something she did. Not on purpose, anyway. Yet, even as she pulled the grant forms onto the screen, she couldn't help overhear their muffled voices.

Normal conversation seldom carried in the clinic when doors were closed. But with no one else around, there were no other sounds to mask what she could hear filtering up the short hallway.

It didn't help that within a minute, Elizabeth's voice rose.

Jenny figured she and Greg must be very near his door. Thinking Elizabeth must have chosen to wait for him at the little conference table rather than his desk, Jenny diligently tried to ignore what she heard and concentrate on the charts on her screen.

"…why can't I have an agent start looking for a house now?" came the woman's faintly exasperated voice. "You'll be through here in a few months. It could easily take that long to find the home we want."

"The home *you* want" was Greg's reply. "We can't afford that kind of house. And if we do decide to buy a place together, we can look after I move back to Cambridge."

Elizabeth apparently chose to ignore the "if" part.

"We can afford anything we want," she insisted. "I have money. My father has money. You have money if you'd just use it."

"Lower your voice."

She ignored that, too. "You don't even know how much that estate is worth," she accused. "I know you needed to prove to your father that you could make it on your own. You've already done that by putting yourself through school and with your stint in this…this…deplorably equipped place," she apparently decided to call it. "You could end your commitment here and return to Cambridge that much sooner if you'd just let go of your pride and use some of your inheritance to pay off your loans."

The drop in temperature felt almost perceptible.

"Elizabeth," Greg grated, his tone careful and dangerously tight, "you've known all along that making my own way is important to me. I don't want your money. I most definitely don't want your father's. And even if it were available to me right now, which it is not," he said tersely, "I'm not touching what my father left me. I'll pay my own debts, and if you can't wait for me to finish the commitment I made here before deciding the housing issue, then we have bigger problems than a difference of opinion over real estate."

Jenny had never understood how silence could be deafening. Until now.

For several long moments she heard nothing. Not so much as a whisper came up the hall. She didn't know if they were staring each other down, backing away from each other, or if one of them, specifically Elizabeth, had reached out to make amends.

The thought of Elizabeth reaching out to him, touching his face, had Jenny yanking her attention back to the screen and praying that something on it would make sense. She needed to focus on work.

The effort was futile.

"…why you're doing it, isn't it? You're staying here to avoid a commitment to me."

Greg's voice fairly dripped exasperation. "My staying here has nothing to do with our relationship. I'm staying because I have a commitment to these people until my contract expires. I'm not backing out on that."

"What about a commitment to our relationship?" she returned. "It's just a house, Greg. If you can't even commit to just *looking* for one, then I don't see how we have anywhere else to go."

Tension fairly crackled in the sudden silence filling the hallway.

That silenced lengthened, stretching Jenny's nerves right along with it. But it wasn't until she realized she was holding her breath that she finally heard something other than the beat of her own pulse pounding in her ear.

She had no idea what Greg had said. Or if he'd said anything at all. She had no idea, either, who had opened the door. She suspected Elizabeth might have opened it herself, though. Within seconds the quick tap of heels sounded on the tiles. Seconds later the female physician slipped past the front office doorway in a blur of hurt and indignation.

The waiting room door opened. Without bothering to close it, Elizabeth moved straight to the front door. The way she rushed out, the bell tinkling madly, made Jenny think she would have left that one open, too, had the mechanism at the top not eased it closed for her.

Greg's approach sounded far less agitated, far more deliberate.

He seemed to be heading for the waiting room door. Not to follow Elizabeth, but to close it. Threading his fingers through his hair as he passed the front office doorway, he suddenly drew to a halt.

Jenny watched his hand fall as he looked toward her.

Embarrassed to have witnessed something so private, her eyes widened as she ducked her head.

It seemed like forever before he quietly asked, "Who else is here?"

She cleared her throat, glanced back toward him. The carved lines of his face betrayed nothing beyond the tension that radiated from him like radio waves from a signal tower.

"No one. It's just me."

The tightness in his jaw remained. "How much did you hear?"

Far more than she ever intended, she thought. "Probably pretty much all of it."

She had no idea what he saw as the cool gray of his eyes moved over her face. She wasn't even sure what she felt beneath that quiet, unnerving scrutiny. She knew only that her heart was beating a little too fast in the long moments before he stepped inside.

Reaching for the other secretarial chair near the computer desk, he turned the back toward her and sat down, straddling it.

"Tell me," he said, his voice deep, his eyes searching. "When you first realized that your life was totally screwed up, what did you do?"

She didn't know which threw her more, the question or that he was coming to her for advice. "I went for a very long walk," she admitted, hating to think he felt as lost as she had. "I figured that was safer than getting behind the wheel of my car, as upset as I was."

"Did it help?"

Not really, she thought. "As much as anything could at that point."

The breath he drew pulled her glance to his broad chest. A moment later, that view slid to the buckle of his belt and the zipper below as he rose like a monolith rising from the sea.

Her anxious glance jerked up as he shrugged off his lab coat.

"Are you all right?" she asked.

Worry washed her features, naked, unguarded. Seeing her unashamed concern, Greg felt that quiet caring reach deep inside him. There was a place in his soul that felt as if it were dying, a dark, hungry place that he usually managed to ignore. She'd touched him there before, given him a taste of comfort that had seemed terribly foreign and more necessary than he wanted to admit.

He knew she understood how it felt when a person hit rock bottom, and she was clearly afraid he felt that way now. Yet, he didn't feel much of anything at all. It seemed to him that he should. The woman he'd once planned to spend his personal and professional future with had just broken up with him, but all he felt was a sense of relief and a vague uncertainty about where he was going to work after he left Maple Mountain. The Cambridge practice obviously was no longer an option. And the doctor who would replace him had already been hired and was counting on the job he'd been promised.

All that mattered just then was that he didn't deserve Jenny's guileless concern.

"I'm fine," he assured her, hanging his lab coat on an arm of the coatrack inside the doorway. "What just happened with Elizabeth was a long time coming. I can't change for her, and she's not willing to accept me as I am." Certainty settled solid and deep. "It's really best for us both."

He looked from where Jenny sat quietly watching him to

what was on the computer screen. When he glanced back to her again, she looked as if she didn't quite know what to say. Or maybe she wasn't sure if she should say anything at all.

"Don't work too late tonight," he murmured. "We need to get that application in, but I know you haven't been feeling all that great lately. Get some rest. Okay?'

He barely heard her softly say that she would. As he turned to leave the room and the clinic, his sole focus was on working off the restlessness he never could seem to shake.

It was after eight o'clock that night when he returned to finish the work he hadn't stuck around to finish before. Thinking to go for a run rather than a walk, he'd changed into sweat shorts and a T-shirt. The jolts to his sore shoulder had ended the idea of jogging after the first half-dozen steps. He'd settled instead for walking the winding woodland paths until dark had settled in, then he'd worked through a couple of sets with his lightest weights to strengthen the healing muscles in his back, arm and shoulder.

The aching joint hadn't helped his mood the past couple of weeks. Neither had the inconvenience of not being able to use both arms. The tenderness was almost gone now and after four weeks of his own therapy, he would be as good as new. In the meantime, being free of the sling felt like a gift in itself.

If he could just get rid of the responsibility his father had dumped on him, he'd been home free.

Wondering how much Jenny had overheard about that, he sank into the old leather chair behind his desk. As he did, he noticed a white clinic stationery envelope centered on his blotter.

It had his name on it.

"Greg." Not "Dr. Reid."

The writing was Jenny's. He would have recognized her open and looping script anywhere.

Paper rustled as he slit open the envelope and pulled out the plain sheet of paper.

There was another thing I did. I bought a bag of Oreos. The kind with chocolate filling. The store is closed by now, so you're welcome to the stash I'm saving for emergencies. You listened to me, so if you need someone to unload on— someone who won't offer unsolicited advice and can keep whatever she hears to herself—I'm here.

She'd signed it simply *"J."*

He sank back in his chair. Read the note again.

He could feel himself smiling as he folded the note and slipped it into his pocket. Her concern felt like a balm to him, quiet and comforting in that same odd way he'd felt with her before. But he wasn't going to show up at her house. He'd make miserable company tonight. Even if he had been tempted, the thought of someone seeing his car—Charlie's truck—out there so late, would have stopped him. Joe had already questioned him about sitting with her on her porch a couple of weeks ago. The eagle-eyed deputy had dropped his teasing when Greg told him that he'd gone there to offer her a job. But he had no practical excuse tonight, and he knew it took next to nothing for rumors to get started around there.

As he opened a file he needed to research a diagnosis, it just felt good to him to know that Jenny was there.

He told her that, too, when he walked into the break room the next morning and found her making coffee.

Jenny stood at the sink of the small, utilitarian room filling the carafe from the coffeemaker with water. She must have just arrived herself. The front office lights weren't yet on, the shades were still drawn in the waiting room and she hadn't yet pulled on her camouflaging blue scrub jacket. The color of the pale-pink shirt that met the waist of her black slacks reminded him of cotton candy. The fit of it over her gently rounded breasts threatened thoughts less innocent in the moments before she turned off the faucet and glanced up.

"Thanks for the note."

With a soft smile, she poured the water into the machine. "You're welcome. I just wanted you to know my Oreos are available anytime."

As he'd done other mornings when he'd come in and found Rhonda or Bess or, now, Jenny going through the ritual of preparing coffee, he did his part to get the process underway. His basic sense of fairness dictated that if he drank it, he could help fix it.

He reached for the box of filters from the cupboard above Jenny as she reached for the can of coffee.

Taking out a filter, he held it while she scooped in the richly scented grounds. As always she added an extra scoop for the first pot, but instead of dropping the scoop back in, she glanced up. "Should I add more? For the extra caffeine," she explained, searching his face before she quickly glanced away. "In case you didn't sleep well last night."

He'd spent half the night tossing and turning. The other half he'd spent in his dark room, developing some of the pictures he'd taken at the town's parade last Fourth of July. He toyed around with his photography mostly in the winter when the long days of summer were gone and the long nights demanded something to fill the lonely hours.

Last night had felt like winter to him.

"Sure," he murmured.

"I know what you said…about it being for the best," she reminded him, adding another scoop, "but I'm still sorry about what happened with you and…what was she? Your fiancée?"

"We were never engaged."

She dropped the filled filter into the basket. As she did, he picked up the plastic lid for the coffee can, snapped it into place. "That was part of our problem," he admitted. "She wanted marriage. I didn't." Picking up the package of filters, he slid it and the coffee back onto the shelf and quietly closed the cabinet door. "I'd gotten the feeling she looked at buying a house together as a way to ease me into the idea. In a way, she was doing to me what Brent did to you."

Jenny's fingers paused above the switch. A knowing look passed through her eyes a moment before she turned back and flipped it on. "Manipulating you," she concluded.

"Yeah."

"I'm sorry."

He started to shrug off what had happened, found that he couldn't. He'd been manipulated before, so it wasn't as if he hadn't had experience with someone trying to control him or bend him to their will. The difference between his father and Elizabeth, though, was that he had respected her, her passion, her dedication. He just hadn't realized until she'd started pushing him for a commitment in their relationship that she hadn't respected *him*. She'd heard nothing he'd said to explain why he felt as he did. Or, if she had heard, his feelings hadn't mattered to her.

"May I ask you something?" Caution entered Jenny's voice. "About your girlfriend. Ex, I mean."

"What's that?"

"You said you didn't want marriage. Did you mean just to her, or to anyone?"

Greg hesitated. Part of him, the part that kept the invisible wall between him and his heart, started to tell her that marriage simply wasn't something he could see for himself and let it go at that. He wasn't accustomed to letting anyone into his past. There were things even Elizabeth hadn't known. But Jenny, the woman he'd practically badgered into confiding in him wasn't after anything from him, and he knew from the shadows in her lovely eyes that she would understand what so many others might not.

"Not to anyone," he finally admitted. "My father had just divorced his fourth wife before he died. My grandfather had divorced three. My mom walked out before I could remember much about her, so I have no personal experience at all with how a good family works. In all honesty," he said, because she'd been so honest with him, "what some people call love looks an awful lot to me like a license to use, abuse or—"

"Manipulate."

He knew she'd understand. "Exactly."

Jenny had caught a trace of his usually well-masked cynicism the day he'd told her how he'd wound up in Maple Mountain. She heard it again in his unexpected admissions. It was difficult, though, seeing that hard certainty glitter in his eyes.

It was like seeing inside herself.

Looking away, she carefully wiped up the dry grounds that had scattered over the beige Formica. There had been a time when she would have insisted his conclusion was terribly wrong. In her naive little heart, she'd felt that there was nothing love couldn't conquer, that knights in shining armor did exist and that happily ever after didn't just apply to fairy tales. She hadn't expected romantic perfection. And she certainly hadn't expected her prince to be perfect, because she was so far from it herself. But she had very much wanted the home, the family and the future that Brent had dangled like bait.

She had learned the hard way that what she'd thought was love had been nothing more than a blinding emotion Brent had used to pull her strings. As sobering as it had been, and as revealing, she had also come to realize that it hadn't been Brent she had loved after all. What she had loved so completely was the illusion he had presented.

It still hurt to know she had been so thoroughly deceived. Yet, she had the feeling from what Greg had just told her that his heart had been abused in far more profound ways. She had merely been used. He had grown up without a mother. And his male role models had gone through women like some men did clean shirts.

"It would be hard to want something you'd only seen as a failure," she murmured. "Having three stepmoms come and go would be difficult, too." A hint of hope slipped into her eyes. "Did you stay close with any of them?"

He'd gone to boarding schools. In summer when he'd been home, only staff had been there. When he'd been home for winter holidays, the women had been busy entertaining, spending and trying to figure out if they should mother him or ignore him. "None were ever close to begin with."

"Oh."

"It's not that big a deal," he said. "They came. They went. They weren't mom material, anyway. They were only after his money."

"No wonder he divorced them."

He didn't want her defending his father. "My father always knew what he was getting," he informed her tightly. "He was the one with the control. He married trophies who seemed to think what his money bought them was *worth* his manipulation. Everyone knew it was his wealth and power that provided the cars, the clothes, the servants. He made sure of it."

The coffeepot sputtered and hissed between them. Needing something to do before his buried agitation surfaced completely, Greg opened another cupboard, took out two mugs.

"He made it just as clear that he could take it all away anytime he chose. From all of us." Ceramic clinked against the counter. "I learned that the less I asked for, the less he had to hold over my head."

He'd learned to ask for nothing, to expect nothing, to count on nothing.

Last night he'd thought mostly of how he never should have let his relationship with Elizabeth go as far as it had. The only reason he figured he had was because part of him wanted what he'd seen other people have, even as part of him balked at the very idea. Nothing about his past had even entered his mind.

Wishing he hadn't allowed it to now, he stared down at the empty mug.

The feel of Jenny's small hand on his arm drew his glance to her face.

"He treated you like that, too?"

At her quiet question, the quick tension spiking through him eased. Or maybe what relieved it was the distraction of her touch. There was gentleness in it. Softness. Warmth.

"Until I left," he admitted.

"When was that?"

"After I told him I didn't want to be a lawyer."

"You were in law school?"

"Not quite. I was in my third year of college."

He wasn't making sense to her. He felt certain of that as she slipped her hand away, self-consciously crossing her arms as if she'd only now realized how easily she'd reached for him.

"There has always been a Reid for a partner in the law firm my great-grandfather started," he explained, drawn by her instinctive need to soothe. "My father had bragged for years that I would be the fourth generation to uphold the tradition. That's why it took me so long to work up the courage to tell him I didn't want to study law. I wanted to practice medicine. When I told him that, I was informed that the choice wasn't mine to make. He paid the bills, therefore he would make the decisions. He told me that if I didn't continue in law school, I'd have to pay for school myself."

His father had also maintained that he would never make it on his own, he told her. In the senior Reid's usual dismissive and dogmatic style, he'd said that Greg was too much like him to ever give up the finer things money could buy, that having come from such affluence, he would never be able to live among the masses. He'd gone on to claim that it was from him that he'd inherited his intelligence, his drive and his name. He didn't much care for the rebelliousness he insisted Greg had inherited from his mother, but he assumed his son would grow out of it once he realized how impossible it would be to make it on his own.

"The bottom line was that I was who I was because of him, that I would be no one without him, and that I would never be able to afford Harvard without his money to pay my way.

"Then he played his trump card." An edge hardened his tone. "He said I owed him my loyalty because he had raised me after my mother had gone. It seems she'd been given the choice of me or a substantial settlement to disappear."

His mother had obviously chosen the money.

"That was the last day I spoke to him. I made it through college and medical school on scholarships, loans and odd jobs." The edge sharpened. "Anything I become, I become on my own. Not because of his influence or wealth."

Jenny watched the muscle in his lean jaw jerk, saw the deep breath he took to blow off what little anger he had allowed past his rigid control. She had the feeling from the way he seemed to constantly check his emotions that he had worked hard to bury the rage he surely must have felt at his father's arrogance. And the hurt. He would have worked just as hard to bury that, too.

Empathy and outrage simmered in Jenny's heart. What she felt most was a deep ache. For him. The way his father had treated him bordered on criminal. There had been no caring, warmth or emotional security in Greg's young life. He'd said little about it, but it sounded as if there had never been anyone there for him. No one he could count on to ease the little hurts or share the little joys. No one to temper the awful coldness and mental abuse he'd been subjected to by his father.

To have revealed that his own mother had chosen money over him had been unimaginably cruel.

"It's no wonder you don't want your inheritance."

His big body seemed to go still.

"Elizabeth said she wanted you to use it," she said, reminding him of the little yelling match she'd overheard. "I had no idea what she was talking about," she confessed. "But I can see now why you want nothing to do with his money."

His arm still seemed to be bothering him. Either that or the tension in his muscles had made it start aching again. He cupped his hand over his shoulder, absently kneading as he studied a spot on the floor.

"I'm not even supposed to have it."

She ducked her head, caught his glance. "So how did you get it?"

He gave a mirthless little laugh.

"By default. One of my father's partners called a few months ago to tell me my father was revising his will to cut me completely out of it. Jack, the lawyer," he clarified, speaking of the man who'd known Matthew Reid through all his marriages and also happened to be Greg's godfather, "wanted to know if there wasn't some way my father and I could reconcile." He edged his fingers toward his neck. "I told him I couldn't see how.

"Two days later he called again," he continued. "This time it was to tell me that my father had been playing golf and collapsed. He'd died of an unexpected heart attack."

"How long ago was this?"

"About three and half months now."

"Did you have to go to Cambridge?"

Mercifully he'd been spared wrestling with that decision. "Even if I'd wanted to go, I couldn't get away. Bess was on vacation and I couldn't leave the clinic unattended. Jack took care of the arrangements and called me a week later. That was when he told me that the new will hadn't been ready to sign and that my father had already destroyed the old one. As his only legal heir, I inherited everything."

He shook his head at the irony of it. "My father didn't know squat about how to treat people, but he was good lawyer. He couldn't have thought anything was ever going to happen to him to have left a gap like that."

Jenny couldn't help but think that such egotism easily fit the man Greg had described. Her interest was more in son than father, though. She finally understood the edginess everyone had sensed in him of late. More important to her, she was beginning to understand…him.

He had gone to the loan program for medically underserved areas not only to help repay his tuition, but because the program assigned doctors to the very sort of places his father had said he would never survive in. He had proven not only that he could make his own way, on his own, as he chose, but that he could manage quite well without whatever high-end creature comforts his father had deemed so necessary.

She couldn't imagine how awful it must have been for Greg to live constantly feeling he had to prove himself.

"So how long before you can get rid of your bequest?"

Her simple query spoke volumes to Greg.

She hadn't suggested that he keep the money. She hadn't tried to come up with a dozen ways to gloss over where the money had come from or, as Elizabeth had, told him he might be carrying a grudge a little too far.

Jenny had immediately understood that he wanted only to be free of what the estate represented. In the past three months Elizabeth had never once grasped that. In one way or another, every time they'd been together or spoken on the phone, she had reminded him that the estate needed to be taken care of and that it was there for his use.

Even Larry Cohen, his attorney and an a old friend from college, couldn't believe how he was balking at filing the necessary papers.

The difference between them and Jenny gave him pause. So did the quiet way she watched him.

Wondering if any woman had ever looked at him the way *she* did, he gave his head another shake. "I have no idea how long it will take. I have a mountain of paperwork from my attorney that I'm avoiding."

He was legally responsible to see that everything was taken care of in probate and beyond. His father's attorney and his own had done what they could in the short term, but they were hamstrung until he read and signed what had been sent him. He told her that, too.

The coffeemaker hissed to silence. Picking up one of the mugs, she filled it for him. Considering how he viewed love, she could see now why he had so little interest in marriage. Considering everything else he'd said about making it on his own and what she'd overhead when Elizabeth had offered her own and her father's money to buy a house, she suspected he also didn't want anyone's help with his personal problems.

She had to offer, though.

"How many documents are you talking about?"

"My bottom desk drawer is about full."

She watched him through the steam rising from his mug. "Is that what's in those manila envelopes that law firm in Boston sends you?"

He hesitated. "Yeah. Why?"

"It just explains why you get so tense when you see one. You know, Greg," she said, making her tone deliberately light as she reached for her own cup. "I know I said I wouldn't offer unsolicited advice, but it seems to me that you're only prolonging the agony. Would it help if I read through the documents for you and gave you a summary? There are bound to be things in there that are more pressing than others. I could filter out what can wait, and then you'd only have to deal with what can't. Then, once you get everything tied up, you could use the money for something constructive."

"I already figured I'd give it to some charity."

The quiet rush of coffee being poured underscored the soft tones of her voice. "Then it might be easier for you to get started on everything if you have something specific in mind. Some specific cause to work toward." She had no idea how much money they were talking about. She strongly suspected, however, that it had a lot more zeros than fit in the average checkbook. "If you make your inheritance stand for something positive, rather than something that reminds you of the past, maybe you could even develop a little enthusiasm for getting everything settled."

Greg's first thought was that she was right. She had said she wouldn't offer unsolicited advice. His second was that he couldn't imagine feeling anything but aversion for the task. Sharing a personal burden wasn't something he was at all inclined to do, either.

He might have told her all that, too, since he seemed to be telling her everything else, when the muffled sound of the bell over the front door jerked their attention to the hallway.

"Where is everyone?" Bess called over the rattle of her keys. "Why isn't the door unlocked and the shades raised?"

Jenny glanced at her watch as Greg stepped back. She hadn't even considered how close they'd been standing to each other until he deliberately widened that negligible distance. In the seconds before the front door opened, she'd noticed only how shuttered Greg's expression had become.

"We're in the break room," she called, realizing she should have opened the clinic ten minutes ago.

He hadn't said what he'd thought of her offer. She suspected from the quick withdrawal she'd sensed in him that he hadn't thought much of it all.

"What did you forget?" he called, stepping into the hall as Bess hurried toward the medicine room.

"Mrs. Belier's insulin," she muttered, stuffing her keys into the pocket of her red sweater. "I forgot that we upped her dosage last week. I didn't have enough with me to get her through until the next."

She glanced up as Greg turned into his office, mug in hand.

Jenny, carrying her coffee, too, headed up the hall.

Catching the disquiet in Jenny's face, the nurse practitioner frowned. "Is everything okay?"

Jenny made herself smile.

"Everything's fine." *Or would be if I hadn't just totally over-stepped myself with Greg,* she thought. She'd just wanted to help. The way he had helped her. "I just...got a late start."

"As long as everything's under control."

"It is," Jenny assured her, and hurried off to open the waiting room blinds as the bell over the front door tinkled again and the mayor's redheaded wife poked her head inside.

"Jenny." Claire Jefferson's overly bright smile clearly indicated she wanted something. "You're just the person I need

to see. Do you remember when you helped make those costumes for the senior class play?"

By seven o'clock that evening Clair's innocuous-sounding request had led to a state of distress Jenny hadn't experienced in
weeks. She couldn't have imagined anything that would have
disturbed her more than Greg's continued silence about her offer,
but that and the depth of his emotional scars were now the last
things on her mind.

The mayor's wife wanted her to help make costumes for the
Pumpkin Festival coming the end of October. Wanting badly to
fit back into the community, she'd said she'd be happy to and
told herself she'd figure out later how to fit the project into her
work schedule.

That was what she'd started to do as she stood at her kitchen
counter staring at the wall calendar she'd just pulled from its
packing box.

She hadn't taken it out earlier because she'd intended to paint
before she hung it. With no social life or appointments to make,
she hadn't needed it, anyway. That lack of activity was evident
in all the blank little squares that followed the last entry for Au-
gust. *Move* had been written in the box for the fifteenth. The only
entries for the two weeks prior to that were for appointments with
her attorney, a Detective Mortensen and for two depositions.
She'd also noted the dates she'd canceled utilities.

It was what *wasn't* there that had her feeling a little sick.

There was no little devil's pitchfork on any of the little squares
for that month. Flipping back a page, she noticed the little symbol for her period missing in July, too.

With all the chaos of Brent's arrest, she had totally forgotten
that her period had been due that following week. When she had
remembered it, she'd chalked its lateness up to stress and stead-
fastly refused to even consider that anything else in her life could
go wrong. With moving, settling in, starting over, she'd managed
to forget about it again.

She couldn't help but think about it now.

As she started counting, she realized that her second period was now over a week overdue.

Chapter Seven

Jenny thought the day would never end. From the moment she'd arrived at work the next morning, the need to know for certain if she was pregnant had plagued her with the relentlessness of a toothache. Had she still lived in the city, she would have bought a pregnancy test last night and put a quick and immediate end to the awful suspicion that had kept her up painting her kitchen walls long past midnight. But this was Maple Mountain. The only place to buy a pregnancy test was the pharmacy inside the gift shop. Depending on who might have seen her, news of such a purchase could have been buzzing on the grapevine by the time she'd made it back home.

Her only options were to drive to St. Johnsbury, which wasn't such a big place itself, or use a pregnancy test from the clinic. She had already slipped her money for one into the petty cash box, since she couldn't figure out how else to pay for it.

Now if everyone would just leave, she could get the test from the supply room. The patients were gone, Bess had nearly finished her charting, and Greg was on his phone in his office talking to a colleague in St. Johnsbury about Sally McNeff's mother. Since the older woman's cancer surgery a few months ago, Greg had been taking care of her chemotherapy. The results of the blood work he'd sent to St. Johnsbury for testing didn't look good.

There were things about working in the clinic that Jenny really didn't want to know. Just as there were things she did want to know but which left her feeling sad in far different ways.

Greg had been trading calls off and on all day with the Rural Health Corps and had asked her to reschedule his appointments for Friday. He had job interviews then in New Hampshire.

"There are days when I just want to wring the neck of every patient I see." Bess, having a bad day herself, made the terse announcement as she put her last patient file in Jenny's in-box for Jenny to file. "One complains of being short of breath, but won't quit smoking. Another doesn't want to take her cholesterol medication because her insurance only covers part of the cost, but won't watch her diet or get extra exercise. And don't even get me started on what insurance will and won't cover. I spent two hours on the phone today after sending documentation and test results, and Marlene McGraw's carrier won't budge."

The day hadn't been good for anyone.

Praying her own wouldn't get any worse, desperately hoping it was just nerves and stress making her period so late, Jenny turned off the printer and the computer and killed the hum of the fan in the corner.

As she did, Bess headed for the bottom drawer of a file cabinet and pulled out her purse.

"I'm just glad this day's over," she said, sighing. "As of right now, all I'm going to think about is going home, getting into my gardening clothes and yanking weeds until the sun goes down. After you get your house fixed up, you might think about working your grandma's old garden." The metal drawer rattled shut. "Best stress reliever in the world."

Jenny appreciated the suggestion. She also tried not to look anxious for the older woman to leave as Bess headed for the doorway. The only thing that would relieve her current anxiety was a negative pregnancy test.

"Have a good evening," Jenny called after her.

"You, too," came the vaguely preoccupied reply. "See you in the morning."

The squeak of sensible shoes on the tiles slowly faded down the hall. The back door opened. A few uneasy heartbeats later, Jenny heard it close with a decisive bang.

She had already closed the blinds out front and locked the front door. The phone had been switched to the answering service Nellie Anderson ran out of her home. Except for Greg, still talking on his phone, she was finally alone.

She knew he had calls to return, dictation to complete. It could be an hour or more before he surfaced.

Her stomach jumping, she slipped into the supply room.

The space was lined with tall gray metal shelves filled with all manner of medical paraphernalia. She knew where the pregnancy tests were because she'd stocked them herself, along with diabetes test strips, tubes for blood tests, syringes and a few dozen other items that had come last week with an order from one of the pharmaceutical supply houses the clinic used.

She took one of the small silver foil pouches marked HCG Pregnancy Test from one box and a specimen cup from another. Refusing to make herself wait any longer, she tucked both into the pocket of her scrub smock and stepped into the hall.

For a few interminable seconds she heard nothing but the tick of the timer on the autoclave Bess had set to sterilize instruments used that day. Finally hearing Greg's voice again, which meant he was still on the phone, she slipped into the bathroom.

She'd barely closed the door behind her before she ripped open the pouch. The test instructions said positive results would be indicated within sixty seconds by two colored bands. Negative results took five minutes to confirm and would only show the top control band.

It took two minutes for her to get everything ready.

It only took thirty seconds for double colored bands to appear.

It took about thirty more for her to move.

The instructions had said to lay the prepared strip on a paper towel while waiting for the results to appear. The towel she'd carefully folded lay on the wide edge of the sink, the dip strip on it.

Still staring at the colored bands, she took a deep breath and stepped back.

Taking another step, her eyes unable to leave the damning strip, she let her back hit the wall. She didn't think she was breathing at all when she slowly slid to the floor.

Her arm bumped the tall white metal wastebasket on her way down. She scarcely noticed the racket. The knot living in her stomach had just turned to lead.

It didn't matter that she had suspected it. It didn't even matter that in her gut she'd felt horribly certain of what the results of the test would be. There was something about having those results stare her in the face that felt terribly final. Before the test, she'd at least had the hope that the result would be negative. Now she had nothing but the numbness that stole through her like a shadow.

That numb disbelief felt familiar. She'd lived with it in Boston from the moment she'd been informed of Brent's arrest and had been taken in for questioning herself. *This can't be happening* had become a litany.

This can't be happening echoed in her mind now.

She drew up her knees, wrapped her arms around them, dropped her head. When she'd left Boston, she'd thought her life couldn't possibly get any more complicated.

She'd had no idea how terribly wrong she could be.

"Jenny? Are you okay in there?"

No, she thought, I'm definitely not.

"Jenny?"

Lifting her head, she reached to the doorknob and unlocked it.

Greg eased the door open. From the corner of her eye, she caught a glimpse of brown loafers and plain brown socks visible beneath the hem of his khakis. No duck socks today.

She'd returned to hugging her knees again when the door opened farther.

In the space of seconds Greg noticed what occupied the edge of the sink across from Jenny and Jenny sitting against the wall by the door. It took about twice that long for him to step inside, note the double lines on the strip and silently swear.

His knees cracked as he crouched beside her.

"I heard something crash," he said, explaining why he'd so abruptly ended his call. "Did you hurt yourself?"

Her boyishly cut hair gleamed in the overhead light as she slowly shook her head. In that bright light, the faint circles he'd noticed before beneath her eyes were more prominent, her delicate features more drawn.

"I just bumped the wastebasket."

She hugged her knees more tightly.

"Are you all right?" he asked, wanting to help her up, not sure she was ready to move. He could only imagine what must be going through her mind—if she was even able to think at all. She looked shell-shocked.

Again she gave her head a slow, negative shake.

"I didn't think you were."

He murmured the words. Reaching out as he did, he nudged back the hair at her temple. He'd never seen anyone look as lost and alone as she did at that moment. Or, if he had, he'd never allowed the depth of that awful helplessness to register. It wasn't as if he allowed it now. It simply happened as he knelt there, touching her. Something twisted inside him. Something that made him feel what she felt and left him nearly as vulnerable as she looked in the moments before he scrambled for the protective detachment that came so automatically with everyone else.

He moved his hand from her cheek, dropped it to her shoulder. Beneath his palm, he could feel her trembling.

"I'll be in my office if you want to talk."

She lifted her eyes to his. Distress filled those haunted blue depths.

"Okay?" he asked.

That same distress robbed the strength from her quiet, "Okay."

The desire to reach for her was strong, to give her back a bit of the comfort he had felt from her. As he gave her shoulder a gentle squeeze, the need to let her decide what help she would accept from him felt even stronger. "Take your time."

He didn't want to move, but he didn't want to crowd her, either.

He would give her two minutes, he decided, reluctantly rising. Then he'd come after her.

Heaven knew that in her current situation, pregnancy was the absolute last thing she needed to deal with alone.

She had just reached her two-minute limit when she appeared in his office doorway. Still looking haunted, she glanced toward him, glanced away.

"I paid for the test. I put the money in petty cash," she explained, her focus on her hands as she rubbed her thumb against her other palm. "I don't want you to think I just took it."

Greg rose from his chair. Of everything she must have on her mind just then, he couldn't believe her first concern was that he not think her dishonest.

"Come on in, Jenny."

She shook her head, crossed her arms over her scrub jacket. "I have to go."

"You don't work at the diner tonight, do you?"

"Not tonight."

"Then, where do you have go right now?" Mindful of her self-protective stance, he slowly crossed toward her. "Anywhere that can't wait for a while?"

Once more she gave a negative shake.

"Were you thinking of taking a walk?" he ventured.

She finally looked up. "Did yours help the other night?"

"Maybe," he allowed, though her note had helped more. "You just don't look like you should be wandering around where someone might see you. Anyone who knows you is going to want to know what's wrong."

Dismay filled her eyes as she lifted her fingers to her face.

"Come on," he said, catching her hand when it fell. Tugging her with him, he backed toward the table with its ever-present collection of medical books and notes. "Sit down for a minute and talk to me."

Her hand felt cold in his. He suspected she might feel that way inside, too, but he made himself let go when he pulled out the nearest chair. As she sank onto it, he pulled over another.

Sitting down facing her, he rested his elbows on his knees and watched her push her trembling fingers through her hair. The motion momentarily exposed the pink, newly healed skin on her forehead. He hardly needed the reminder of all she'd been through—or of how she diligently moved on from each crisis—as the shake of her head had her bangs falling right back over it again.

"This isn't happening," she insisted. Leaning forward herself, she hugged her stomach. "I keep telling myself I'm going to wake up any second and find out this is all a bad dream."

If pressed, Greg would have conceded that there was indeed a certain nightmarish quality to her life of late. "Do you know how far along you are?"

Jenny knew exactly how far along she was. Brent had taken her to dinner after she'd worked late the week before his arrest. The date had been on her calendar. They'd gone to her apartment afterward, as they had so often done. That had been the last time they'd been together.

"Seven weeks." Nearly two months, she thought. In another couple of months, she'd be showing. "Our protection obviously failed."

She could feel Greg's eyes on her. She just couldn't make herself look up to meet them.

"Do you know what you want to do?"

"Not really. I mean I'll have it. And I'll keep it," she decided, her heart and her instincts reaching conclusions even as she spoke. "Beyond that...I don't know."

For a moment Greg said nothing. With her head lowered, he couldn't see the distress he was sure must be in her eyes. He could hear it, though. And while he hated that it was there, he knew there was really nothing he could do to alleviate it.

He'd dealt with unmarried pregnant women before. He knew their emotions ran from despair to anger to guarded excitement and back again. He'd had women come to him wanting an abortion, which he wouldn't do, or his help with an adoption, which he gladly had. If adoption had been Jenny's choice, he would have supported her in it. He would have helped any way he could. But even before he'd asked what she wanted to do, he had suspected what her answer would be. As caring and as compassionate as she was, as committed as she was to dealing with the consequences of her actions, he wouldn't have expected anything else.

He just hated to think of the added struggle ahead of her.

"What about Brent?"

Confusion colored her tone. "What about him?"

"This is his child, too," he reminded her. "He needs to know he's going be a father. If nothing else, you need to let him know so he can pay child support."

The thought of dealing with Brent made Jenny feel sicker than she already did. "He's in jail."

"It doesn't matter where he is. He still has a financial responsibility."

He sat back, fully aware of the sharp surge of resentment he felt toward the man who'd gotten her into this mess. Brent Collier had taken everything from her but what she'd salvaged of her pride. And now he'd left her alone and pregnant.

Greg had taken an oath to heal, "to first do no harm." But he suspected that the words of his Hippocratic oath might well have been forgotten had Brent Collier been in the room just then. Harm was exactly what he felt like doing to the man.

A vivid image of grabbing him by the throat and slamming him up against a wall flashed in his mind an instant before he reined it back. He didn't do so well restraining the protectiveness he'd felt ever since he'd heard the clank of metal against the bathroom wall. He'd thought Jenny had slipped, fallen. Or, as pale as she'd looked today, passed out.

Someone needed to look out for her. Someone who knew all that she had gone through. She'd trusted him with her secrets. As long as he was there, it might as well be him.

"Just think about talking to the guy," he finally asked. "If you don't want to talk to him, talk to his attorney." Not wanting to talk about Brent at all, he changed the subject. "Do you need to take tomorrow off?"

Either she thought him terribly kind for offering or she was as anxious as he to move on. "What I need is to stay busy," she told him, tugging up a smile from somewhere inside her. "I don't do so well when I have too much time to think. Besides," she added as the low ring of the telephone sounded from the front office, "you have rounds tomorrow, and that would leave Bess here alone."

One of the lights on Greg's phone started to blink. Glancing toward it, Jenny saw that the call was coming in on the line used by hospitals, other doctors and whoever else he had given the number to.

Guilt had her rising.

"Do you want me to get that?" she asked. She shouldn't be dumping this on him. His silence on her offer to assist with his father's estate made it clear enough that he didn't want her help with his little problem, so she had no business turning to him with more of hers. As kind as he was being, and as practical, she needed to work this out on her own.

"I've got it." His chair legs bumped against the carpet as he rose and headed for his desk. "I'm expecting a call about my interviews. Hang on."

She heard him answer the phone then ask the caller to hold for a moment. Hitting the hold button, he turned to where she'd moved between the table and the door.

"I'll be another hour here tonight. Then I'm going to see Mrs. McNeff. Her family is taking her to St. Johnsbury for more extensive tests in the morning so I won't see her on my rounds." He hesitated. "Are you okay to drive home?"

He was letting her know he was available if she needed him.

As reassuring as she found the thought, she didn't think it terribly wise to start counting on him any more than she already did.

"I'll be fine."

"Are you sure?"

"Positive." Still feeling numb, she tried for another smile. "I have my emergency Oreos."

Her original bag was almost gone by Saturday. By Sunday night she was down to two cookies and trying to figure out where to get more because the general store didn't carry the chocolate-filled kind. She really needed another bag, too. She'd taken Greg's advice and contacted Brent.

She wished now that she hadn't.

Cellophane rattled as she started to pull out the next-to-the-last cookie, then changed her mind and left it. The way her life had been going lately, she'd best save what she had. It was always possible that something worse could happen.

Carefully folding the bag, she tucked it behind the cans of tuna and soup in the cabinet. Her stash was barely hidden before she turned around, listening.

Beneath the creaks and groans of the old house settling in for the night she heard the rumble of a vehicle coming up the drive.

She glanced down at her clothes, brushed at the front of her shirt. She had worked at the diner until four, then changed into her old gray sweats with the stretched-out neckline. For the past few hours she'd sat on the back porch, alternately blanking her mind as she listened to the crickets and the distant babble of the stream and sanding the rickety wood table and chairs she'd found in the storage shed out back. She needed a table in her kitchen.

Not caring to think about everything else she needed, she tried to imagine who would be coming to visit so late. It was nearly eight o'clock. Even in Maple Mountain people didn't just drop by at that hour.

Her front porch light now worked. The doorbell didn't.

Greg didn't have a chance to knock, though, before he saw Jenny look from behind the oval of glass on the door.

He had debated for most of the two-and-a-half-hour drive from the airport about whether he should stop to check on her or wait until he saw her at the office to see how she was holding up.

He'd actually driven past the house with its muted glow of light from the porch and the kitchen window when he swore, hit the brakes and turned back.

The moment she opened the door, a smile sneaked into her eyes. "Are you just now getting back from Montpelier?"

"My flight was late."

She stepped aside, tugging up the neck of her sweatshirt from where it slipped off one shoulder.

"You don't have a phone," he said, dragging his glance from where she'd just covered a delicate pink bra strap. "If you had, I would have just called."

The light from the kitchen illuminated half of her face as she tipped her head. With her dark hair cut so short around her ears, the line of her neck looked as smooth as alabaster. "What for?"

Because I worry about you out here, he grudgingly admitted, despite having told himself a dozen times that she'd be fine. Much of the population of Maple Mountain had miles between them and their neighbors. There were miles between all the little villages and miles between many of the people who lived in them, too.

"Because you were pretty shaken up the last time I talked to you," he said, since that reason seemed more relevant. "I didn't know if we'd get a chance to talk in the morning."

He'd come by to make sure she was all right. The thought did something strange to Jenny's heart as she reached behind him and closed out the mosquitoes before they could make their way through the holes in the screen.

"Tomorrow will be busy," she agreed. "Chaotic, actually. I had to work four appointments from Friday into your schedule."

"No rest for the wicked."

"So they say. Come on in."

Greg stepped past her. The only other time he had been inside the house had been her first night there. The living room was still bare, but the kitchen had been transformed. As much as it could be, anyway, considering the wood rot around the window frame over the sink, the tattered weather stripping under the back door and the rather desperate need for new linoleum.

The cracked walls were now a golden Tuscan yellow. The scarred and scrubbed beige countertops held a couple of Bristol-blue canisters, a red cereal bowl of wild berries and a canning jar filled with the flowers that still struggled to grow at the side of the house.

It was the row of boxes below the sheet-covered window that had his attention, though. That and the neat pallet of bedding near her cardboard nightstand and dresser.

"Soap and paint only go so far." She shrugged, apparently hoping her philosophical approach would remove his quick frown. "So," she continued, motioning to the little refrigerator he knew Rhonda loaned her. "Can I get you anything? I only have milk and orange juice, but you're welcome to either."

"I'm fine. Thanks." Stuffing his hands into his pockets, he glanced inside an open doorway near the woodstove.

He had no idea what horrors lurked in her plumbing, but as he stepped closer he could see that the bathroom with its clawfoot tub and pedestal sink had been scrubbed clean. It also smelled of her soap and shampoo.

"It's better than it was," he heard her say.

His glance slid from the defense in her expression to where the faded gray sweatshirt covered her stomach. It did look better, he thought. Brighter, definitely. But she had a long way to go to get the place ready for a child. This was the only area she was using, the only part of the house even halfway livable. She was sleeping on the floor. Her only furniture was the wooden stool she'd painted the same warm color as the walls.

Not wanting to sound as critical as he felt, he rubbed the frown from his forehead. "Mind if I ask what kind of heat this place has?"

"Oil."

"Does it work?"

It was her turn to look displeased.

"No." She had asked the electrician about it. Oil furnaces hadn't been his area of expertise, but he had one himself. As for hers, aside from needing a new motor, the empty oil tank had water in it and had rusted. "But the woodstove does. Grandma used it all the time."

"You have firewood then?"

"Some," she said, thinking of the lean-to that used to always hold a winter's supply. "Less than a cord," she amended, since he looked as if he were about to ask how much. "I'll have to buy more."

"At least you're not planning to cut it yourself," he muttered. He checked behind the sheet over the window. "What about storm windows?"

Jenny's brow furrowed. "They're in the storage shed."

"And?"

Something in her expression must have given her away. "Most of them need to be replaced. The frames warped and the panes broke."

She thought he might ask why they hadn't been put on the house before it had been boarded up. She would have had to tell him she didn't know. She might have also told him his inspection wasn't necessary. She was well aware of all the structural deficiencies. Most of them, anyway. But he'd just hitched his thumb toward the living room. "Mind if I look around in there?"

Tugging at her sweatshirt, feeling as uneasy as she had the first time she'd considered what he must think of how she was living, she motioned for him to go ahead.

Clearly on a mission, he disappeared.

From where Jenny stayed beside her kitchen counter, she listened to him cross the hardwood floor and open the door that led upstairs. Since the door closed a few moments later, he'd apparently chosen not to go up. It was just as well, she thought. Between the cobwebs and the water damage from where the roof sagged over the bedrooms, the space was fairly frightening.

When he walked back in, his features were drawn in the same thoughtful expression she'd seen when he was about to break uncomfortable news to a patient.

"This really was a good house." She wanted him to know that. As a child she'd had so many wonderful times there. Holidays. Birthdays. Ordinary days that seemed special just because her family had been together then. That was probably why she didn't see it as the disaster Greg must, why she felt safe where no one else would.

"You need some serious work here, Jenny. I know you don't want to talk to Brent," he admitted, stopping an arm's length away, "but you really should call his attorney."

"I already did."

That seemed to surprise him. "What did he say?"

The Oreos in the cupboards seemed to whisper her name.

The man with the broad Bostonian vowels hadn't wanted to help her at all. At least, not until she'd told him why she'd wanted to talk to his client. Even then he'd said that the best he could do was arrange for Brent to call her from the jail during one of his visitation times, and then only if Brent wanted to talk to her.

Since the only place she could be reached during the day was at the clinic, and since the only time she could count on Bess not being there was on their lunch hour, she'd asked if he would call her then.

She honestly hadn't thought the man would call her back. And he hadn't. When the phone had rung at ten in the morning with Bess, mercifully, busy with a patient, it had been Brent himself.

"I talked to Brent Friday," she finally admitted. Feeling an urgent need to move, she picked up the dishcloth from the edge of the sink to wipe the chocolate crumbs from the counter. "Aside from learning that he's in the process of plea-bargaining himself from twenty years in jail to ten, he said that I'll have to prove paternity." She swiped at the counter, shook out the crumbs. "I'm not about to fight him."

She could still feel the sting of his insinuation. The man had to know the child was his. She had been with no one else. Ever. Brent knew that. But Brent was a man without character. The fact that he acted as if she had none tore her to the quick.

"I don't have the money to go to court," she continued, tossing the cloth into the sink. "I have enough legal debt because of him as it is. And don't tell me I should fight anyway," she hurried to insist, because that was something Greg would do. He was used to fighting. He'd done it all his life. She was too new at it to survive its cutthroat rules. "He has no assets, no job and no means of paying me anything. This child is mine. No one else's."

For a moment Greg said nothing. When he did, his quiet apology made her go still.

"I'm sorry, Jenny."

She studied him as he stood there, taking up the middle of the golden-yellow room. She couldn't tell if he was sorry for what Brent had said, or if he'd apologized for almost insisting that she contact Brent in the first place. She didn't care. As empty as she felt inside, she would take either one.

"Thanks," she murmured. She was sorry, too. "But you know what really upsets me?" she asked, because the matter tore at her, too. "When I'd left Boston, I was escaping a scandal. The minute it becomes obvious that I'm pregnant, I'll be right in the middle of another one. I'd thought I was safe here. I thought I could come back and blend in and just be like everyone else. But that can't happen now. I'm going to be the girl who went to the city and came back pregnant. I don't care how nice people will be to my face, I know what they'll be saying behind my back."

Greg took a step toward her. "Jenny…"

"You know Emmy Larkin, don't you?" she asked, stepping back, not wanting him to stop her. "She runs her parents' maple sugaring operation in the spring and a B and B in the summer and fall. I feel so awful for her whenever she comes into town. It's been years and people still talk behind her back. She didn't even do anything herself. The scandal was with her dad and the man who was supposed to be his best friend, but there are always whispers about how sorry people feel for her and how she's going to die out there an old maid. People won't be nearly so kind talking about me, but I'll know they're doing it. I don't want people talking about me as if I don't know what they're saying. And I definitely don't want it for my baby."

"Jenny…"

"What?"

"Come on," he coaxed, reaching for her. Wanting to ease her agitation, his hands curved over her shoulders. Beneath his palms, her slender muscles felt rigid with tension, her bones amazingly delicate. "You're not the only single woman to ever have a child."

Jenny felt the gentle kneading motion of his fingers and the heat of his hands seeping into her. Part of her craved that contact, the quiet support she felt in it. Another part wanted desperately for him to fold her against his very solid chest and simply hold her until the awful emptiness went away.

The rational part of her simply wanted him to understand.

"How many single mothers do you know in Maple Mountain?"

"There's Lorna Bagley."

"Her husband died."

"Penny Prescott."

"Divorced."

"There has to be someone else."

"Carrie Higgins's sister got pregnant in high school and her parents shipped her off to relatives in Maine. She never came back. It's not like I can leave here myself, either. I need the medical insurance that comes with my job at the clinic."

She stopped herself. Moving back from the arms he wasn't offering anyway, she shoved her fingers through her hair. She didn't mean to unload on him. It was just that with Greg it always seemed so easy to do.

"I'm sorry," she said, needing to pull back from where her thoughts had gone. She was better off to focus on one day at a time. One week, max. "You didn't come by to hear me rant." She wanted to hear about him, to just talk with him about something that wasn't distressing. "How did your interviews go?"

He wasn't ready to drop the subject. She could tell by the quality of his silence. Desperately needing to move on, she tried again.

"Did either place appeal to you?"

"Brayborough," he finally replied. "It's about the same size as Maple Mountain, and they're desperate for a doctor. They offered me the position on the spot."

"What did you think of the offer?"

"I accepted."

She needed to take lessons from him, she thought. Something could get to him, but he could bury his reaction to it a matter of seconds. She had no idea how long it had taken him to learn how to do that. A lifetime, she suspected. But she definitely needed to study his technique. The best she could do now was force a smile and hope her quiet "That's great" didn't sound as disheartened as it felt.

It must not have. Or if it did, Greg didn't seem to notice. He left a few minutes later, after telling her he was relieved to have the job and that he should go so she could get some rest.

A minute after that Jenny dug out what was left of her Oreo stash and slowly unscrewed a cookie.

Chapter Eight

Within days, change permeated the air. Jenny could feel it in the sudden coolness of the past few evenings and in the mornings that, almost overnight, turned crisp. She could see it, too, in the leaves. Touches of gold and bronze appeared in the birches lining the wide fertile fields and meadows, and crowning the ridge tops. Before long, maples would blaze crimson.

As much as Jenny loved the change of seasons, as much as she'd always looked forward to them when she'd lived in Maple Mountain before, she felt more anxiety than anticipation now. In the past couple of months, she had experienced enough change to last her a lifetime and nothing would have made her happier than to find a routine and settle into it for…forever. There had been a time in her life when she'd thought she would dry up and die without the prospect of something new and exciting to look forward to. But she had since learned that there was a lot to be said for security and that a person had to be very careful what she wished for.

Every morning now brought the reminder of more change to come. Every sunrise meant she had one day less to prepare herself for the responsibility of a child, and that she was one day closer to the time the little secret she carried would become apparent. Each day that passed meant she had one day less to repair the old house, and that she was twenty-four hours closer to the time the ice and snows would turn it drafty and cold.

Her to-do list changed, too.

She could go without buying a bed, but she needed a crib.

She could go without a dresser for her clothes, but she needed warm clothes for the baby. And blankets. And a car seat. And a snowsuit and mittens and a cap. The baby's list grew.

The baby.

The thought of a child had brought panic before. Now that distress was still there, but so was a guarded sense of anticipation. She was going to be a mom. Life grew inside her. Life that was too tiny now to even feel, but it was there. And it was hers. The new little person wasn't responsible for any of the circumstances surrounding its existence, the very existence that complicated the daylights out of her mother's life. But she would be loved for who she was simply because every child deserved no less.

She, Jenny found herself thinking more and more. She hoped her child was a girl, mostly because a girl would be easier than a boy to raise without a father. Yet, boy or girl, she would promise her child that she would somehow keep it safe and remind it not to be in a hurry to grow up because being grown up wasn't nearly as much fun as it appeared to be when a person was only four feet tall.

She needed a rocking chair.

The thought hit as she left the clinic Thursday afternoon, so she added one to her mental list right below a washer and dryer. She'd decided those had to be priority, especially once the weather grew too inclement to dry clothes outside.

She winced as she remembered something else she needed

to add. Firewood. Greg had reminded her of it Sunday night while discussing her heating situation, but she'd forgotten to write it down. There were acres of trees on the property, some fallen from previous storms. She could barter half of whatever was cut for the labor. People did that sort of thing around there all the time.

Dodging the slow-moving stream of visitors' cars on her way to the diner, she wondered who she knew who owned a chain saw. If no one wanted to trade, maybe she could borrow the saw and cut the wood herself. Greg had said he was surprised she hadn't already considered that, though his muttering had sounded more like an odd sort of frustration to her than mere observation.

The memory brought a faint frown. He had seemed different to her all week. More watchful, somehow, but far less inclined to make small talk. She knew he had a lot on his own mind, but she missed his casual interest in the ongoing saga of her house repairs. Each morning he still asked what she'd accomplished the night before. Yet his response to her having sanded another chair and fixed the frame on one of the unbroken storm windows had been nothing but the pinch of his lips.

His strangely restrained manner had been evident, too, when Bess had been on her rounds a couple of days ago. Jenny had been changing the paper sheet on an exam table after a patient left when he'd walked in and asked if she was taking any sort of vitamin supplement. After she'd replied to the seemingly odd question by telling him she wasn't, he'd handed her a bottle of prenatal vitamins and told her to take one a day. He'd also given her a slip of paper with the name and number of a St. Johnsbury obstetrician because he figured she'd be more comfortable getting her care away from the clinic and Maple Mountain.

Wondering at his thoughtfulness for her unborn child and his sensitivity for her, she hadn't been able to think of a thing to say other than, "Thank you."

He'd said nothing more himself. He'd just given her a nod,

pushed his hands into his slacks pockets and walked out without another word.

Someone called her name.

Plastering on a smile when she saw Claire McGraw wave at her on her way out of the quilting shop next door, Jenny waved back. Ever since Greg had alluded to how easy her emotions were to read when she worried, she'd made a conscious effort to keep her thoughts away from her troubles when she was around those who knew her.

She was about to face a few more of those who knew her now.

Dutifully keeping her smile in place, she headed up the stairs Dora had lined with early-harvest pumpkins and pots of red and gold mums and pulled open the diner's screen door.

Greg stood at the reception room window watching Jenny wave to someone he couldn't see before she disappeared inside the diner. He'd returned from his rural rounds a half hour ago, earlier than usual because he hadn't had as many calls, but he'd yet to start his dictation.

He hadn't been able to shake the thought that Jenny was sleeping on the floor. She was using a comforter for a mattress.

Until he'd followed the impulse and stopped at her house, he hadn't given any thought to what she might be using for a bed. Mostly, he suspected, because thinking of Jenny in any horizontal context would have conjured thoughts of her sweet little body and how he'd like to be horizontal with her. All she had to do was walk into the room and he could feel his body responding in ways that had him feeling more frustrated than he did already. But casual sex was the last thing she would want or need. Aside from the emotional beating that had undoubtedly left her frightened and fragile inside, she was carrying a child. She had a roof with holes. She didn't have a decent place to sleep.

He'd been thinking of that for the past five days. He'd spent those same five days trying to figure out a way to make her house more habitable.

For all her efforts, she was simply applying bandages when major surgery was needed. He had no idea what kind of damage the elements had done through the sagging roof upstairs, but he'd felt a breeze and smelled fresh air when he'd opened the stairway door. The night she'd helped him realign his arm, she'd had a pot on the kitchen floor to catch the rain.

He'd called a roofer in St. Johnsbury himself to see how much a roof would cost and how soon the work could be done. After he had described the approximate size and condition of what was there now, the guy had given him a ball-park figure of ten thousand dollars, give or take a few thousand either way. He wouldn't be able to tell him for sure until he saw it himself. With the jobs he was trying to finish before the rains started, he also wouldn't be able to get to it until next spring.

Greg had no money to speak of himself. Like Jenny, he was in debt and would be until his work with the Rural Health Corp helped him pay off the last of his student loans. That was why he'd jumped at the job in Brayborough, much as he had at the one in Maple Mountain. He had his salary, which adequately met his personal needs, but there was little left to spare. Certainly, not enough for a roof and furniture.

For a rather disquieting and totally unexpected moment, he'd even thought of giving her some of his father's money. But even if it had been accessible to him, which it wasn't because it was tied up in real estate and investments and he'd yet to sign a single document that had been sent to him, money wouldn't solve her bigger problem. In her kitchen the other night, it had been clear that what bothered her even more than the condition of her house was how people would perceive her once her pregnancy became apparent. After everything that had been taken from her, her good name in Maple Mountain was all she had left.

He could think of only one way to help her.

He didn't have money to give her, but he did have space.

The idea of having her move in with him had hit two nights ago on his way through his spacious living room to his study.

The house he lived in had been built for a family. There were extra rooms. Extra beds.

He had promptly dismissed the notion, however. The idea wasn't nearly as straightforward as it first seemed. And what it would take to make it work was the epitome of extreme. Aside from that, though he could see the logic in it, Jenny might easily think he'd lost his mind.

"Something interesting going on out there?"

He jerked his glance to Bess, looked back out the window again. Despite the radical edge to it, the idea kept returning, taking firmer root.

"Just watching the tourists," he replied, since the street was scattered with them. The fall foliage season had started to arrive and with it the first of what the locals called leaf-peepers. He'd just spotted a license plate from Rhode Island.

As he wondered where the people with the out-of-state plates were staying and how long they would be, he frowned at himself. He was getting as nosy as Amos and Charlie.

Bess lifted one of the blinds' white slats so she could see better herself. "I heard you ask Jenny if she knew what the specials are at the diner tonight. Thought you might be debating whether or not to go for dinner before the tourists took over the place."

Food had actually been the last thing on his mind. When he'd asked Jenny about the menu a few minute ago, he'd just been making conversation. "I have work to do yet. I think I'll just stay here for a couple hours, then go home and thaw something in the microwave."

"Well, if you're of a mind for something more palatable, we're having pot luck at the community center while we set up for the chicken dinner tomorrow night." Turning in her sensible shoes, she headed for the far side of the room to close the blinds. "There won't be any visitors there. At least not until tomorrow, and then I hope they come in droves. We need their money to buy wood and supplies for the extra booths I'm helping paint for the Pumpkin Festival. Come over about seven. I'll be there. So will Amos, the Sheldons and the Moorehouses. Mary is bringing her lasagna casserole."

The fund-raising chicken dinners at the community center were nearly as popular as the town's seasonal celebrations themselves. More important at the moment, Mary Moorehouse made amazing lasagna.

"You're painting?" he asked absently, writing off a frozen dinner for potluck. "I thought you always baked pies for the festival."

"I'm doing that, too. Claire McGraw talked me into the other." She turned to straighten the magazines on the small table. Since Jenny had been in a hurry to get to the diner today, Bess had told her she would lock up. "She's got Jenny working on pumpkin costumes."

Mild interest turned acute. "When will she have time do that?"

"You'll have to ask her," his nurse-practitioner replied. "I already think she's bitten off more than she can chew trying to get that house in shape. Not that I can't see why she's doing it," she confided, one professional to another. "If she rebuilds it, she rebuilds her life, so to speak. And the busier she stays, the less time she has to think. Between you and me, I don't think she's doing so well with what happened to her in the city."

Greg felt himself hesitate. He had no idea what Bess knew. No idea how much, if anything, Jenny had confided in her. "What do you mean?"

"Her being attacked by that man who tried to rob her," she said, frowning as if she couldn't imagine what else he thought she'd be talking about. "Being mugged scared her enough to bring her back here," she reminded him. "She says she's just fine when I ask, but I don't think she is. She's trying to handle too much on her own." Her tight salt-and-pepper curls barely moved when she shook her head. "I worry about that girl."

Greg couldn't fault Bess's psychology or her metaphor. As he followed the older woman through the reception room doorway, he conceded that he might have reached the same conclusion himself had he not known that Jenny was in the process of moving home when the mugging had taken place. Or had he not been privy to the events that had really brought her back to Maple Mountain.

"Oh, for Pete's sake," he heard Bess say as she opened a file drawer for her purse. "I thought she seemed distracted when she left here. She forgot her jacket."

"Leave it." Since Bess had suggested he ask Jenny where she'd find time to work on the festival, he planned to do just that. She barely had time to sleep as it was. "I'll drop it off for her on my way home."

The closed sign swung in the door's window as Jenny shut the diner's door behind her. Inside, Lorna had just finished mopping the kitchen and Dora was snapping out lights.

Shivering as the cool air hit her skin, she crossed her arms over her thin white blouse and started down the stairs.

Had it not been for the chill keeping her shoulders hunched, they would have sagged as the fatigue of the day set in. She'd hadn't slept well last night, not that she did any night, and had been at a dead run since she'd arrived at the clinic that morning. The thought of now having to go to her cold, creaky house and build a fire to get warm and be back at the clinic first thing in the morning made her want to sit down and cry. But if she sat down, she wouldn't want to get up, and crying wasn't something she allowed herself to do—even though she felt like doing just that more every day. She was afraid that if she started she might never stop and she needed to learn to be strong for her baby.

"You really don't ever want to play poker."

There were no streetlights in Maple Mountain. In the glow of the half-moon and the entrance light from the building behind her, she saw Greg walk toward her. With his hands deep in the pockets of his casual corduroy jacket, something dark looped through one arm, he met her at the edge of the street.

"Long day?"

She couldn't tell who was asking. Greg her boss. Or, Greg the man who had somehow become her confidant and who totally, completely confused her.

"Is that a trick question?"

"A redundant one," he replied, letting her off the hook. "I can see you're beat. Here." He held out her jean jacket. "You forgot this."

Grateful that she wouldn't have to go in and get it or drive home cold, she thanked him and slipped the flannel-lined denim over her blouse.

"Are you just now leaving work?" she asked, crossing her arms against another shiver as she started to warm.

"I worked until about seven, took a dinner break, then put in another hour."

"And you brought me my jacket," she concluded, touched as she always was by his thoughtfulness.

"You needed it. Come on. I'll walk you to your car."

Jenny glanced up at his profile. He seemed distracted, as if his mind hadn't yet left work and he was still thinking about a patient or concerned about one. There was a deep-in-thought, pensive quality about him as they angled across the road and headed for the lot behind the clinic. She always left her car there when she worked at the diner. It seemed silly to drive it across the street.

"Is Mrs. McNeff doing worse?" she asked, thinking Sally's mom might be who occupied his thoughts. The older lady had been in the hospital for a week now.

"Actually, I talked to her oncologist a couple of hours ago. He thinks she's responding well to the new chemo protocol."

A faint smile tugged at Jenny's mouth. That was really good to know. "I just thought you might be thinking about her," she explained. "You had that look."

"That look?"

"The one you get when something's on your mind."

"I don't have a 'look,'" he insisted, frowning.

"Yes you do. You say you can always tell when I'm worried.

Well, I can tell when you're preoccupied. You get two little lines. Right…" She started to reach up and touch the spot between his eyebrows. For a variety of reasons, starting with the fact that they were in full view of whoever happened to drive by, she touched between her own instead. "Right here."

"So," she said, still wondering what was on his mind since he wasn't saying. Not that he'd confided in her much lately. If she'd had the nerve, she might have asked why he seemed to be keeping his distance from her. But she was afraid she already knew. When she'd discovered she was pregnant, he had offered to be there for her if she needed him. And she didn't doubt that if she asked, he would be. Just as he would be for anyone else. He just didn't want her to think he was offering anything more than that.

She didn't want anything more herself. All she wanted was his friendship. And maybe, once in a while, to have his strong arms wrapped around her.

"So," he echoed. "What hours do you work this weekend?"

She shook off her thoughts, hating how needy she felt, and hugged herself tighter. "I work lunch and dinner Saturday and lunch on Sunday. Why?"

"And your house," he said, ignoring her question as they walked. "What do you plan to do there when you're not at the diner?"

"Caulk."

"Caulk?"

"You know. Put that gooey insulating stuff around the windows, the bathtub and the sink. Mostly the windows. I want to get them done before it rains."

"So when do you plan on making costumes for the harvest festival?" he asked mildly.

The deep tones of his voice made him sound merely curious. Still, Jenny couldn't help but hesitate. "I'm only doing two. And I have six weeks to get them done."

"That doesn't answer my question. What about sleep?" he

continued in that same deceptively quiet tone. "When do you plan to do that?"

Confused by his questioning, she tried not to sound defensive as she tipped up her chin. "I sleep."

"But not well," he countered. "And not enough. You try to hide it, but you're tired all the time, Jenny."

Probably because I'm pregnant, she thought, but decided not to say. He knew that. And she *was* tired. She hardly needed him to point that out to her. But her concern at the moment was why he felt it necessary to mention her fatigue at all.

Lights from a passing car illuminated the short driveway beside the clinic. At the back of the square white building, a yellow security lamp glowed near her car. Uneasy, she glanced toward him.

He towered beside her as they moved along the quiet and darkened structure, seeming as tall and strong as the oaks and maples behind the lot. And suddenly just as silent.

"The tiredness will go away," she assured him. At least she hoped it would. If it didn't, she'd be dragging by the time the baby came next April. "Rhonda managed."

"Rhonda wasn't working two jobs and rehabbing a house."

"She has four children. She does now that she has little Amy Lynn, anyway. That's a job and half right there."

"She has a husband and sister who help her, too. You don't have anyone."

Now there was a reminder she could live without.

Unfortunately she had no way to counter it. The best she could do was say, "I'll be fine. I'm fine now," and head to her car.

She had her fingers on the handle when she looked up to thank him again for her jacket and tell him good-night. She needed to go. She really did. She had no idea why he was saying what he was, but she was feeling too dispirited to hear it. The last thing she needed was him making her feel more discouraged than she already did.

The feel of his hand covering hers stopped her cold.

"You don't have to do that with me, Jenny. You want to be okay. And you pretend you are. But you and I both know you're not."

Greg lowered his voice even more. They could be seen if someone really looked, but now no one could hear them.

"You need to give something up," he insisted. "You're trying to do to much."

His big hand engulfed hers, his heat permeating her skin. The side of his jacket brushed her shoulder. As close as he stood, she could almost feel the heat of his body, too.

He was right. Something had to give. It was just difficult to think of what that something might be with him taunting her with his big body and jerking around with her flagging morale.

"I'll ask for a smaller project for the festival," she said.

"I was thinking more of your job at the diner."

In the glow of the pale light he saw pure panic slip into her eyes.

Pulling her hand away, she drew back, quickly recrossed her arms.

"I can't quit there. I need that job. You know that."

"I know you're trying to do too much," he repeated.

"My work at the clinic is okay, isn't it?" she hurried to ask. "I haven't come in late and I don't leave early. Except for tonight," she amended, seeming to think her job performance was the issue. "But I had everything done before I left, and Bess said she didn't mind locking up."

"Jenny—"

"It's just that with all the tourists, Dora needed me as soon as I could get there."

"Tonight wasn't a problem."

"Then what is? Did I set someone up for the wrong test? Am I making mistakes in your transcription? Bess is helping me with the words I'm not sure about and I'm trying to get the terminology memorized—"

He couldn't stand her panic. Unable to bear that he'd caused it, he reached toward her. Nudging back the soft hair at her temple, he said, "You haven't done any of that. Your work is fine."

Fear and fatigue strained her features as her eyes searched his. "Then, why do you want me to quit the diner? What I make there is the only way I'll be able to pay for a new furnace."

The crisp night air he breathed brought the scent of burning pine from someone's fireplace and a hint of her herbal shampoo. The smoke barely registered. The blend of balsam and sweet herbs always did. And, as always, breathing in that soft, seductive scent, he felt a twinge of pure visceral awareness low in his gut.

He let his hand fall.

"I think you should forget about the house, too," he told her, needing to keep his libido out of this. "It's taking too much of your energy. You need to take care of yourself," he explained, his voice softening. "If not for you, then for your baby."

"I can't forget about the house." She looked as she sounded, utterly amazed that he could think she would. "I don't have any choice but to do what I'm doing. You know that, too."

It was because she had little choice that the idea he'd had simply refused to go away. He just hadn't considered that he would really suggest it until he'd felt her distress clutch his chest. He'd never intended to alarm her.

"Actually, you do. You can marry me," he said, because he needed her to know he was trying to make things better for her, not worse. "Temporarily."

Bewilderment disappeared in a slow blink. Now she just looked stunned.

"I would suggest that you just move in with me," he hurried to add, wanting her to know he'd explored all the options and found his proposal the only viable alternative. "That wouldn't work, though. There's a morals clause in my agreement with the community. Housing here is only for the physician and his legal dependents. Bertie Buell and her friends on the city council would be the first to come pounding on my door to remind us of that, too." Heaven knew the old biddy had a nose for improprieties. "Just living with me wouldn't solve your other problems, anyway.

"If we're married," he explained, "we can share the house and you can forget about the work on yours. Being married would save your reputation, too. You're a little more than two months along now. I'll be leaving here in just over another two. You should be able to hide your pregnancy for that long."

Jenny slowly shook her head. "Marry you?"

"For a while," he reiterated.

Still struggling to believe what Greg was so calmly suggesting, Jenny threaded her fingers through her hair. "How long is 'a while'?"

"A couple of years. That's the length of my new contract. When we move from here, everyone in the new place will assume the baby is mine. I can help you with it after it comes," he told her, because in the past few days, he'd thought about that, too. "And you can help me run the office while we're there. The way you do now. That way you'll have the references you need so when my contract expires, we can both move on."

From a few blocks beyond them came the hoot of an owl. Up toward Greg's house, his neighbor's dog barked in response. Those distant sounds were all that broke the stillness as Jenny stared at the man she knew didn't believe in marriage, didn't want to be married and was proposing it to her all the same.

"Why would you want to do this?"

Greg actually had several answers to her baffled question, every one of which he'd mulled over and discarded, then analyzed and argued all over again. But he didn't want to tell her that he felt sorry for her. Or that her quiet sensuality was driving him crazy and that he wanted her in his bed. The last thing he wanted was to make her feel bad or scare her off.

"Because I figured we could help each other out," he replied, giving her the more logical reasons he'd come up with. "You've got to admit you could use a break, Jenny. If you do this, you won't have to work so hard, your reputation wouldn't be trashed and you can stop worrying."

He rubbed the side of his nose. Not all of his reasons were altruistic.

"I've also been thinking about your offer, and about what you said. About my father's estate," he clarified, because he'd been wrestling with that, too. "Maybe you're right. If I can focus on selling off everything to use it for something positive, I'd be more inclined to deal with it. I figured if you would do what you offered to do and go through those papers for me, you could help me figure out where the money should go."

Jenny felt some of the tension slowly leak from her shoulders.

"Are you still interested in doing that for me?" he asked.

Of course she was, she wanted to say. But when she opened her mouth, all that came out was a confused rush of air.

"I know," he said, rubbing the side of his nose again. "It's a lot to think about. It just seems like a good way to help each other out."

Looking as if he didn't want to crowd her, or maybe feeling crowded himself thinking about the documents in his bottom drawer, he reached past to open her car door. "You don't have to answer me now," he said. "Just take a few days and think about it. Okay?"

Just think about it, Greg had said.

All day Friday as they worked more or less side by side and for the rest of the weekend, Jenny thought of little else. Only when she was working and distracted by the need to answer phones and questions and take orders for blood tests, X-rays and blue-plate specials was Greg's offer not at the forefront of her mind.

His offer was most definitely there when she returned to her house after finishing the lunch shift Sunday afternoon.

It was a little after four o'clock by the time she changed into jeans and a pullover sweater and picked up her to-do list from the counter. After staring at it for nearly a minute, she carefully set it back down.

If she accepted Greg's offer she wouldn't have to do anything else on that list. At least, not now.

His offer. That was how she'd been thinking of what he had

suggested, for it certainly wasn't a proposal in the traditional sense. It was more of an arrangement, she supposed. One that would benefit her far more than him. But the fact that he wanted her help with his father's estate, that he trusted her with something so intensely personal and painful to him, had eased the awful feeling that she'd overstepped the bounds of their relationship.

What he had offered also left her vacillating between numb disbelief and the heady prospect of reprieve.

In a little more than six months, she would give birth to the life growing inside her, the child who would depend on her for absolutely everything. She had gone from weeks of living each day doggedly looking only toward the future, to accepting that she would now never be able to escape parts of her past. She lived each day dreading the gossip to come, and worried constantly about how she would care for a child in a house she couldn't afford to heat even if she did get a furnace and new tank. Without storm windows to help insulate the drafty old place, the cost of heating fuel would go through the roof, right along with the heat.

It seemed as if there was always one more expense or problem out there waiting to bite her. Afraid to wonder what that next thing might be, she picked up a roll of duct tape and headed for the crack in the living room window, hoping distraction would help shake the feeling of helplessness that grew inside her like weeds after a spring rain.

That feeling was usually most noticeable in bed at night when there was nothing to divert her thoughts. It tended to come when she was trying to not think about how she'd gotten where she was and the awful emptiness inside her because of it. She felt hollow, as if part of her simply no longer existed. Part of her no longer did, she supposed. The enthusiasm and energy that had once driven her were long gone. But the sense of helplessness bothered her more.

With a quick rip, she tore off a piece of duct tape and knelt by the crack. She had never been one of those weak, dependent women who always seemed in need of being rescued. She'd known what she'd wanted, gone after it and even though her marvelous plans had blown up in her face, she had never felt as if she couldn't somehow scrape her life back together by herself.

But it wasn't a matter of just taking care of herself anymore. She had a child to consider. As for putting things back together, she wasn't doing such a hot job on that score with much of anything.

She'd carefully touched one end of the tape to the crack. She'd just as carefully pressed halfway along the diagonal fissure when the bottom half cracked farther up and simply…fell out.

Slowly sinking back on her heels, she stared at the gap in the window pane.

It was a hole. That was all. Not even a minor blip on the crisis scale, but something about having the glass do the very thing she'd been trying to prevent only compounded the disheartened sensations living in her chest. She hated the powerlessness she felt. Hated the awful void. She hated trying to do everything alone. But Greg was offering her a way to not have to do everything on her own. And even though what he offered was only temporary, and even though he was only offering as a friend, she desperately needed the lifeline he'd thrown her.

Her first priority was her child. Her reputation and her pride aside, what she needed more than anything was to take care of her health while the baby was growing and have a decent place to take it after it was born. If that meant marrying and ultimately moving on to Brayborough with him, then that's what she needed to do.

There was no relief in her decision. Not yet. It was too soon to feel any sense of ease, too soon to let herself believe that she no longer had to worry. As she moved outside to clean up the chunk of glass that had shattered on the porch boards and tape cardboard over the hole, her only thoughts were of where Greg would be at five o'clock on a gorgeous fall afternoon.

She needed to know he hadn't changed his mind.

If she'd had a phone, she could have called him. But she didn't, so it was either drive to his house or wait until morning.

Ten minutes later, worried more by the second that the Fates were only toying with her and that Greg had come to his senses, she hurried to her woodpile to get the wood she needed for heat that evening. She wouldn't go out to get any once it was dark. The back porch light didn't work making it too hard to see. Once she had the wood, then she'd go find him.

She had just filled her bucket with kindling and reached for a split log when the familiar rumble of an engine joined the rustle of the breeze in the leaves. Because certain parts for Greg's damaged SUV were on back order, he still drove Charlie's truck. She'd come to know the sound of the vehicle as well her own heartbeat.

From fifty feet away she watched the truck pull up to the house and saw Greg step from the cab. He had barely started toward her porch when he stopped. As if he'd felt her presence, he glanced to where she stood beneath the canopy of trees.

The nerves in her stomach jumped as he walked toward her, leaves crunching beneath his boots. The faded jeans and crew-neck sweater he wore did incredible things for his lean, athletic build, but it was his expression she noticed most as he drew closer. He looked as guarded as she felt.

Setting the log she'd picked up back on the pile, she offered a quiet, "Hi."

"Hi, yourself." Greg swept his glance over her face as she brushed off her hands. Behind her quiet smile she still looked troubled. He'd hoped that what he'd proposed would have eased some of that. "I thought you might come by after you got off work. It's hard to talk at the office."

"I was just coming to see you. After I got the wood in," she explained as her glance fell to his chest. "I thought…I mean, it's always possible that you got to thinking about what you said, and maybe now that you've had chance to think about it yourself, you've…well…"

She shook her head as she cut herself off. Taking a deep breath, she looked up and started over. "I just needed to know if your offer is still open."

He heard the faintest hint of hope in her voice, but whatever hope she felt, she held most of it back. All that really showed was her anxiety. It clouded her eyes, robbed her of the optimistic spirit that had once been so evident.

Wanting that anxiety to go away, not trusting why it tore at him to see it there, he reached toward her.

"Of course it is," he said, touching his knuckles to her jaw. "I haven't changed my mind, if that's what you were worried about."

"I wouldn't blame you if you did."

Still afraid to believe him, her head moved almost imperceptibly toward his touch.

"Well, I haven't. And I won't," he assured her, feeling that motion against his knuckles. She tried to be strong. She was strong, but at that moment she seemed to need the comfort of that small contact as much as she needed his reassurance. "This will work for both of us, Jenny."

Hope still didn't want to break free. She drew an unsteady breath, gave him a faltering smile. "It sounds like it should. And I really want it to…"

"But?" he asked when her voice trailed off.

Jenny's eyes held his. He looked so certain. So sure. "I'm scared."

"Of me?"

"No. No," she murmured, her eyes suddenly stinging. Loath to let him see tears, embarrassed that they were there, her glance fell to his chest.

"What then?"

Blinking to clear the moisture welling along her lashes, she touched her fingers to the heavy cotton covering his heart. His arms looked so strong, his chest so solid. From the moment she'd met him, she'd been drawn by his strength. She would give anything just to be surrounded by it.

She felt the steady beat of his heart. Realizing what she was doing, realizing what she so desperately wanted just then, she ducked her head lower and drew back her hand.

"I'm afraid to believe it'll be this easy, I guess."

His hand cupped the side of her face a moment before he tipped up her chin.

The tears were gone. She'd blinked them back. But he knew they'd been there by the brightness that remained. He'd seen enough people's tears to float a small armada. He'd seen tears of fear, pain and hurt. Tears of frustration and anger. Tears of sadness and joy. There were times when he thought he'd become immune to them, and in many ways he had. It was the struggle that could get him, though. The honest attempt to control whatever might cause them. He respected that. He'd just never felt the way he did seeing Jenny fight for that restraint.

She had a multitude of reasons to simply let go, yet he'd never once seen her cry. That he had nearly made her do what she so valiantly avoided, squeezed hard at his heart.

"Hey," he murmured, slipping his hands over her shoulders.

He'd never seen her look so badly in need of being held. Not caring to consider how much he wanted her in his arms, telling himself he was thinking only of her, he drew her toward him.

"You have nothing to be afraid of. Nothing," he promised, when personal promises weren't something he made to a woman.

It never occurred to him to question what he said. Something eased inside him as she slowly sagged against his body, seeking his solace, making him think of how small and fragile she felt. The bones of her back seemed as delicate as a child's beneath his larger hands, and when he felt her sigh at the comfort he offered, he was aware of nothing so much as his need to protect her.

That need might have felt dangerous, too, had he not just breathed in the scent of her hair. With her hands fisted against his chest, his hand at the back of her head, he became aware of the heat slowly rising in his blood.

Her thighs skimmed his as she drew closer. Her stomach brushed lightly against his zipper.

"So," he said, because he needed to think of something other than the feel of her slender body against his. "We're going to do this?"

Jenny's forehead rubbed against his sweater as she gave a small nod.

"Please," she asked, though all she really cared about at the moment was that she was finally where she wanted to be.

She had suspected how it would feel to be in his arms. She'd longed to be there, more often than she could even recall. But she'd had no idea how safe it would feel to be held by him. It was as if nothing more could happen to her there. She was protected, sheltered and she wanted nothing more than to stay exactly where she was for as long as he would let her.

She desperately craved the security he was offering. However temporarily. She just didn't trust the strength of the need she felt for him just then. Nor did she want him to know that that soul-deep need was there.

It took every ounce of fortitude she had to keep herself from seeking more of his hard body. The desire to lean on him, to simply cave in and let him take over completely was almost as strong as the sharp pull she felt low in her stomach when she eased back and met his eyes.

With his eyes locked on hers, she was suddenly aware of his body in far different ways. Awareness seemed to burn into her everywhere they touched. As his glance fell to her mouth, she felt her body quicken, her breathing become more shallow.

She wasn't at all prepared to deal with the sensual pull she felt toward him. He was offering her comfort. Nothing more.

Caution filled her as she eased back.

Greg eased away, too, letting her go before she could pull away herself. The incredible feel of her was not something he should be thinking about. He shouldn't be considering how beautifully her soft curves would fit beneath him. He shouldn't been thinking, either, about how tempted he was to pull her back.

"It really will be all right," he said, thinking it might be wise for them both to focus on practicalities. "There's plenty of room in the house, so it's not as if we'll always be bumping into each other."

He offered the assurance for himself as much as for her. Winter nights could be long, and while he would appreciate her company, a little distance would be a good thing. "We just need to decide if we want to get married this week or next. The sooner we do it, the easier it will be for people to assume the baby is mine if someone does start to suspect you're pregnant."

He had a point. He also had a way of keeping her slightly unsettled. The thought of how close they would have been for such a possibility to exist did strange things to her already sensitized nerves. He was a man with an unrelenting need to serve his purpose, yet he could be incredibly sensitive. He would be an amazing lover.

The unbidden thought had her heart jerking hard as her glance shied from his. "I'll leave that up to you. I'm sure you'll need time to have a prenuptial agreement drawn up." She needed to be as practical as he was being. And just as straightforward. As grateful as she was to him for all he had done, for all he was doing, she needed him to understand she expected nothing from him but temporary use of his shelter and his name. They would be married. Though they hadn't openly discussed the details, each knew the marriage would end. Considering that he would certainly want to keep his property and earnings to himself—especially considering that he'd inherited an apparently not-so-small fortune—a formal agreement would definitely be in order.

From the way he'd hesitated, it seemed he'd thought of everything about their arrangement but that.

"I'll have Larry e-mail me something," he told her, stacking logs in his arm to carry inside for her. "In the meantime, I'll see what we need to do to get a license, and you can decide when to give notice at the diner."

Picking up her bucket of kindling, she followed him inside. "I can't totally quit on Dora." The woman had given her back her old job without question. She owed her. "The next six weeks are the busiest time of year for her. Especially on weekends."

"Then help her until she can replace you."

She planned to do just that. She also knew that Dora had received calls from a couple of high-school girls in the area looking for temporary work. Once the weather turned and the visitors left, Dora and the Bagley sisters could easily handle the diner on their own.

"You're welcome to sleep at the house tonight if you want," he said, eyeing her bed on the way in. "Amos is tied up next Tuesday, so he and I are playing checkers tonight instead. I won't be home until nine, but I'll give you my key."

Jenny gave him a sideways glance. They were no more playing checkers than she was flying to Mars. Tonight would be another reading lesson. Everyone in town would know that.

"Bertie and her friends will have enough to talk about when we show up married," she replied. If she stayed at his house now, her car would be seen and rumors of an affair would start flying. "I'd really rather not get them started until then. If I stay here until we're official, they won't have much to criticize."

"Then, tell you what," he said, leaving the logs by the old woodstove. Pulling out his keys, he headed back to the front door with another glance to the comforter and blankets on the floor. "Forget about next week. We'll do it this Friday. Since the office closes early on Friday, anyway, see if you can get someone to cover for you at the diner and we can go to St. Johnsbury then."

Chapter Nine

Jenny had always thought she would be married in a white gown, a veil with yards of tulle and carrying flowers in every imaginable shade of bright. She'd thought her older and only sister would be her attendant, that the cake would be multi-tiered and that there would be friends and family everywhere. She'd imagined every detail carefully planned and nothing left to chance.

It never entered her mind that the woman standing up with her before a justice of the peace would be the justice's wife, that the man standing up for the groom would be a total stranger or that she would be saying her vows in a slate-blue business suit to a man she'd never even kissed.

"Now that the fee is out of the way, do you have the license?" The justice of the peace, a tall, thin gentleman with a rather prominent Adam's apple peered at Greg over the top of his rimless half-glasses.

"Right here."

Greg removed an envelope from inside his suit jacket. He had picked up the license at the courthouse yesterday when he'd stopped at the hospital to check on Mrs. McNeff and Edna Farber. Three days ago Edna's stubborn old mule had kicked her in the head after the cantankerous and equally stubborn old woman lost her footing trying to push him out of her garden. Her neighbor had been with her at the time and rushed her to Greg, but he hadn't been able to bring her around. Fearing hemorrhage and not wanting to wait for the ambulance, he and Joe had raced her to the hospital themselves.

Paper rustled as Greg handed the document to the lanky, sixty-something Cletus Jasper. The clerk at the courthouse had suggested they call him when Greg had said he was looking for a quick and simple ceremony.

"Thank you for doing this on such short notice."

Mr. Jasper motioned that it was nothing. "Me and the missus do weddings all the time. Done hundreds of 'em over the years. Best part of the job."

"If you'll step over here?" The man's wife, a pleasant looking woman who reminded Jenny of Mrs. Claus, motioned to a spot in the corner of the antique-filled office off the side of their home. "This won't take any time at all. Cletus has this down to less than three minutes."

The knot in Jenny's stomach tightened.

She didn't know why she felt so nervous. It wasn't as if she and Greg were really marrying. At least, not in the emotional sense. And it wasn't until death did them part. Theirs was strictly a marriage of convenience. An arrangement. She and Greg were friends. Nothing more.

Still, she felt as nervous as a real bride as she glanced from the well-meaning woman to the handsome man at her side. She'd never seen Greg in a suit before, but he wore formality as easily as he did jeans or a lab coat. The charcoal pin-striped fabric turned his eyes more silver than gray, and he wore suspenders rather than a belt. The touch was both trendy and old-fashioned conservative, and though she knew she shouldn't be thinking such things, made him look incredibly…sexy.

Her nerves jumped as he threaded his fingers through hers and leaned down to her ear.

"Smile," he whispered, his breath warm on her skin. "I'm just marrying you. Not amputating a body part. We'll be out of here in no time."

He lifted his head. In the lean angles of his face she saw nothing but the disarming confidence that always seemed to surround him. That and a certain impatience to get this over with. He had a consultation with Edna Farber's neurologist in twenty minutes.

The justice of the peace cleared his throat. His wife stopped smiling at them long enough to motion in the balding older gentleman who apparently attended such nuptials whenever the groom hadn't brought his own witness.

Jenny had thought that Greg might ask Joe to stand up with him. She'd realized after she'd thought about it, though, that Greg wouldn't ask his friend to stand with him for the same reason she hadn't asked her sister. They were only performing a legality. Friends and family weren't necessary for moral support and sharing.

A faux Roman pedestal supporting a bushy fern served as the ceremony site. Standing beside it, Cletus Jasper held a small book and asked Greg to take Jenny's hands.

With her fingers trembling slightly in Greg's firmer grip, the man cleared his throat again.

"You have come before me and these witnesses today to enter into the union of matrimony. Is there any reason this union should not take place?"

Short and to the point. They were getting what they'd asked for. Greg said, "No."

Jenny, staring at the subtle pattern in Greg's tie, shook her head.

Apparently satisfied, the sober-looking man then asked Greg if he took her, Jennifer Dawn Baker to be his lawfully wedded wife.

She heard him say, "I do."

"And do you, Jennifer Dawn Baker take Gregory Matthias Reid to be your lawfully wedded husband?"

She glanced up, made it as far as the cleft above his upper lip and murmured, "I do," too.

"Do you have the rings?"

Her eyes met Greg's. Buying rings hadn't occurred to either one of them.

"We aren't exchanging them," he said, making it sound as if the subject had been discussed and dismissed.

"Oh, well, then…" He flipped a page, cleared his throat again. "Do you have anything you want to say to each other?"

One of Greg's dark eyebrows arched at her. "Do you?"

She shook her head, hanging on to his hands more tightly. "Do you?"

He mirrored her motion, gave her hand a squeeze that almost felt sympathetic and looked back to the man watching them both.

"We don't."

He flipped another page, glanced at his wife. Mrs. Jasper checked her watch. The surreptitious thumb's-up she gave him seemed to indicate he was about to set a new record.

"In that case," he said, "by the power vested in me by the State of Vermont, County of Caledonia, I now pronounce you man and wife." He looked to Greg as he closed his book and his wife glanced at her watch again. A smile threatened above the slash of his glasses. "You may kiss the bride."

Jenny hadn't thought about this part. She didn't know if Greg had, either. But with the three people clearly waiting for them to get on with it, she didn't have a chance to consider how awkward the moment might have been. Greg let go of her hands to touch her cheek. His expression seemed to say it would only be a moment before this little formality was over as he dipped his head toward hers.

Her eyes had barely closed when she felt the brush of his lips.

They were warm, tender and far softer than they looked. She also felt a jolt of heat that shot from her breasts to her womb and caused her breath to stall in her lungs.

Greg felt her go still. He went still himself. It was just a kiss, the mere touch of skin to skin, but his heart jerked against his breastbone. When he dragged in the oxygen he suddenly craved, her intoxicating scent came with it.

Heat smoldered through him, catching him off guard with its intensity, making him lift his head.

His eyes held the unmistakable confusion in hers as he skimmed his hand to her neck. With his thumb resting at the hollow of her throat, he could feel the erratic beat of her heart. She'd felt that heat, too. He could swear it.

"Congratulations," he heard the man beside him say as Mr. Jasper stuck out his hand.

"Congratulations to you, too, dear," his wife echoed. "Now, if you'll just come over here and sign your certificate, the two of you can be on your way."

It only took a couple of minutes to dispense with the last of the necessary procedures. With Mr. and Mrs. Jasper wishing them well, and feeling like a hypocrite because the older couple honestly thought they'd just sent another happy bride and groom on their way, Jenny moved ahead of Greg out the door.

"I think we made their day. Quickest ceremony on record," he said, watching Jenny as he tucked the folded certificate into his inside jacket pocket. The afternoon sun shimmered in her hair as she glanced toward him.

Determined to be as unaffected as he apparently had been by what he'd done, Jenny gave him a quick smile.

"Are you okay?" he asked.

"Of course," she replied, reluctant to let him think otherwise. "Are you?"

"Yeah," he murmured. "Sure. Look," he continued, wondering if he should explain why he'd done what he had, or just let it go. A glance at his watch solved the dilemma for him. "I need to see Edna's neurologist in about five minutes. I want to check on Mrs. McNeff, too. The hospital is less than a mile away. Just drop me off at the front entrance, then meet me there after you go to the office supply place. I shouldn't be more than an hour."

He watched her reach for the handle of the truck's door. Beating her to it, he opened the door for her and forced his glance from her long legs and strappy high heels as she hiked her slim skirt to climb in.

When he'd kissed her, it had seemed a whole lot easier to just do what was expected than make a big deal out of something that was as much a custom as the ceremony had been. Easier, anyway, until he'd heard the way her breath had stalled, seen the awareness in her eyes.

"I'd like to see Mrs. McNeff, too," she said, glancing at him while she modestly tugged her skirt to her knees. "It won't take me long to pick up what we need for the office. Why don't I meet you in her room after you do what you need to do?"

The regional hospital in the rural little town of St. Johnsbury was small by big-city standards. But it served the scattered communities and villages of the Northeast Kingdom and beyond with much of the latest technology, and provided the sort of advanced care a country doctor needed for his sicker patients. Provided he could get them there in time to utilize their expertise.

Jenny hadn't honestly appreciated how critical the availability of such care could be until she'd started working at the clinic. The need for such services wasn't often, given the relatively small population the clinic served. Yet, as she sat with Mrs. McNeff while waiting for the man she'd just married, she found herself thinking of times when that care had simply been too far away.

"I'm just so glad it isn't winter." Sally McNeff's seventy-five-year-old mother spoke quietly, her eyes tired, but clearly inquisitive. With her round glasses and her silver hair pulled into its neat bun, she reminded Jenny of a librarian, which she practically was. The woman had owned the town's only bookstore for over forty years and had probably read every title to ever grace its shelves.

"It's such a long way to come here," she continued, "and I worry about Sally having to drive me if I have to come back every three months like they say. We can certainly wait for a day or two if the roads are especially bad, but I can't help think of the things that happen where people can't wait. Like when Harlan Waters had his heart attack last year. They say he might have made it if the ambulance hadn't taken so long to get to him. And Amos's daughter when she had her first baby a few years back. She was too early and Dr. Wilson couldn't stop her labor, you know. Everything turned out fine, but it had to be a nightmare for them getting in that accident. Her husband still has a limp.

"Forgive me," she murmured, waving a weathered hand. "When my eyes get too tired to read, that leaves me with nothing to do but think." A wry smile lit her pale eyes. "When an old person thinks, it tends to be about all the things that can go wrong out there. That's why so many of us spend so much time on our knees. Those of us who can get down on them, anyway."

Jenny offered a sympathetic smile. "No apologies necessary," she said, thinking of her own experience with the need to hurry.

She would never forget the frantic rush with the boys at the quarry.

And only days ago Greg had dropped everything to get Edna the help he couldn't give her without access to sophisticated equipment and specialists.

As if thinking of him conjured his presence, Greg appeared in the doorway.

"Mrs. McNeff," he said, walking into the room with its wheeled tray at the foot of the bed and IV monitor clicking away. "I'll see you back in Maple Mountain. Your oncologist said that if you're feeling strong enough, you can go home tomorrow.

She'll be here in a while to tell you that herself." Totally dwarfing the diminutive woman, he reached for her thin arm and gave it a squeeze. "It'll be good to have you back home."

There was no doubt from the lady's smile that it would be good to be back home, too. "Thank you," she murmured. "And thank you, Jenny," she said as Jenny rose from the chair by the bed. "It was so nice of you to sit with me. Tell me, will you always accompany Dr. Reid on his rounds?"

Jenny opened her mouth and promptly hesitated.

"She's with me because we just got married," Greg offered easily. He glanced at his watch. "About an hour ago."

The pale arcs of Mrs. McNeff's eyebrows rose above the rims of her glasses. "You did? Well, how wonderful," she said, placing her blue-veined hand delicately at the neck of her pink bed jacket. "You'll have to forgive me, but I don't recall hearing that you were seeing each other. Not feeling well has kept me somewhat isolated from everyone's news."

"No one would expect you to keep up with everything." Gentle as always with his more frail patients, Greg patted her arm again. "We've kept it quiet, anyway. And thanks very much," he said, sounding far more at ease than Jenny felt as they both stepped from the bed.

Thinking the woman looked slightly perplexed, or maybe it was just curious, Jenny edged toward the door. "You take care."

Mrs. McNeff assured her that she would, but her faintly distracted air seemed to warn Jenny. It was entirely possible that once they were gone, she would be on the phone at her beside, if for no other reason that to fill herself in on whatever else she might have missed. Depending on who she called, their news could be all over town by the time they returned home.

She mentioned that to Greg as they started down the brightly lit hall.

"I know," he muttered.

A few steps later, he glanced at her with his brow lowered. Two steps after that he stopped.

Looking somewhere between apologetic and preoccupied, he said, "We have a little problem."

Her heart seemed to stop. He already regretted what they'd done. She could feel it.

"A problem?" she asked, priding herself on how calm she sounded as a pair of visitors and a nurse walked by.

"We have to take Edna back with us. She has a goose egg on the side of her head, but her CAT scan looks great and her other tests are all fine. Dr. Dickson said there's no reason to keep her here, and she's driving the nursing staff crazy. Her nearest relatives are over in West Pond and they can't come until Sunday. So, she either asks someone from Maple Mountain to get her, which makes no sense with us here, or she comes with us now."

Jenny's breath leaked out like air from a slowly deflating beach ball. She didn't know if it was the sense of insecurity she'd acquired over the past couple of months or the hormonal swings that came with being pregnant, but there was an intensity to her reactions that hadn't been there before. Or, maybe, she thought, they'd been there all along and she was only now acknowledging them. "Why is that a problem?"

The look he slanted her clearly said he couldn't believe she'd had to ask. "Because the woman never shuts up."

Jenny found a certain advantage to having the spry and wiry Edna sandwiched between her and Greg in the cab of the truck. For one thing, thinking about what she'd just done was impossible. Edna was the same age as Mrs. McNeff, but she was far more outspoken and far less introspective. It also took more than getting kicked by her mule to slow her down.

Clutching her purse as if one of them might snatch it, Edna jabbered pretty much nonstop all the way to Maple Mountain.

It wasn't until they had pulled into the driveway of her tiny house, two miles from Jenny's, that she finally slowed down long enough to tell them she thought it awfully nice of them to give her a ride and mentioned that they were both dressed as if they'd been to a wedding or a funeral.

"So which was it?" she asked, looking fully prepared to ask who had wed or died in her absence.

"Wedding," Jenny replied.

"Ours," Greg added, since the question was coming. "Come on, Edna. Let's get you inside."

They left a half hour later, after going out with Edna and her flashlight to make sure her mule and her chickens had been watered and fed by her neighbor, and heating her a cup of tea and a bowl of soup. They had also confirmed to Edna that, no, they hadn't known each other but a little over month and that, yes, their marriage was pretty sudden. Since it was after eight o'clock when they pulled up in front of Greg's house, he ushered her inside before they encountered anyone who might stop them with similar questions.

Because it was getting late, and because they hadn't been able to leave the clinic as early as they'd intended, they had decided on the way from Edna's to fix something quick for dinner so he could get to the dictation from his patients that day and she could get settled in. The plan had sounded fine to Jenny until she stepped into his foyer and he closed the door behind her.

The nervousness she'd felt with him earlier threatened to return. Which, she told herself, was ridiculous because she'd been alone with him countless times before. Wanting to ignore the fact that she hadn't been alone with him since the mere touch of his lips to hers had turned her insides to mush, she glanced from the stairs straight ahead to the entry mirror and table by the door. She had just noticed what looked to be a cozy study off to her left when the scents of lemon polish and pine cleaner registered.

"Lorna has been here." Greg offered the observation as he tossed his keys into a brass dish on the table and motioned her to the double doorway on her right. "She cleans for me on Friday mornings."

Not sure if she should leave her purse by his keys, not totally sure what any of the protocol was now that she was here, she wrapped her fingers around its thin shoulder strap and crossed the hardwood entry floor.

"I can do that now," she offered. The tap of her heels silenced as she stepped onto the thick toast-colored carpet. Greg moved ahead of her. "Clean, I mean."

It was the very least she could do. Especially since he wasn't letting her pay rent. He'd told her to use the money to pay off her lawyer. She started to mention that, too, only to have Greg cut her off.

"She needs the work."

Jenny's contention died on her lips. She'd been thinking only in terms of what she could contribute to their arrangement. Greg was clearly thinking of Lorna. The late-thirty-something widowed mother of two worked full-time at the diner, but she had also cleaned for Dr. Wilson and his wife since she was sixteen. Apparently, she'd more or less come with the house.

As a single parent, Lorna definitely needed the extra income.

Thinking she could definitely relate to her situation, and thinking it very much like Greg to consider the woman's needs, Jenny looked from his broad back as he flipped on the brass table lamps on either side of two armchairs. Overstuffed furniture in shades of sage and brown and throw pillows printed with sprays of pine needles lent a definite north woods feel to the comfortable space. The slate fireplace that took up half the end wall promised warmth on long winter nights.

A collection of photography and news magazines on the maple coffee table caught her eye. So did the framed photos of pinecones, tree bark and leaves he'd hung in a line above the couch.

She'd seen the photographs in his office, thought how beautiful and detailed they were. She just hadn't realized until Mrs. McNeff had mentioned it during their visit that he'd taken them himself.

She had little time to consider how truly talented he was, or to wonder how a man who had been raised in such an emotional wasteland had emerged with so much compassion and such an eye for beauty. She had barely noticed how each photo had a single heartbeat in it—a butterfly, a beetle, a ladybug—when he disappeared through the doorway ahead of them.

It occurred to her as she followed that she needed to look at the landscape photographs in his office again. It seemed there was a single figure in the distance in each of them, too. She remembered a tiny fawn in one. A single bird in flight in another.

It was almost as if he didn't simply freeze the beauty of the world. He captured a sense of how alone some were in it.

"The kitchen is in here," he said, shedding his jacket on the way. "It came with all the basics. Stove, fridge, microwave. Freezer on the back porch. Wash and dryer through there."

He indicated another door off the spacious country kitchen and left his jacket on the back of a chair at the big pine table in the breakfast nook.

The tie came off and landed on the jacket.

"That side hall goes to a bathroom and a room I've converted to a darkroom," he said, nodding toward it as he opened the refrigerator. "The door on the left is to my study. If you go through that, you're back in the front hall."

The tour of the downstairs apparently complete, he looked to where she'd stopped by the table. "Are you okay with eggs?"

The thought that his photographs might be images of how he felt himself had caused an odd catch in her chest. It also raised her internal defenses. She already knew he isolated parts of his heart. As kind as he'd been to her, as kind as he was to everyone, she needed to remember how deliberately he distanced himself.

He was also making things easy. Enormously grateful to him for that, she shook off her disturbing thoughts, dropped her purse on her chair and shed her jacket, too.

"I'm fine with them." Heading toward him, she smoothed the front of her slate-blue shell and absently skimmed her hands over the sides of her hips to make sure her skirt was straight. "Let me do that."

Greg followed the movements of her hands. As unaware as she seemed, skimming her hands over her clothes, he was dead certain she didn't know how enticing the action was. His eyes were drawn to the gentle fullness of her breasts, her small waist, her trim hips. Then, there were her legs, he thought, when his glance reached the short hem of her skirt. They seemed to go on forever.

Thinking she'd be easier to have around in her baggy lab jacket or sweats, he shrugged as if to say suit yourself and opened a cabinet above one of the long green Formica counters.

"I put the suitcases you dropped off this morning upstairs," he said, taking out two plates. He would help her bring the rest of her things over tomorrow. Right now it just relieved him to know she would be sleeping in a bed tonight instead of on a floor. "There are two extra rooms up there. Both have sets of twin beds. I put you in the one in back. It's bigger."

It wasn't bigger by much. A foot, maybe, if anyone bothered to measure. But it was also the farthest from his. He'd put her there even before he'd so briefly kissed her, before he'd felt the sharp heat of carnal need that threatened to play total havoc with his sense of objectivity.

She would be sleeping just down the hall from him. She would be showering on the other side of his bedroom wall, getting the bathroom all steamy and filling it with the scents of her soap and shampoo.

As aware of her as he'd been before, he was infinitely more so now. He also knew he wasn't going to do a single thing about the undeniable physical desire he felt for her.

Her sense of trust had been shattered. Yet, despite the caution he'd sensed in her since they'd left chatty old Edna behind, he knew she trusted him. He wasn't totally sure why that was. If he'd believed in anything cosmic, he might have thought they were simply kindred spirits. Two cynical souls who'd bumped into each other at a time when each needed something the other could give. She needed his shelter and protection. He needed the sense of calm he often felt with her so he could tackle the estate that hung over his head like Damocles's sword. But he didn't believe in soul mates any more than he believed in the myth of undying love. He knew only that he wouldn't shake her trust by making any moves that would cause her to think he expected anything more than what they'd agreed on.

Or, so he was telling himself when he saw her give him a quiet little smile. "I'm sure the back one is perfect. Thank you."

"There's only one bathroom up there, though. You might want to take over the one down here."

He handed her a bowl from the cupboard above her head.

"Whatever's most convenient for you," she said, her focus on the crisp white shirt covering the breadth of his very solid chest. Hugging what he'd handed her, wanting her awareness of him to go away, she turned to the eggs.

He took a step back himself. "That would probably be best."

"Then, that's what I'll do."

"Utensils are on your left."

"Do you have the prenuptial agreement?" she asked, not sure if he was getting tense or if it was just her as she looked around for something to use for an apron. "And a dish towel?"

Other than a few small appliances, a basket with fruit and a bottle of dish soap by the sink, the counters were bare. Nothing hung from any of the knobs, or the handles on the stove or fridge.

"I should have probably signed it before we went to St. Johnsbury," she continued, unable to bring herself to say *before we got married.* "But it's not like it has a time stamp on it, so as long as I sign it today it should be fine." She frowned. "Except it probably needs to be notarized, doesn't it?"

Greg opened one of the doors beneath the sink, pulled a white dish towel from the chrome bar on the other side of it and held it out.

"I would imagine it does."

Thanking him, she turned sideways to wrap the rectangle of cotton around herself. "Is Joe a notary?"

"I don't think so. Joanna at the post office is. And Lois at the sheriff's office." He watched her as she tucked the short ends of the towel into her waistband at the small of her back. Her motions drew her blouse tight across her breasts, accentuated her still-flat stomach. "But I didn't get around to calling Larry," he admitted, forcing his glance away to open the refrigerator again. "I'll do it next week. Do you want milk?"

It seemed to her that the agreement was something he would have wanted to make sure was in order. She would have mentioned that, too, and asked if he wanted her to remind him to make the call Monday, had he not just so clearly dismissed the subject.

There was something else she needed to ask him about, too, she thought after telling him milk would be great. Yet, as he went about pouring two glasses and dropping bread in the toaster while she scrambled the eggs, she couldn't quite work up the nerve to bring up the subject.

Nerve wasn't necessary. The eggs had just set when he mentioned what was on her mind.

"We got off easy with Mrs. McNeff and Edna." He set plates beside her, turned to butter the toast. "No one is going to expect us to just suddenly be married. How do you want to explain it?"

"What you said to Mrs. McNeff is good." As good as anything she could come up with, anyway. "Saying we wanted to keep things quiet will explain why no one has seen us acting like we were dating."

"And what about Edna's comment? About it being so sudden."

"It is sudden." There was no way around that one. Keeping her focus on her task, she scooped their dinner onto the plates. "There's only one explanation I can think of that people wouldn't question."

His arm brushed hers as he took his plate and fork, then

stepped back to lean against the sink. He took a bite of toast, washed it down with milk. "What's that?"

She didn't know whether he usually ate standing up, or if he was just in a hurry to get the meal over so he could get to his work. Whichever, she picked up her plate and moved to lean against the counter across from him.

She cleared her throat. "Love at first sight."

Greg watched her glance fall to her plate a moment before she started picking at her eggs. She wasn't nearly as comfortable with this particular conversation as she wanted him to think. A hint of color touched the soft skin of her cheeks, much as it had the time she'd inadvertently admitted that she'd hung on to her virginity waiting for the right man. For all her guts and spirit, even considering that she was standing there pregnant, she was the only female he knew over the age of sixteen who still blushed.

Leaning against the counter with her long, shapely legs crossed at the her slender ankles, the dish towel wrapped around her short, businesslike little skirt, she also looked as tempting as sin itself.

Lust at first sight he could buy.

"I suppose there are those who believe such a thing exists," he conceded, not being one of them. "And it's good because it's too subjective for anyone to question." He scooped up a bite of fluffy egg, his attention on his plate to block the view of her legs. "I'm okay with it if you are."

Jenny watched him finish his dinner in a few bites and rinse his plate in the sink. In a little over a minute he'd annihilated what she'd barely touched.

She was about to ask if he wanted hers when the ringing phone had him reaching for the instrument hanging beneath the cabinets.

"Greg Reid," she heard him answer as he dried his hands on another towel. His motions slowed, his brow dropping sharply. "No, it's not a problem. Is the guy conscious?"

Jenny set her own plate aside, her thoughts shifting automatically to wonder who had been hurt and what had happened. She heard Greg ask more questions as he tossed the towel aside. His hands moved down the front of his shirt, slipping buttons from their holes. He'd reached his belt and tugged his shirttails from his slacks, when she heard him say, "I'll meet you at the clinic in ten minutes."

He hung up and turned to face her, a slash of hard muscle visible between the sides of his shirt.

It had seemed like an eternity had passed since the night she'd helped him with his shoulder, but she could still remember the feel of his naked chest beneath her hands.

Pulling her drifting glance from his hard belly, she consciously ignored the strange tingling sensation in her palms.

"They're getting an early start out at The Dig," he said, unbuttoning his cuffs, now that his hands were free. "Joe's bringing in a drunk with a few gashes and a split lip. Apparently he ran into a beer bottle."

"Anyone we know?" she asked as he headed down the hallway and through his study.

"Some itinerant worker here for the apple harvest."

"Do you want me to help?"

"The guy's drunk and belligerent, Jenny. It's possible he's also strung out on something more heavy-duty than alcohol." He moved through his study, stopped at the base of the stairs. Turning to find her behind him, something moved into his eyes. Protectiveness possibly. Or, maybe, simply gratitude for the escape. "You stay here and get unpacked. Joe will help me handle him."

He turned and jogged up the stairs before she could say a thing. Then jogged back down minutes later, presumably having changed his clothes. She didn't know for sure because she didn't see him go. He just called from the entry that he'd be back in a while and left her where she stood at the sink, washing the dishes they'd used.

The task took no time at all. Neither did unpacking her clothes and putting them away in the closet and the dresser of the room decorated predominantly in blues. She had curtains on her window, white to match the bedspreads and the tiny flowers on the delft-blue wallpaper. The braided oval rug covering most of the hardwood floor had been woven in shades of sapphire and periwinkle.

She'd noticed Greg's room as she'd passed it at the top of the stairs. Loath to invade his privacy any more than she already had, she stopped in the doorway only long enough to notice the burgundy-covered double bed, which had to be far too short for his tall frame, and the stacks of books on his nightstand, before moving to the room at the end of the hall.

She passed his room again when she headed back downstairs to wait for him to return.

Curled up on his sofa, she tried valiantly to stay awake by watching his satellite dish television. But the emotional ups and downs of the day, the month, caught up with her just before midnight. Because Greg had alluded to his patient being potentially dangerous, she'd wanted to stay up and make sure he was all right himself. He was a big man, and Joe was even bigger, but unless they'd wrestled the guy into restraints and knocked him out with an injection, it was possible that one of them could get hurt, too.

Greg, however, looked just fine to her when she woke to find him standing over her.

Chapter Ten

Greg stood over Jenny, his hands on the hips of his drawstring sweatpants. "I just wanted to make sure you were still breathing."

She hadn't heard him come in. She didn't remember him covering her with a blanket, either. But he'd obviously done both. She could feel the pleasant weight of warm fleece from her cheek to her toes.

Pushing away the blanket, she eased herself upright. The neckline of her favorite sweatshirt promptly slid off one shoulder.

"How is your patient?" she asked, tugging it back into place.

"Resting comfortably in jail."

"Did he give you a hard time?"

"Not once we restrained him."

That was good, she thought, because restraints meant Greg had been safe, and he was the one she'd been most concerned about.

"What time is it?"

"Ten."

Her eyes widened. "In the morning?"

He lifted his hand toward the two multipaned windows across from her. He'd already drawn the heavier drapes back. Sheer curtains blocked the view of passersby on the street, allowing muted sunlight to filter through.

Jenny sat a little straighter. She had an hour and a half before she had to be at the diner. She hadn't given Dora notice yet. When she'd requested to have last night off and arranged for Tina Waters, the high-school girl Dora often employed, to cover for her, Dora had asked for no explanation and Jenny had offered none. She hadn't said anything to anyone about what she was doing. Mostly, she supposed, because she hadn't totally believed it would happen. But there she was, looking up at the man she'd married yesterday.

The thought seemed a little unreal at the moment. She couldn't remember the last time she'd slept so late. She couldn't remember the last time she'd slept straight through the night, for that matter.

Thinking it might have something to do with sleeping on something soft rather than hard floor, she swung her sock-clad feet to the carpet—only to immediately slow her motions at what felt like a wave of seasickness. For weeks, she'd told herself the sensation was only fatigue, because she always woke so tired. She now knew that fatigue couldn't be blamed for everything.

"Queasy?" he asked as she eased one hand to her stomach.

"A little. The feeling is usually gone by the time I wash my face and get something to eat."

"I haven't noticed you drinking coffee lately. Are you off it on purpose or does the smell bother you?"

She was fine with its aroma. And she was dying for a cup. "I read in one of the brochures we give our pregnant patients that caffeine should be avoided. I've switched to herbal tea."

"The smell of food doesn't bother you in the morning?"

"Not so far."

She didn't know what caused his quick frown. She just knew she wasn't awake enough yet to be into subtleties.

"Then you probably won't be bothered much more than you are," he told her.

Pushing her fingers through her hair again, she watched him lower his big frame to the sofa. He'd apparently just returned from his morning run. A dark vee of sweat stained the neck of his gray sweatshirt. His hair, damp at his temples, looked as if it had been combed by the wind.

She smiled across the cushion separating them. A night's growth of beard shadowed the lean line of his jaw. "Really?"

"Really," he echoed, smiling back. "Morning sickness often starts around the fourth to sixth week and is usually gone by the twelfth to sixteenth. Some women never get rid of it. But if this is as bad as it gets for you, the worst is probably already over."

Her sleepy smile brightened. "Then I have nothing to complain about. It really hasn't been bad at all."

Greg held his own reaction to that news in check. As his glance swept her face, he also wondered if she was only masking how bad she did feel. Knowing her as he did, he wouldn't put it past her. She didn't look as if she were ready to bolt for the bathroom, though. And her color wasn't as pale as it might have been had the nausea been as severe as some he'd treated. If anything, as she sat with her hair tousled and tugging her shirt higher on her shoulder she simply looked…appealing.

She had a sleep crease in one cheek. Her clear-blue eyes, like her smile, still looked languid and drowsy from having just awakened. But even just waking up, that smile seemed to come easily. He felt relieved to see it.

What gave him the most relief was that her old optimism seemed to be waking, too.

What Jenny felt awakening was her curiosity. Since Greg didn't seem in any hurry to rush off, and she wasn't feeling quite ready to stand up, she figured she might as well take advantage of the knowledge in his handsome head. There could be definite advantages to living with a doctor.

"What causes morning sickness, anyway?'

He didn't even hesitate. "Hormones. As best we can tell," he qualified, sounding like the physician he was, looking like a regular guy taking it easy on a Saturday morning. "They mess with everything when you're pregnant."

"I thought they just messed with mood."

"They can definitely do that. I've had pregnant patients tell me it feels as if their body has been taken over by their evil twin. Things irritate them that never bothered them before. They cry at the drop of a hat. But hormones affect everything from digestion and sense of smell to libido and energy level."

She'd noticed certain of those effects already. Those on her energy level and libido, anyway. Pulling her glance from his broad shoulders, she murmured, "And that's all going to go away?"

"Sure," he offered with confidence. "Within a few months after the baby is born. Then you just have to deal with your normal hormonal state."

Jenny opened her mouth, closed it again when she saw his smile. She couldn't tell if he was being sympathetic or if he was teasing her. Either way, their discussion was over.

He rose to stand over her. "I'm fresh out of herbal tea. Do you have any at your grandma's house?"

"It's packed."

"Then I'll throw in some toast for you and go grab a shower. Whenever you're ready, we'll go get the rest of your things."

Throwing the blanket aside, she scrambled after him to the kitchen, slowing a little when she became aware of the queasiness again. "You don't need to do that. I can make my own breakfast."

"I'm getting coffee anyway," he called back, totally ignoring her insistence that she could do it herself. "Stop being stubborn."

She wasn't being stubborn, she just didn't want him to feel she needed to be taken care of.

Or maybe what she wanted, she realized an hour later, was for him to stop doing things that made her care about him any more than she already did.

She'd told him she could get the boxes from the house after work tomorrow. She only worked lunch shift then. Today she had lunch and dinner. In turn, he'd told her that lifting heavy boxes wasn't a good idea for a woman in her condition. He'd seemed to know she didn't want to impose on him. He also seemed to suspect that she would slip over and accomplish the task by herself, anyway—which was probably why he'd ushered her out the door to help her get them before her shift that day.

He'd already carried out three.

"Do you want the flowerpots on the porch?" he asked, picking up the last box from the now empty counter.

As Greg started away, she moved to the stool at the end of the counter, positioning it just so.

The floor of the bright kitchen was now bare of bedding and boxes. Everything from the cupboards and bathroom had been packed and stowed with her two remaining pieces of luggage in the back of Charlie's pickup.

"Please," she said, unable to leave the flowers to die. "But I'll get them."

He stopped, looked back. "Have you asked anyone to help board this back up?"

"Not yet."

"I'll do it."

She gave a nod, murmured a quiet, "Thank you."

It relieved her enormously to know she wouldn't have to live in a kitchen with a leaky roof, plumbing that rattled, and survive the winter by the heat of a woodstove. As she glanced around the now-empty room, it was hard to see any improvement she'd made beyond the paint. The sink was still stained. The window over it was still cracked. That crack did now sport a slash of duct tape, but the silver-gray bandage actually made the window look worse.

Even with all the advantages of moving, the thought of leaving her grandma's house empty again made her feel incredibly…sad.

Wanting the feeling to go away, she refused to look around anymore. Aware of Greg watching her, she pulled the overhead cord to turn out the light on her way from the kitchen. With their footsteps echoing in the empty living room, she headed with him for the front door and locked it behind them.

It wasn't until the box was in the back with the others and they were in the truck heading up the road that he asked, "Are you okay?"

She could blame the sadness she felt on fluctuating hormones, she supposed. She might have done that, too, had the explanation not felt disloyal somehow.

"I'm fine. I was just thinking about the house." She picked a bit of lint from her black skirt, absently smoothed her hem. "Living there reminded me of how safe I'd always felt when I was a child. There was always this wonderful sense of security at Grandma's house when I was growing up. At my parents', too," she told him, thinking of how little thought she'd given the gift back then. "It was the freedom to just be who I was, I guess. And a sense of belonging that sort of followed me everywhere I went around here."

Her hormones were definitely fluctuating, she decided. She was getting maudlin. That thought alone would have had her trying to laugh off her melancholy—had she not just caught the look of total incomprehension Greg shot her.

He couldn't relate to a thing she'd said.

The realization turned her odd mood into a different sort of sadness. He'd had none of what she'd simply taken for granted growing up. He knew nothing of being raised with security and freedom. His own childhood had held little beyond constant control, reproach and a total lack of affection.

She remembered Greg telling her of the claim his father had made, that he had been too privileged to ever make it in a place like Maple Mountain. Considering that now, she couldn't help but wonder if one of the reasons Greg took jobs in isolated places was more than a need to prove his father wrong. She wondered if maybe it was because he was searching for the sense of belonging he had never known.

"Do you feel that in Maple Mountain, too?" she asked, still unable to accept the benign indifference he'd claimed toward the town. "That sense of belonging?"

His focus remained on the road, his expression as matter-of-fact as his tone.

"I've never felt I belonged anywhere in particular," he admitted, ruling out Maple Mountain along with every other place he'd ever been. "I only knew where I didn't. I know some people need that," he offered, sounding as if he knew how much she did. "But being a permanent part of a place isn't something that's ever mattered to me.

"Are you okay to go to work?" Casually dismissing a need most other people would consider essential, he glanced toward her, then checked his watch. "You were due there three minutes ago."

Every time she encountered the wall his emotional scars had built, a voice of caution sounded in the back of her brain. Mindful of that voice now, she assured him she was fine and focused on acting as if having married a man who never allowed anyone to get truly close had been the most natural thing in the world.

"You know Lorna will have heard," Greg warned, waving at Joe when the deputy's Jeep went by in the other direction. "She's friends with Sally, and Sally calls her mom every morning, so Mrs. McNef would have mentioned it by now."

"I think Joe heard, too." Jenny motioned the rearview mirror, catching brake lights in it as the Jeep suddenly slowed.

Glancing into the mirror himself, Greg passed the Welcome to Maple Mountain sign. "Yeah. He did," he concluded, seeing the Jeep turn around. "Either that or he needs something."

The trail of weekend cars on Main caused Greg to slow a couple of blocks before he came to a stop in front of the diner. By then the Jeep's bumper was mere yards from theirs.

Jenny reached for her door. She was about to thank Greg for the ride, when his brow furrowed.

"Tell you what," he said, as if he only now realized he should tell her where he'd be. "I'm going to drop your things off at the house. Then, depending on what Joe wants, I'll either be at the clinic or out at the Larkin place. I told Charlie I'd help them with the branch thinning."

Behind them she heard Joe's door slam. Her heart jumped with the sound. Greg also knew they were about to have company, and if they wanted everyone to believe they had married for the usual reasons, then he might do exactly what had been expected of him after their little ceremony yesterday.

Surprised by how quickly her heart beat at the thought of him cupping her neck and drawing her into a kiss, however brief it might be, she prepared to meet him halfway. But all Greg did was glance from the image of Joe grinning in his side mirror and give her a quick smile of his own.

"Good luck," he said, and kept both hands right where they were.

Caught between feeling awkward and embarrassed, she ducked her head and grabbed the clean apron she'd left on the seat between them. "You, too."

Glancing up, she wiggled her fingers at Joe standing at Greg's window and slipped out, calling back to Joe that it was good to see him, but she couldn't visit because she was now officially late.

The quick embarrassment she'd felt gave way to a different form of unease as she hurried past the pumpkins and mums on the diner's steps. It was such a little thing, but not knowing what to expect from Greg made her feel as off balance as she had before he'd offered her the use of his home and his name.

Trying to shake the suspicion that she'd just traded one set of anxieties for another, she hurried inside, smiled at the teenage Tina waiting on the eight occupied tables and headed into the kitchen to wash her hands.

Dora stood at the grill, her silvering blond hair in its usual figure-eight bun covered by a hairnet. Jenny had no more opened her mouth to apologize for being late, than Dora turned from the grilled cheese sandwich she'd just flipped and planted her fist, spatula protruding, on her ample hip.

"I can't believe you didn't ask for the weekend off."

"You can't?" she asked, tying on her apron before she shoved her hands under the faucet.

"You just got married! You're supposed to be on your honeymoon." Dora's green eyes danced. "Tina is covering your shifts this weekend. I asked her as soon as I heard your news from Lorna. And speaking of which, why aren't you and the doctor off somewhere nice and romantic?"

Jenny's motions slowed. She and Greg hadn't discussed that one.

"Tina is taking my shifts?" she asked, evading.

"Well, of course. I couldn't imagine that you'd want to spend your time around here. And by the way," she added, a smile rounding her cheeks, "I had a feeling there was something going on with you two. I could see by the way Dr. Reid watched you when he'd come in for dinner that he had a real thing for you."

She offered the claim with a definitive nod, quite proud of her powers of observation. "Lorna, she saw it, too. Amos missed it though," she continued, turning to flip two more sandwiches and scoop up the first. "The man just about lost his dentures in his coffee cup when I told him this morning."

She grinned, then turned to slide the sandwich onto the cutting board. With the deft whack of a wicked-looking knife, she sliced the sandwich in two and slipped it onto a plate.

She looked back at Jenny.

"Go on," she said, making shooing motions with her hands.

"Get out of here and go spend the day with your husband. I'll see you tonight at the community center."

"The community center?" She and Lorna had thought Greg had a thing for her? "What's going on there?"

"Your wedding reception, of course. You might be able to sneak off and get married, but there's no way you're going to deny us a party. Joe's wife is organizing it. Anyone who sees you is supposed to tell you to be there at seven o'clock. I'm closing my doors at eight sharp, so I'll be there by eight-thirty. Don't leave before I get there. I want to hear all about this."

Joe told Greg about the reception that morning. Jenny knew because Smiley mentioned it when he dropped off her mail at Greg's house that afternoon. But Greg didn't return from the Larkin place until six-thirty that evening.

Hearing him come in, she figured he had just enough time to shower and change clothes before they had to leave.

She was actually grateful for his need to hurry. She'd spent the day in the house, debating if she should put her cookware in his kitchen or leave it packed and fixing the supper he hadn't returned in time to eat. When he poked his head around the doorway, much as he did at the office, and told her he was home, his glance when straight to the nicely set table and the pork chops, mashed potatoes and salad she had just started to put away.

The look on his face made it clear that he hadn't considered letting her know he'd be late, or that he'd thought she would have gone to such trouble for a meal.

Feeling even more awkward than she had when he hadn't kissed her that morning, she turned away, reminding him as she did of how little time he had to get ready.

He said he would hurry and headed straight upstairs.

Jenny quickly took care of the rest of the food and the dishes, feeling foolish for presuming they would share their meals together, feeling even more foolish for having him realize she'd thought they would. For all practical purposes—and the entire arrangement had been born of practicality—when she and Greg weren't in public they were nothing more than roommates.

She reminded herself of that as she hurried upstairs herself, checked the makeup she'd already spent too much time on and changed into the off-white cocktail dress she'd last worn to a company dinner. It was the only thing bridelike or party-ish that she owned. The Feds had taken most of her good clothes, those with the better labels that she'd bought on sale. The only reason she had the dress and the suit she'd worn yesterday was because they'd been in the dry cleaners at the time her other things had been confiscated.

Hurrying back down minutes before seven, she pulled her black dress coat from the closet. She'd just finished buttoning it when Greg appeared in gray slacks and a navy sport coat, took one look at the strappy white heels on her feet and announced that they'd drive rather than walk.

She had no idea where Dora and Lorna got the idea he had a thing for her. Except for her feet, he barely glanced at her as they climbed into Charlie's truck for the minute-long drive to the center.

Because they only had that long to get their stories straight, she mentioned the little glitch she'd encountered at the diner. "Dora asked why we didn't go on a honeymoon."

"So did Joe."

"What did you tell him?"

"That we didn't have time. What about you?"

"I sort of skipped over it and didn't answer."

"Then, let's stick to what I told Joe."

She lifted her chin to agree, only to frown as he turned the corner and the large, white clapboard building came into view. "There are an awful lot of cars there."

Greg thought so, too. Distracted as he was by the woman beside him, he simply figured there must be something else going on.

He felt like a heel for not having called her. Joe had told him that Tina had covered Jenny's shifts for her, so it wasn't as if he'd thought she was working. It just hadn't occurred to him that she would have spent her first real day off in ages in his kitchen.

They needed to talk. If she enjoyed cooking and that was how she relaxed, he had no problem reaping the benefits. If she felt she needed to cook for him, or if she had the idea that he was looking for anything domestic in their arrangement, he needed to let her know that wasn't part of the deal. He knew she felt grateful to him, but he expected nothing from her other than what he'd asked, her help with the estate and, later, in the new office.

Now just wasn't the time to bring it up, he conceded as they left the truck a minute later and headed for the center's main door Not with half of Maple Mountain turning toward them as they stepped into the large main room and bursting into applause.

His hand rested lightly against the small of Jenny's back. Beneath the wool of her coat, he felt her go stock still.

He didn't move himself. Being married to her seemed to be getting more complicated by the minute.

"Well, come on in you two!"

Amber Sheldon, Joe's pretty blond wife, emerged from the wall of people ahead of them and motioned toward Jenny. "Joe, get her coat. Let's get you both some punch."

Jenny felt herself being pulled forward as her coat was slipped from her shoulders. She glanced behind her to thank Joe, but it was Greg holding her coat.

He was also staring at her bare shoulders.

The silky white dress she wore covered her from neck to knee in front, but bared her shoulders and half of her back. In the space of a second his glance ran from the tiny strips of white fabric criss-crossed between her shoulder blades, skimmed her backside and jerked to her eyes again.

"Great dress," Amber exclaimed as Jenny felt her heart skip. "Is that what you were married in?"

"Ah...no," she murmured, still feeling his eyes on her back as Amber tugged her forward. "I wore a suit."

"Oh, well. I'm sure it was nice, too. This is just so exciting," Amber continued, oblivious to Jenny peeking back to see Joe nudge Greg and take her coat from him. "I don't know how you managed to keep your relationship a secret. Not that you really did, I guess. I hear Dora suspected something. And Joe said he knew there was something going on from day one. But the two of you running off like that caught everyone by surprise."

Jenny pushed aside the thought that she had rather liked the faintly stunned look on Greg's face. Feeling slightly stunned herself, her glance moved from the white crepe paper twists running from the huge paper bells in the middle of the low ceiling to the long white-draped table Amber guided her toward. She caught a glimpse of plates, silver and a wedding cake behind the people gathered around it. Flowers and tea lights had been placed at the center of each white-colored table around the dance floor.

"I can't believe you did all this."

"It was fun." Balancing her own plastic cup of pink liquid, Amber flashed the smile that had earned her the title of Sweetest Personality in high school. "After Sally called me this morning, I called Claire. You know how good she is at getting things organized," she reminded Jenny in her always thoughtful way. "I told her I still had all the stuff from Joe's and my wedding. So, Carrie Higgins and my mom and her aunts started decorating. Claire got Agnes to bring over the punch makings from the store. Smiley and Bud strung the lights. Bess made the cake. And here we are."

Joe's wife had every reason to look as pleased with herself as she did. She'd pulled off in one day what some would have taken weeks to plan.

The main table had been strewn with white ribbons and red roses from someone's garden. A punch bowl and silver coffee service that looked suspiciously like those from the Community Church anchored each end. In the middle, the cake, three tiers covered in butter cream and leaning slightly to the left, had the same fresh blooms on top and cascading down one side.

Greg seemed to be well-liked and she had grown up knowing nearly everyone there, so she told herself she shouldn't feel as amazed as she did by what everyone had done. When people in Maple Mountain felt they had reason to celebrate, that's what they did. What totally bewildered her, however, was that people honestly seemed to think she and Greg had been involved with each other all along.

"Congratulations, Dr. Reid," she heard her friend Carrie say from behind her. "And you," Carrie continued, stepping around Jenny to wrap her in a hug and a cloud of her boys' bubble-gum scented bubble bath. "It's no wonder you never had time to come out for dinner. But my gosh, girl!" she exclaimed. "Isn't this a little sudden?"

Jenny had felt Greg's presence even before she glanced up to see his charming smile on Carrie. Wondering if he felt as overwhelmed as she did, doubting it because nothing seemed to rattle him, she hoped for something convincing to say.

"Some things shouldn't wait," Greg supplied for her. He lifted one broad shoulder in an easy shrug. "We couldn't see any point putting it off once we decided we were getting married."

Carrie put her hand over her heart, her glance sliding back to Jenny. "And you knew that this soon?"

"It did catch me by surprise," she admitted, being as honest as the man at her side.

Carrie gave her heart a little pat. "Oh, that's just so romantic. You hear about love at first sight, but I never knew anyone it actually happened to before." She took a deep breath, let it out on a sigh. "I just can't believe you didn't tell me."

Jenny didn't know which bothered her more just then. Seeing her old friend look so happy about an emotional situation that didn't exist, or wondering if Greg was standing there thinking about how love gave people a license to use and control.

"We didn't tell anyone, Carrie."

"No one," Greg confirmed.

"Not even me."

Bess, clearly miffed, planted herself beside the enthralled mother of three. The silver brooch on her royal-blue pantsuit matched the frames of the glasses that gleamed from their neck chain. The smile that had been in everyone else's eyes seemed conspicuously absent from hers.

"I can't believe that one of you didn't say something to me before I left yesterday. You didn't even give me time to bake you a proper wedding cake. You can't make a cake like that the day you need it. You have to give it a day to firm a bit. That thing over there's already got a tilt to it, so you'd better cut it before it falls over."

Jenny's glance flew to Greg's an instant before he looked to the slightly listing creation. Bess truly didn't appear to be happy with either of them.

"It looks beautiful," Jenny insisted. But Bess didn't seem interested in compliments, and Jenny didn't have time to figure out if she was more upset about the cake or of not having been informed. Joe had just stopped behind the woman who didn't look as if she wanted to talk anymore, anyway.

"There you are." Having dispensed with Jenny's coat, he smiled over Bess's tight curls. "Amber tells me it's not proper to congratulate the bride. Something about the guy gets congratulations for winning the prize and the woman gets best wishes for having to live with him. Or something like that."

As Bess left them, lips pursed, to tend to her cake, he touched his plastic punch cup to the one that had materialized in Jenny's hand. "So best wishes, Mrs. Reid. I told Greg this morning that I knew there was something between you two the first time I saw you sitting together on your grandma's porch. He tried denying it back then, but it's pretty hard for him to do it now."

"Well, I knew there was something going on last week when I saw him walking her to her car after work," Claire declared, joining them. "I just can't believe how quickly things happened."

"That's because it took Ed three years to propose to you," Bertie Buell supplied. She stuck her hand out to Greg.

"Congratulations, Doctor. Best wishes to you Jenny. I've never been in favor of long engagements."

Greg could pretty much imagine why, too. The woman was old-school to the core. Had shunning not gone out with the pilgrims, she would have wholeheartedly supported the wearing of scarlet PS for those who engaged in premarital sex.

The congratulations continued. So did the stories everyone seemed to have about when they first suspected there was something special between Greg and the woman his glance kept straying toward. It threw him to know that people thought they were involved more than they were, but their assumptions served his and Jenny's purpose far better than the stories they'd agreed on about a courtship that had never existed. And when it came to questions he hadn't anticipated, he found the simple truth served well enough.

Earlier that day all he'd had to do was agree with Joe and with Bud, the electrician who'd checked out her wiring, that it was good she was out of that old house. When Charlie said he supposed they'd wanted to be married before they left Maple Mountain because it would make the move to their new community easier, all he'd had to do was agree with him, too.

Now, with Jenny turning to him to nod toward Bess and whisper that they might want to cut the cake so their co-worker could stop frowning at them, he agreed with that, too.

He'd been to enough weddings—two of them in Maple Mountain—to know what was expected after the first slice had been cut.

Aware of several dozen pairs of eyes on them, he leaned down to whisper in her ear. "How do you want to approach this?"

She seemed far more at ease than he suspected she felt.

"It has to be dignified," she whispered back. "You're the doctor around here."

"Dignified?"

"You know," she murmured. "No shoving or smearing. You

do either and your morning coffee will look like tea for the rest of the month."

He liked that she had a little of her sass back. "Got it," he said, and grabbed her by the hand to lead her to the cake that was beginning to resemble the leaning tower of Pisa.

With everyone gathered around the long table, he held his hand over hers on the beribboned knife. There were comments about how he might have been more comfortable with a scalpel. Charlie, whom he'd worked with thinning trees all day, said he'd seemed right comfortable to him with an ax. The teasing was good-natured and helped distract Greg from the feel of her skin beneath his, the scent of her shampoo. There wasn't much, however, to distract him from the shape of her lush mouth when he held a small piece of cake to her lips. Or the feel of her finger catching the icing at the corner of his mouth after she did the same for him.

"Hey, Doc! Kiss the bride!"

Kissing her was inevitable, he supposed. And kissing her would hardly be a hardship. She looked incredible in the little slip of a dress she wore. It flowed over her gentle curves, caressed her body with her every move. With her short hair shining, her blue eyes sultry, her lips glossed a pale shade of ripe peach, she looked sexy and demure. Sensuous and innocent. The combination had seized his attention all night.

She also seemed a little more prepared than she had in the moments after they'd been pronounced man-and-wife-in-name-only. When she looked up at him, she blinked as if to say she was sorry she'd put him in this position and offered a soft little smile.

Certain she felt more distressed about it than he did, he tipped her chin with his finger and lowered her head to his.

The jolt was there again. Even with a roomful of people clapping and murmuring around them, he felt it tug low in his gut. With her sweet mouth touching his, he felt her lips part slightly with her quick intake of breath. The tug pulled a little harder.

She felt something, too. It was there in her eyes when he edged back. But he could have sworn the smile that slipped in to hide it looked only like relief, now that the little ritual was behind them.

Over the applause and what sounded like a couple of teenage giggles, the music started.

Amos and a few of his friends had a little band that hadn't learned a new song since they'd played together in high school. The strains of "Only You" began as the overhead lights dimmed and the white twinkle lights strung around the stage at the end of the room flickered on.

"The first dance is yours." Amber made the announcement as she nudged them away so Carrie and Bess could take over the cutting and distribution of the cake. "No one knew if you had a favorite song, so Amos just picked one. You two are going to look so nice out there."

Greg had no idea how they appeared as they dutifully moved toward the empty floor. He was conscious only of Jenny when he took her in his arms and she slid her hand to his shoulder. Her thighs brushed his. The gentle roundness of her breasts pressed his chest. He could feel tension in her body, but what he noticed most was her grip on his hand.

It was almost as if she needed him for moral support.

"I feel really guilty," she whispered, finally looking up.

Because the music was loud, he dipped his head toward hers. "About what?"

"All of this. Everyone went to all this trouble because they think we're really married."

"We are married," he reminded her.

"You know what I mean."

"We can't control what they want to see or choose to believe, Jenny. Our reasons for doing what we did are no one else's business. We're not doing anything wrong, and we're not hurting anyone."

"Not everyone is crazy about what we did."

"I know," he muttered. His hand inched a little higher on her back, his thumb brushing bare skin above soft fabric. "Do you think Bess is really upset with us?"

"I'm not sure." She swallowed at the feel of Greg's hand drifting back to splay over the fabric lower on her dress. It was almost as if his touch to her bare skin had been inadvertent, something he really hadn't intended to do. "I heard her tell Agnes Waters that you're probably the reason I was mugged. She said Fate brought me back here so I could meet you."

Jenny had found the thought terribly kind and insightful, considering her co-worker's displeasure. When Agnes had repeated Bess's conclusion to her a few minutes later, Jenny had simply smiled and agreed that it was entirely possible. In many ways Greg had turned out to be more of a knight in shining armor than any man she'd ever known. She didn't believe in the fairy tale anymore. She knew he never had. And he wouldn't have considered himself anywhere near as noble as she'd found him to be. But there was no denying that he had come to her rescue.

She ducked her head, conscious of the feel of his strong arms, the way their bodies flowed to the music. She had no idea what he'd said to the men who'd gathered around him while the women had alluded to how well she'd done for herself. But the friendly questions and comments tonight had made her even more aware of the enormous sense of gratitude she felt toward him.

She just wasn't prepared for the rest of what she felt in his arms just then. She'd seen the look in his eyes when they'd gone through the cake ritual. She'd felt that disturbing tingle along her nerves when he'd kissed her. As reassuring as she found his solid presence, and with the way everyone had been wishing them well all evening, it would be terribly easy to get caught up in the idea of them as a real couple.

The thought had her steeling herself against the feel of his hard muscles as he turned her on the dance floor. That kind of thinking would only get her hurt again. Greg had made it clear from the moment he'd proposed that their situation was temporary. And temporary was all she needed. With the way her luck had gone lately, the last thing she wanted to do was to put her heart on the line again. Especially with a man whose own heart had a wall around it a mile high.

"Relax," he whispered in her ear.

"Sorry," she murmured back. "I must be more self-conscious than I thought. About everyone watching, I mean."

Self-consciousness hadn't brought the fine tension to her muscles. At least, not the kind she was talking about. Greg would have staked his license to practice on that. What she wasn't comfortable with was the awareness he felt shimmering between them like flame.

Their bodies fit beautifully, hard angle to soft curve, and they moved together to the music with an ease that should only have come after hours in each other's arms. That thought had others drifting into his mind as he held her. Thoughts of her bare shoulders and how beautiful the rest of her body would be stripped of her enticing little dress. Thoughts of her body, naked and moving against his as slowly as they moved with each other now.

He eased her back a bit, consciously distancing himself from that exquisite torture. The last thing he wanted was for Jenny to feel uneasy with him or with what they had done. He had signed on as her protector.

Nothing more.

Chapter Eleven

"I don't want you to think that I'm not happy for you, Jenny. Like I said the other day, your moving back here would seem to be the best thing that could have happened to you. You have a fine man in Dr. Reid and, even though I think you both could have given yourselves a little more time, you're both adults and your personal life is none of my business.

"Now, I'm sure you've had other things on your mind. Any new bride would," Bess allowed, her tone clipped. "That's why I've waited the past few days for you to bring this up. Since you haven't, I will. Have you given any thought to who's going to replace you since you'll be leaving Maple Mountain, too?"

The moment Bess had started to speak, Jenny had turned from the computer she'd just shut down to see her co-worker standing in the front office doorway. The woman with a smiley face pinned to her lab jacket had her hands on her hips. Displeasure pinched her expression.

"Rhonda's not going to like having to come back," she continued. "She was hoping to take a year off."

Jenny rose from her chair, stuck her hands in the pockets of her scrub jacket. Bess was right, she had had other things on her mind. "I'm not leaving for another couple of months," she assured the clearly disgruntled woman. "If Rhonda really doesn't want to come back for a while, I can train someone else. Who filled in when she took maternity leave before?"

"No one I want back here. Except the oldest Waters girl."

"Then, I'll call her."

"She moved to Portland."

"So, I'll find someone else."

"If that's what you're going to do, you'd best get word out that the clinic is hiring. And start soon. It's going to be bad enough having to get a new doctor used to the way we do things around here without having to worry about incompetent office help."

Looking as annoyed as she did when faced with an uncooperative patient, she collected her purse from the file drawer and turned back to the door.

"See you in the morning," she muttered.

Jenny blinked at the woman's back. Despite Bess's surprisingly easy acceptance of her and Greg as a couple, she had been unusually reserved the past few days. Jenny hadn't known what to make of her manner. When she'd asked Bess if she was all right, she'd said only that she had things on her mind. Listening to the woman walk away, Jenny finally understood what those "things" were.

"Have a good evening," she called after her.

She heard her grumble a goodbye to Greg on her way to the back door.

Moments later he appeared in the open doorway.

"What's the matter with her?"

"I don't think she's very happy with us."

"She's not still annoyed that we didn't give her more time to make us a cake, is she?"

The cake had certainly seemed to be the problem at the reception. The heart of the woman's dissatisfaction, though, went far deeper than the delicious confection Jenny had thanked her for in person and by note.

"I think she feels we sabotaged her."

Frowning, he headed for the supply cabinet above the files. "How?"

"Because we're both leaving." Now that she thought it through, it was no wonder Bess had been so displeased. She had been with Dr. Wilson for three decades before he retired. And Rhonda had worked there ever since she'd graduated from high school. Nothing had changed for Bess until Greg had arrived.

"Bess just got you trained," she explained, certain the veteran of thirty-plus years in Maple Mountain's medical trenches felt she had done just that. "Now you're leaving and a new doctor is coming in for her to deal with. She just got used to working with me, and I'm leaving, too." Sympathy for the woman softened her voice. "Everything is changing for her."

"Change isn't always a bad thing, Jenny."

"It is when you've had too much of it."

His glance caught hers. "I hadn't considered that," he conceded and, still preoccupied with work, looked back to the cabinet. Taking out a pack of batteries, he peeled out two fresh ones for his calculator. "I guess all we can do for her is make the transition as smooth as we can."

He offered the conclusion as a simple matter of fact. What was done was done. You simply moved on from there.

He wasn't a person who looked back. Jenny knew that. She also knew that when faced with the past, he did his best to ignore it. At the moment she was more concerned with the fact that there were a lot of things neither one of them had considered— such as how getting married would alter their relationship.

Keeping that uneasy thought to herself, she simply agreed with his conclusion, then returned to closing up the clinic while he headed for his office.

Their relationship had definitely changed. Jenny felt it as surely as she did the reserve that had hung in the air between them ever since they'd left their reception the other night. The only time she didn't notice that subtle distance was at the clinic. There the demands of the patients and the routine allowed a sense of familiarity that made working with him nearly as effortless as it had always been. Because their roles were so well-defined at the office, she felt comfortable with him. She knew what to do, how to act around him. And almost always there were other people around.

The problem was at his house. Without the buffers, the routine, the defined roles, she had no idea what he required of her. Or, if he required anything at all.

The one thing she knew he hadn't expected of her was that she cook for him. He'd told her that the day after their impromptu reception, after he'd returned from helping Charlie again.

He'd already told her she didn't have to clean. He wouldn't accept rent. Unable to imagine how she would ever feel comfortable living with him if she didn't contribute somehow, she'd told him she would be cooking for herself anyway, that it was as easy to cook for two as for one, and that it made absolutely no sense to mess up the kitchen twice. Since he'd used pretty much the same argument on her the morning he'd fixed her toast, he hadn't had much else to say.

With at least that much settled, she had gone to the house after work the past few nights, prepared dinner and left his half in the oven to keep warm while he stayed to finish his dictation and she started working on pumpkin costumes.

Had he brought up the matter of his father's estate, she might have worked on that, too. With all he'd done for her, she felt desperate to contribute something more substantial to their arrangement than preparing meals, but she didn't want to push where his father's assets were concerned. From what Greg had told her, it had been clear that the senior Reid had valued his wealth more than he ever had any relationship, including his own son's. Aware of the mental abuse that estate represented to Greg, and suspecting how he'd rankled whenever Elizabeth or his attorney brought it up, she knew he needed to come to her with it in his own time.

By the end of the week, however, he hadn't even mentioned it. A couple of evenings into the next, she was beginning to wondered if he'd decided not to accept her help with the matter. She knew it was on his mind, though. He'd had that familiar edge about him the past couple of days, and a restlessness she'd come to recognize as a need to escape thoughts he would much rather avoid.

The front door opened and closed.

From where she stood at the maple table in the dining room, she glanced up from unpinning pattern pieces for the second pumpkin costume to see Greg in the entryway. Thinking his jaw looked locked tight enough to shatter teeth, she watched him shrug out of his causal tan jacket and hang it over the coat closet's knob.

He didn't turn from the closet, though. Cupping his hand to the back of his neck, he lowered his head and drew a breath that stretched the fabric of his blue oxford shirt tight across his broad shoulders. For several long moments, he just stood there threatening the seams of his shirt before he rotated his head as if to work the knots from his neck. When he finally turned around, he looked no less edgy than he had when he'd first walked in.

"Your dinner is in the oven," she said as he entered the living room. "Do you want me to get it for you? Or would like a glass of wine first?" They had the bottle Dora had given them as a wedding present. She wouldn't share it with him because of the baby. But there was no reason he couldn't enjoy it. "You look like you could use one."

Still rubbing his neck, he continued through the room, turning at the end of the sofa to pass the dining table. "It's been a long day."

"That doesn't answer my question."

She offered a smile. He didn't seem to notice. Obviously preferring to wait on himself as he always did, he said, "I'll get it," and disappeared into the kitchen

She heard a cabinet open and close. Then, a drawer. The sounds weren't unusually loud, but there was a sharpness to them that spoke of impatience, irritation or both.

She knew Larry Cohen, his attorney, had called. Twice, actually. She had dutifully taken the messages asking Greg to return the calls ASAP and left them with his other messages on his desk.

With her back to the doorway, she returned to unpinning tissue from bright-orange felt. "Do you want to talk about it?" she ventured, hoping he would confide in her. If he would just share his thoughts, some of his restiveness might ease.

She wondered if he had any idea how unsettling his tension could be. At the clinic he managed to mask the worst of it. Here, he obviously didn't feel the need.

"Not really."'

Hope died. "Okay."

She hated this. She hated that he was closing her out when it seemed that all he had to do was give her the papers in his bottom drawer and let her help him get his past behind him once and for all. But she had the feeling there was even more going on with him than he'd confided in her, and she wasn't going to be one of those who pushed him. All that would do was cause him to avoid her the way he was avoiding his attorney. When he didn't want to deal with something, he simply…didn't.

The movements in the kitchen stopped. Feeling the fine hairs on the back of her neck prickle, she glanced around to see him watching her from the kitchen doorway. He held a bottle of cabernet in one hand, a corkscrew in the other.

She didn't know if he realized he was being unfair, or if he'd changed his mind about talking. Either way, he looked positively forbidding as he frowned at her mouth.

"I need to call Larry."

Pulling the two straight pins he'd noticed from between her lips, Jenny poked them into the red-fabric tomato Claire had loaned her. If it hadn't been for the wall of tension surrounding him, she might have felt relieved that he'd finally brought up the matter. As it was, all she felt was caution.

"I know."

"It's apparently worth around five million." A muscle in his jaw jumped, his expression grim with the thought of being forced to deal with what should have never been his responsibility. "I just want to be rid of it."

She knew that, too. "Have you thought of where you want it to go?"

His terse, "No," was as flat as the green-felt leaf on the table. All he could think about was that the estate had to be liquidated first. That was what he didn't want to deal with, getting from point A to point B. Getting rid of it would be the easy part. But before he could do that, he would have to deal with the real estate, stocks, bonds, boats, cars and jewelry his father had personally selected. "All I know is giving it to charity is a good idea. Anonymously, if possible."

He sounded as if he knew his father would have hated that. The wealth he had so cherished would simply...disappear.

"Anonymously certainly would be possible," she told him, willing to encourage him any way she could. "You just use untraceable paper. Something like a cashier's check," she explained, having assisted at the brokerage with the investment of such donations. "Once you liquidate, you can have your attorney turn the funds over to you that way. One check. Several smaller ones. No one would have to know who you give them to."

Not by a twitch did his expression change.

"Would you consider using it here?" she quietly asked.

She still thought that if he could find a cause he believed in, he could focus on that rather than all the dark emotions that had him so blocked now. She was also dying to run an idea by him that had occurred to her sitting with Mrs. McNeff in her hospital room.

He shook his head, his dark hair falling over his wide brow as he walked past her and set the bottle on an empty spot between two pieces of orange fabric.

"That wouldn't even make a dent in the money. I'll be glad to send Bess a check to get a new computer and printer. The clinic in Brayborough could use those, too," he added, already thinking about needs he could fill there. "But that would only take twenty or thirty thousand dollars."

"I was thinking a little bigger than that."

He jammed the corkscrew in the cork. "If you're talking about getting more sophisticated medical equipment, the problem there is that putting money into expensive diagnostics doesn't make sense. In a community this small, the machines would be unused most of the time. And that's even if you could find trained technicians to run them when they were needed."

"What about something that doesn't already exist? What about something that could be used both places?" she asked, because she'd been thinking ahead, too. "And everywhere in between?"

The furrows in his forehead deepened. "Such as?"

A hint of her old enthusiasm bubbled in her chest. Afraid to sound as if she were pushing the idea on him, especially as resistant as he was being, she shoved it down.

"I asked Bess about all the medical crises the clinic hasn't been able to handle over the years. I told her Mrs. McNeff had mentioned a few," she explained, so he'd know how she'd brought up the subject. "Mrs. McNeff also talked about how hard it is sometimes to get to St. Johnsbury in winter even for scheduled treatments. There have to be people like her in remote places for hundreds of miles around here. Bess said not having quick access to a trauma center or treatments is just something people who live in rural areas accept. But maybe you could help them get where they need to be that much quicker."

The quality of his frown shifted at the light in her eyes. "So what are you thinking?"

"That you could fund an air rescue program. I did some research and found out that some smaller cities in the middle of the state contract with companies that have the capability to airlift patients from one hospital to another. Maybe your fund could contract with them to expand to St. Johnsbury. They could fly out of there and be here in half an hour instead of an hour and a half. I didn't know what kind of money you were talking about, but now that I do, another option would be to purchase a helicopter outright and lease it to a company and contract for their pilots. There would be insurance and administrative costs, but the services could always be free to the patients who need it. The project could even grow to serve all of rural New England."

For a moment Greg said nothing. He just stood watching the light in her eyes transform her face and wishing he could feel even a trace of her enthusiasm.

"So, for emergencies like heart attacks and the kind we ran into at the quarry, it would be a rural air rescue," he concluded, pulling the cork from the wine bottle. "For people like Mrs. McNeff who need critical treatments, it could double as a medical shuttle service."

"Exactly."

Something about the appealing brightness in her eyes seemed to loosen the knots in his stomach. "Who would administer the fund?"

"I know you'd want nothing to do with it, so maybe after you liquidate the estate, you could have your attorney turn the whole thing over to the hospital, and their board of trustees could handle it."

He'd thought before that there was no way on God's green earth that he could feel anything even remotely redeeming about the wealth his father had used like a leash to control those around him. The connotations with it were all overwhelmingly negative, and even with Jenny's assertion that putting a positive spin on it would help, he had seriously doubted anything could change his mind or his heart about what he'd felt.

He liked what she'd suggested, though. The need for such a service was definitely there.

He just hated that his father was still jerking with him from the grave. He had to handle the man's estate, whether he liked the idea or not. The responsibility was one he didn't want, should never have had. But he'd never turned his back on a responsibility in his life. Never had he allowed anyone else to solve his problems. And he'd certainly never relinquished control over any of his personal affairs. There was something threatening about handing over control in any form. It meant failure to cope on his own, to measure up, to handle the pressure, the responsibility.

The more he'd thought about bringing the papers in his bottom drawer home to Jenny, the less he'd been able to get past the feeling that he would be doing just that. Handing over control and failing to make it on his own.

"Will you think about it?" he heard her ask.

She was talking about a rescue fund. "Yeah," he murmured, picking up the bottle to go find a glass and his supper. The idea really was a good one. "I will."

The relief Jenny felt that Greg had finally at least spoken about the estate didn't last. As one day moved into another, he said nothing else about the rescue fund or the estate. When they were alone, conversation touched only on the necessary, the inconsequential and the baby.

Talking about the baby seemed to relieve the caution that underscored their hours alone. Sharing her dreams for her child, talking about how she would teach her to ride a bike and sew and play T-ball felt safe, too. Far safer than thinking about how awkward she felt having him put a roof over her head when he still wasn't allowing her to repay him in any substantial way— or how he wouldn't be around to coach those games or hold that bike himself

By the time her child was old enough for those things, she and Greg would have gone their separate ways.

She didn't want to let herself think that far ahead. She didn't want to think about how hard it would be on her baby to leave the only father he or she would have known when that time came. She'd had to make a choice to do what was best for her child now. There would be plenty of time later to deal with the consequences of that decision.

She just wished she had someone to talk to about her concerns, her fears, and the lingering sense of loneliness that had yet to go away. But she had no one. The one person she would have talked to before was the very one she couldn't talk to now. Greg was part of the reason that loneliness had become more acute.

The night she had accepted his offer to marry, she had felt so protected when he'd held her. There were even moments now when it felt as if he were sheltering her, watching out for her. Elusive moments when he would take care of something he knew needed to be done, as when he'd enlisted Charlie's aid and boarded up the house. Or when he would ask how she felt, if the queasiness was better or worse. If she was resting better.

She knew in those moments of thoughtfulness that it was possible for the void to be filled. But it had almost been easier to get from one day to the next before he'd teased her with the comfort of his arms because he hadn't offered them again. As for the void, if not for thoughts of her child, that hole in her soul might have felt even bigger than it already did.

Taking a deep breath, she tried to shake her disquieting thoughts. They seemed to hit at the strangest times, waking her from sleep, catching her in the middle of doing ordinary tasks. Just now, they had caught her doing the only task she'd been able to wrest from him.

She stood by the sink, her hand on her stomach, where it had protectively settled moments ago. In the minutes before Greg had come home, she had changed into a sweater and jeans and headed straight to the kitchen to put on water for pasta. It was Tuesday, and he and Amos were scheduled to "play checkers" in a little over an hour.

"What's the matter?" he asked, walking in to see her hand at the waist-length hem of her white sweater.

She gave a dismissing shake of her head. "I was…just thinking."

"When you look that concerned, you're usually doing more than that." His narrowed glance slid down her torso. "Are you worried about the baby?"

Her hand returned to her stomach. There was no reason he had to know the exact nature of her worry. Any one of her myriad concerns would do. Especially since there were things about her child she had no problem discussing with him at all.

"I keep waiting, but I haven't felt it move yet."

Greg felt a smile threaten as he rolled up the cuffs on his chambray shirt. The woman looking up at him with her lovely blue eyes struck him as an impossible blend of sophistication, cautious cynicism and childlike innocence. When it came to running the office, she was as sharp and savvy as any woman he'd ever met. When it came to anything personal, however, she seemed infinitely more vulnerable.

When it came to her child, she seemed most vulnerable of all.

"For one thing," he said, stopping in front of her, "you're only eleven weeks pregnant. You won't feel movement for at least another five or six.

"For another," he said, reaching toward her, "your hand is too high."

He circled her wrist with his fingers. Taking her hand from where her fingers splayed in the vicinity of her navel, he slid it down.

"The baby is nestled right about here."

Greg's body dwarfed hers. His big hand engulfed her wrist, holding her hand low on her belly. Had she been prepared for what he was going to do, the intimacy of their positions might not have been so disturbing. But she hadn't been prepared. Any more than she was prepared for the heat that seemed to move from his hand through her palm as she murmured a quiet, "Oh."

Beneath his fingers, Greg felt her pulse skip.

His own jerked a few times, too, in the moments before he slowly, deliberately released her wrist.

Their ease with each other seemed harder and harder to find. And touching her only strained what little they had left. Had he been thinking, he wouldn't have touched her at all. He would have just motioned to where her child grew and ignored the way his fingers itched to smooth the little furrows from her brow, to sink into the silk of her hair.

He couldn't believe how quickly she could affect him. He'd done nothing more than take her wrist and catch the scent of the shampoo that drifted into his bedroom every morning, and he was aware of little beyond her and the slow burning heat settling in his groin.

"You worry too much," he told her, taking a step back.

She shrugged, tried a smile. "I'm afraid it's become a habit."

"Well, work on breaking it, would you? One of the reasons you're here is so you don't have to do that."

His frustration with himself must have put more of an edge in his voice than he'd realized. With the single blink of her dark lashes, the smile died and uncertainty clouded her expression.

Taking a step back herself, she quickly turned to the counter. "I'll have dinner ready in a few minutes."

In the suddenly silent room, the click of the pot she picked up from the counter practically echoed when she set it in the sink to fill.

Swearing at himself, he reached toward her, only to pull right back. Touching her again would only taunt him more and he'd taken enough cold showers as it was. There hadn't been a night since she'd been in his house that he hadn't lain awake in his bed wondering if she was awake in hers.

Beneath the cables on her sweater, he saw her shoulders rise as she drew a deep breath. She was trying to regroup, mask whatever it was he'd just caused her to feel.

Swearing again, he reached for her, anyway.

"Hey," he murmured, turning her around. "I didn't mean that the way it sounded. It's normal for you to be concerned."

She aimed a forgiving smile at his chest. "I'm being overly sensitive. Blame it on hormones."

No problem, he thought. That was certainly what he blamed for his reactions to her. "Yeah, well, I'm a guy. We're known for not being sensitive enough."

The sensation of silken warmth whispered along his nerves. Her sweater dipped at the neck in short vee, just deeply enough to expose the delicate line of her collarbone. He hadn't been aware of his thumb brushing her skin until he'd felt its texture. Apparently even his subconscious felt that need to touch.

"Is there anything else you're worried about?"

Her glance stayed on the middle of his chest as she murmured. "No."

Hooking her chin with his crooked finger, he tipped up her head. "Look me in the eye and say that."

She couldn't look him in the eye and lie. He apparently knew that. But looking at him just then didn't feel safe. He saw too much. He always had. With him standing so close, with him touching her as if he couldn't stand not to, she was afraid he'd see far more than she wanted him to know.

It was one thing to want him to hold her. It was another entirely for him to know she did.

"Did you make an appointment with the obstetrician yet?"

"I go in three weeks. Right after the harvest festival."

"Would you feel better if you went sooner?"

Still focused on the buttons on his shirt, she shook her head. "I told the nurse how far along I was and what kind of prenatal vitamins I was taking. Since I'm not even three months, she said there's no hurry to come in."

"So what's wrong, then?"

"Why does something have to be wrong?"

"Because I know you," he coaxed, his voice as gentle as his touch when he retraced the path of his thumb over her collarbone. "We know each other's secrets, remember? Maybe I can help."

That elusive sense of being protected was there again. The caring and concern that stopped just short of offering her the respite she had felt before in his arms.

She turned her head away, refusing to let him see what she wanted when he held back so much himself. She hated that she felt so needy when he seemed to need nothing at all.

For days, she had waited for him to either give her the estate papers or tell her why he'd changed his mind about trusting her with them. She hadn't wanted to bring it up for fear he would withdraw from her.

She hated that, too.

Slipping from his hands, she turned to the cabinet where he kept plates.

As frustration collided with the need to protect herself, she turned right back to face him.

"The day you offered me the job at the clinic," she said, her tone far calmer than she felt, "you said you were doing it because I'd helped you with your arm. You said you don't like owing people," she reminded him, "so that made us even. But from that point on, it's only been you helping me. And you won't even give me a chance to repay you."

Absolute incomprehension lowered his brow. "What are you talking about?"

"I'm talking about the way you won't let me do anything for you. You've given me a decent roof, a decent bed, the protection of your name and a way to support my child. All you accept from me is dinner. Lorna does the major cleaning on this house. She does your laundry. You're so insanely neat about everything that you don't even leave anything for me to pick up after you."

"It bothers you that I'm neat?"

For an intelligent man he had totally missed the point. "It bothers me," she clarified, bracing herself, "that you won't let me keep my end of our agreement."

"How am I not doing that?"

"You're not letting me *help*."

"But there's nothing I need help with," he tried to explain, only to remember what he'd asked of her the night he'd more or less proposed.

Greg felt his incomprehension slide into oblivion. She was talking about the estate. What he didn't understand now was why she'd let herself stew about for so long.

"Why didn't you just ask me about it?" he inquired.

Her arms snaked around her waist. "Because I don't want you to think I'm pushing like Elizabeth did and Larry is doing now. And I'm not," she explained. "If you've changed your mind about trusting me with it, that's fine. But at least let me do something to repay you."

"It has nothing to do with not trusting you, Jenny."

She stood with her arms crossed, looking as if she were protecting herself somehow. The thought that she felt she needed to protect herself from him barely registered before he saw her arms relax.

"Then let me pay rent."

"I told you to use your money to pay your lawyer."

"See what I mean?" Her arms flew out to her sides, the gesture a blend of helplessness and pure frustration. "You're not the only one who doesn't like feeling obligated, Greg."

"I don't want you to feel obligated."

"Well, I do."

Well stop, he wanted to insist.

He cupped the side of her neck with his hand, eased his thumb over the pulse beating at its base. "I know none of this is easy for you. But it doesn't have to be so hard, either. For what it's worth," he confided, "I wanted you here because I worried about you living out there in that house. If you're looking for trade-offs, you've already paid me back in the sleep I haven't lost since you moved in."

Incredulity touched her expression. "You lost sleep over me?"

You have no idea how much, he thought.

"Some," he conceded.

Jenny had no idea what he saw in her eyes at his quiet admission. Something shifted through his, though. Something that left them dark and inscrutable.

"Don't look at me like that," he murmured.

"Like what?"

His jaw seemed to tighten. *Like you wouldn't stop me if I kissed you.*

The thought jerked hard at his self control. He couldn't be anywhere near her without wanting her. Touching her made denying that impossible.

His glance moved over her face, drifted to her mouth.

Behind Jenny, the faucet dripped into the sink. From across the room came the steady hum of the refrigerator. All she really noticed was the man holding her frozen with nothing more than the touch of his hand. Greg's features seemed to tighten as his eyes roamed her face. She didn't know if he was questioning her or himself, but there was no denying that struggle was there as he traced the line of her jaw with his knuckles.

She felt his fingers slip past her ear, slide up into her hair. As if drawn by its texture, or his own memories, he let the pad of his thumb caress the corner of her mouth.

He felt her breath tremble against his hand.

She wouldn't stop him. The stark realization overrode resolve, dissolving it completely as he cupped the back of her head and slowly lowered his own. He'd meant to keep his hands to himself. And he would. Soon. All he wanted was to know the taste of her. He'd been denied that before in the brief kisses they'd shared. One kiss and he would let her go.

Jenny's breath stalled as his mouth settled over hers. The feel of his lips was unbearably gentle as he eased her toward his big body—and the possibility of being held once more.

Aching for what was suddenly so close, she flattened her hands against his chest, slowly fisted his shirt in her fingers. At that small capitulation, his tongue touched hers and he slowly began to rob the strength from her knees. That deliberate, sensual invasion had her sucking in air, clutching his shirt more tightly to keep from sinking to her knees.

She didn't know if she sagged against him or if he drew her closer. She knew only that his arms were suddenly around her and that she was finally, exactly where she'd yearned to be. He was holding her, kissing her, and she could almost feel the awful insecurities plaguing her life loosen their grip.

She knew that didn't make a lot of sense considering he was one of the reasons those insecurities were there. But she wasn't feeling particularly logical just then. All she cared about was that he cared for her, that he trusted her. And all she wanted was to sink into his strength and obliterate the void inside her.

Greedy with that need, she lifted her arms, curved them around his neck. As she did, he angled her head to take her deeper, dragging a moan from her throat at his blatant invasion of her senses. He drew another whimper from her when his hand slid down her back to press her against the daunting bulge behind his zipper.

Wildfire.

Greg felt it rip through his veins, sear a path along the nerves at the base of his spine. With her slender body seeking his, her little moans of need nearly undid him. She tasted like warm honey, felt like pure heaven, and letting her go was the farthest thing from his mind.

He drew her up, molded her shape to his. He'd thought before how fragile she felt. She still did. Yet there was a strength in her supple muscles that turned fragility to pure feminine power. If she were to set her mind to it, she could have him begging at her feet.

He already felt precariously close to doing just that when a hint of sanity slithered through the red haze of heat threatening his control. Needing to slow down, needing more logic and less temptation, he edged her far enough away to break contact with her body.

His heart felt as if it could beat right through his chest when he tipped her head up see her face. Her mouth was shiny with his moisture, her cheeks flushed.

It was the look in her eyes that ruined his attempt to be noble.

She seemed to know he was about to let her go. Beneath the desire, she looked lost.

"Hey, honey," he murmured. "What is it?"

"Don't you ever need anything?" she asked, her thready tone almost accusing.

"What do you mean?"

"Don't you ever need…closeness?"

He'd never considered the question before. But if she was talking about the basic need to touch and be touched, the answer was easy. "Of course I do."

"Then why did you stop?"

The plea in her quiet question twisted at something deep inside him. "Because I have to." Knowing that tore at him as he brushed her cheeks with his thumbs. Her skin felt like satin beneath his touch. She would feel like that everywhere. "If I don't, this won't end here."

At his blunt admission, she lowered her head.

"What is it you need, Jenny?"

Her fingers settled over his pounding heart. "For you not to stop."

He caught her face between his hands, made her look into his eyes. The fire had barely begun to subside. Seeing the naked need in her expression, it nearly flashed out of control.

Greg bit back a groan as he took her mouth once more. Had she given any indication at all that she wanted him to slow down, he would have ignored the razor-sharp desire clawing at him and managed somehow to walk away. But she seemed to crave his touch as much as he did hers. That knowledge sharpened the edge and turned thoughts of nobility to steam.

He suspected that what she wanted had more to do with seeking comfort than with physical desire. But the line between raw need and getting lost in the heat seemed too fine to differentiate just then. He wasn't sure which one of them felt the greater hunger as he slipped his hands under her sweater and drank in her sigh at the feel of them on her bare skin. Beneath his hands he felt her shiver. Or maybe that tremor was his. He wasn't totally sure as his tongue tangled with hers and he sought the fullness of her breast.

Jenny's knees nearly buckled at the feel of his palm covering her. She'd thought that all she wanted was his arms around her. She was wrong. She needed the sweet oblivion he created as his hands memorized her shape, toyed and teased. He urged her closer, carrying his touch over her back and down, molding her to the hard lines of his body. With his mouth moving over hers, she felt parts of her going tense, others growing soft. Low in her belly her insides turned liquid at the feel of his hardness seeking her through layers of cotton and denim.

There was something terribly freeing about knowing he wanted her. Something that made it far easier than it should have been to finally acknowledge what she'd suspected all along.

She was falling in love with him. Probably already had.

The thought shimmered through her consciousness as he turned her toward the hallway, backing her down it and through his office, the shortest route to the stairs. He let her go only long enough to take her hand and lead her up the stairs before turning her in his arms again and backing her toward his bed.

Her knees hit the edge of the mattress. In the light from the hallway, he stopped there with her and tucked his hands under her sweater again.

He asked her to raise her arms, and the sweater hit the floor.

Lifting her hand to his chest, he murmured, "Your turn."

Her fingers trembled as she worked her way down the buttons on his shirt. When she reached the buckle of his belt, he took over for her, unfastening it so she could tug his shirttails from his pants. Compelled by the need to touch, she slipped his shirt over his shoulders. It had barely reached the floor when she skimmed the tips of her fingers over his chest.

Remembering the pain he'd been in the night they'd met, she traced over those sculpted muscles and along the hard line of his collarbone. The bruising she'd seen for weeks above the collars of his shirts had finally faded.

"Does it hurt anymore?" she asked.

His carved features were beautifully taut as he shook his head. "It hasn't for a while."

She kissed his shoulder, anyway, and the spots where she'd once seen the bruising start.

Something feral slipped into his expression when she raised her head. But the diamond brightness of his eyes barely registered before his mouth claimed hers. A ragged heartbeat later, his hands were at the clasp of her bra, and filmy lace joined the growing pile of clothes.

For long moments he held her at the side of the bed, gently stroking her tender breasts, making her weak with need, before turning her sideways so he could throw back the comforter. Easing her onto the cool sheets, he followed her down to trail a path of heat from one beaded nipple to the other. Her flesh there already felt fuller, heavy and terribly sensitive, but his gentle ministrations seemed to soothe even as he coaxed sensations from her that she'd never known existed.

Stretched beneath him, she felt his fingers drift down to work at the snap of her jeans. Kissing his way to her belly, he stripped denim and pink lace down her legs, then went to work ridding himself of the last barriers between them.

Greg's glance swept her beautiful body. Having wanted her for so long, impatience battled the need to savor. Impatience had the edge. He was ready to die from wanting, and the feel of her soft hands roaming his shoulders, urging him over her was almost more than he could bear. He could feel the enticing shivers in her body as he suckled her, could hear the little moan she made when he slipped his hand to the downy thatch between her legs to caress her there.

He wanted nothing more than to slip inside her and bury himself in her heat. But the small part of his brain that still functioned above animal instinct reminded him of the need for protection. A surge of resentment for that need swept through him. He didn't want it with her. He wanted nothing between them.

The thought had no sooner occurred than he realized the need for protection wasn't there. A sense of possession swept through him, unfamiliar and demanding. Tucking his hand beneath her hip, aligning her to him, he bit back the urge to drive himself deep.

She whispered his name, the sound urgent and ragged.

He whispered hers back as he eased inside her, gritting his teeth against the silken feel of her, fighting for control. But control was lost. And he honestly didn't care. In the moments before he felt her convulsing around him and his brain shut down, he was aware of nothing beyond the woman who made it impossible for him to hold back and the white-hot heat that melted the lock on his soul.

Chapter Twelve

The light from the hallway spilled across the bed. In that soft glow, Greg eased his weight off Jenny and rolled to his side. With one arm beneath her head, their legs tangled and their breathing ragged, he let his hand roam from her breast to her belly.

For a fleeting instant, he found himself wishing the child she carried was his. In the next heartbeat, he felt himself go still.

He didn't know which shook him more. The unexpected thought, or the way the protectiveness he felt toward her had gotten all knotted up with physical desire.

He was in unfamiliar territory here, caught up with something that felt utterly foreign and wholly capable of moving beyond his control. Feeling distinctly threatened by that, he told himself the only thing he really felt was guilt. Sex had never been part of the deal.

He could tell by the sudden tension in Jenny's body that reality had hit her, too—and that she felt no more certain than he did about what they had just done.

The phone beside the bed gave a quiet ring.

The tension in her supple muscles increased.

Being the only doctor for miles, he never had the luxury of ignoring a ringing phone.

"Stay where you are," he said, and raised up to reach across her.

Jenny heard Greg's deep voice rumble above her as he answered the call. But the uncertainties waiting to be felt had barely piled up when she heard him say, "Sure. I'll tell her," before he offered a remarkably normal-sounding goodbye and hung up.

He eased back to his elbow, his arm still under her neck. With her head tucked toward his chest, he could see nothing of her expression.

"That was Claire." With the tip of his finger, he nudged back the fringe of hair around her ear. "She said she knew I had plans tonight so she invited you over to work on the festival."

He'd forgotten all about Amos until just then. It seemed he'd forgotten pretty much everything. His intention to keep his hands to himself. His common sense.

Jenny blinked at his beautifully muscled chest, not quite able to meet his eyes. "Does she want me to call her?"

"Only if you can't make it."

She gave a little nod.

His voice dropped. "Are you all right?"

Jenny wasn't sure if she was or not. She felt shaken to the core by the need she'd felt for him. As the cold light of reality shed it's painfully bright light on their intimate position, what disturbed her more was his mental withdrawal from her. She'd felt it as surely as she did the weight of his heavy thighs trapping her leg. Yet his tone held nothing but concern.

She lifted her head, forced a faltering smile. "Sure," she lied, desperately hoping it was just insecurity making her imagine the vaguely shuttered look in his eyes. "You?"

His glance swept her face. Leaning down, he gently kissed

her forehead. "Yeah," he finally said, but the distance was still there.

The void around her heart suddenly opened again. Desperate to hide the effects of that awful empty sensation, she kept her tone as light as she could. "Then, you'd better get up and get dressed. You're going be late if you don't." She glanced at the clock on his nightstand, grateful for the excuse to turn from his quiet scrutiny. "You don't want to keep Amos waiting."

Jenny curled away from him as she sat up, the sheets falling away. With her back to him, she reached for her sweater, pulled it over her head without bothering with her bra. Grabbing his pants, she handed them to him and reached for her panties and jeans.

She could practically feel his hesitation.

"Are you okay if I go?" he asked quietly.

The concern in his voice sounded suspiciously like obligation. It was bad form to bolt from bed after making love with a woman. But the last thing she wanted was for him to stick around because he felt he had to. Or, worse because he was feeling sorry for her. She hadn't exactly begged him to take her to bed, but she'd come close.

"Of course I am."

Bedclothes and khakis rustled as Greg threw back blankets and pulled on his pants. Jenny kept her back to him while she fastened her jeans. But he had the feeling it was far more than modesty preventing her from facing him. The spontaneous combustion in the kitchen had revealed needs she hadn't wanted him to see, needs she didn't feel comfortable with even now.

The guilt jerked harder, along with a sharp tug of responsibility for the woman totally messing up his peace of mind. He really had wanted to make things better for her. Now it seemed he'd just made them worse.

He reached toward her, only to let his hand fall when he realized she might pull from his touch. "I'd never intended for that to happen, Jenny."

His quiet words froze her where she stood. She didn't want to hear him apologize. Having him say he was sorry he'd made love with her was just a little more than she could handle just then.

Frantically searching for the brave smile that served her so well, she turned before he could.

"I hadn't, either," she told him, handing him his shirt. "Let's just blame it on hormones. Okay?" She motioned to the clock on her way to the door. "You won't have time for dinner, but you should go soon. You don't want be late meeting Amos. And I need to get ready to go to Claire's."

He'd always known what to say to her before he'd married her. Now he hadn't a clue.

Greg sat in Charlie's truck in front of Amos's old farmhouse with his wrists draped over the wheel, staring at a pasture he didn't really see. He had no idea how he'd thought he could live with Jenny without wanting her. He was a healthy, red-blooded male with a normal, healthy libido. She was an attractive, desirable woman whose spirit intrigued him, whose body drove him wild and whose smiles warmed his heart.

Having made love with her, knowing how she moved beneath him and the little sounds she made when he'd caressed her, only made him want her more.

Were she anyone else he'd been that attracted to, he would have had no qualm adding a little mutually fulfilling sex to their relationship. They would be together for a couple of years, and as good as they'd been together that one time in bed, sex would be incredible with her. But the situation was different with Jenny.

She wasn't the sort of woman who could have a physical relationship and walk away from it unscathed. The fact that she had invited such intimacy between them told him her heart was involved already—and he refused to leave her feeling hurt and used the way Brent Collier had.

He sat back, ran his hand down his face. His relationship with her seemed to get more complicated by the minute, but he had no intention whatsoever of complicating it any further by letting her think they could possibly have a real marriage. From now on, he'd keep his hands in his pockets and do nothing else to take advantage of how truly vulnerable she was right now. The last thing he wanted was to shake her trust in him.

With Amos standing on his porch, hollering at him to come on in, he didn't let himself wonder why he wanted that trust so badly.

Jenny had thought before that it would just take time for her and Greg to find their way around each other. She'd even thought they were making headway—before she'd let her emotions ruin everything.

There was no mistaking the need they both felt to get past what he'd never intended to have happen. Or the subtle distance he put between them. At the clinic they managed well enough. But on nights he didn't have other commitments or weekends when she wasn't at Claire's, he either stayed later at the clinic than usual or worked on the festival booths in Joe's garage.

Greg was a man who filled needs where he could. She didn't know if he'd simply been born with an amazing natural generosity, or if he filled those needs because doing so answered a need in him. She had no idea what that need might be, since he seemed to have very few. But he did it with nearly everyone. He did it with Amos and Lorna and with the kids he coached in the spring. He did it with Charlie. What he was doing for her was truly extraordinary, far beyond the scope of anything anyone else had ever done for her before. But she knew he hadn't taken her in because he wanted to be part of something. And she knew without a doubt that he didn't want the commitment her heart was beginning to crave.

That didn't stop her from loving him, though. Or from worrying about him—which was exactly what she was doing a few hours after he'd been called out to tend an elderly patient with breathing problems in North Stratford.

The night was miserable. Windy, cold and wet with the kind of driving rain that made it nearly impossible to see. She knew how dangerous the winding mountain roads could be in the dark. Especially when a person drove too fast, and Greg had definitely been in a hurry when he'd left.

He finally had his black SUV back, the one he'd been driving the night he'd shown up on her grandma's porch, drenched and in pain. The vehicle looked safe enough. It was as rugged as Joe's Jeep and had new tires. And Greg had told her that the accident the night he'd met her was the only one he'd ever had. Still she worried. As he'd pointed out, she did it well. When a person was good at something, she might as well perfect it.

Or so she was telling herself as she paced the living room in her blue robe and fuzzy slippers a little after two o'clock in the morning.

She'd paced another lap from the entry to the middle of the living room when she heard his key in the lock.

Greg stepped inside and glanced up the stairs. The light in the upstairs hall was on, but the rest of the house was dark.

Dripping on the entry rug, he closed the door with a soft click and hung his raincoat on the coat tree by the mirror so it could drip on the rug. As he did, he heard the shuffle of feet in the living room.

He had been up since six o'clock the previous morning, driven what felt like a thousand miles on the rounds he'd taken for Bess so she could take his rounds Thursday, and just put on another sixty to North Stratford and back. A headache brewed at the base of his skull from lack of sleep and the glare of headlights on the winding pavement, and he had to leave at the crack of dawn for a four-day rural medicine symposium. Yet at that moment he was aware mostly of the odd sense of comfort he felt when he saw Jenny standing there.

She'd waited up for him. He'd never had anyone do that for him before.

"How is your patient?" she asked, her arms crossed over her long robe.

"One of her nieces set her oxygen too low. She'll be fine."

She held his eyes, shook her head. "I'm sorry."

Anyone else might have thought her response terribly unsympathetic. But Greg knew she wasn't thinking of his patient just then. She was thinking of him and of how often his services were called on for problems that weren't problems at all, or for situations that were but which easily could have been avoided.

He was more drawn than he wanted to admit by her caring.

Knowing she needed her rest, he motioned toward the stairs. She moved ahead of him, her steps seeming almost weary, then turned when they reached the top of the landing.

She shouldn't have stayed up, he thought. In the glow of the overhead light, she looked pale and tired herself.

"You don't need to wait up for me when I'm called out like this, Jenny."

"I know." She gave a small shrug. "I just wanted to."

That touched him, too. "But it's really not necessary."

It made no sense for them both to lose sleep. She didn't seem to understand that was all he was saying, though. A pang of hurt shifted through her eyes, something she quickly tried to hide with her injured smile as she stepped back.

"I won't keep you up. 'Night," she murmured, and turned down the hall.

Within seconds she'd slipped into her room and closed the door.

It was clear to him by her expression that she thought he'd simply rejected her concern. With the distance he'd kept between them the past week, her reaction wasn't entirely illogical.

He wanted nothing more than sleep. He had to be up in less than four hours to drive to Montpelier for the start of the conference at nine o'clock, and each passing second robbed him of the rest his body craved. But he hated the hurt he'd seen in her eyes. He hated more that he'd put it there.

Even with fatigue clawing at him to drag him to his bed, he moved down the hall and stopped at her door. Something inside him wanted nothing more than to gather her in his arms and ease that hurt away. He did want her concern. It was beginning to scare him just how very much he did want it. And her.

He'd touched his hand to the knob. He didn't know if it was simply acknowledging what she might mean to him, or the un-expected realization that he'd let her get that close that made him hesitate. But in that moment, he could practically feel his sense of self-protection crumbling. Unnerved by the sensation, unpre-pared for what he'd just begun to understand, he dropped his hand from the knob.

Jenny heard the muffled sound of his fading footsteps on the runner in the hall. She'd all but held her breath when she'd heard him outside her door. Hearing him walk away now, the quiet click of his door closing, she dropped her robe at the foot of her bed and sank to the edge of the mattress. Feeling as tired and dispirited as she had in weeks, she crawled beneath the covers and curled into a ball.

Emergencies like tonight aside, she knew the reason Greg worked late and stayed away so much was because she was there. She hated the way that made her feel. This was his home, and her presence was driving him from it.

The knowledge tore at her as she shifted positions to ease the slight ache she suddenly felt in her lower back. There had to be something she could do to make their situation better. Some way to let him know that she would do anything to get back the ease they'd once had with each other.

She knew he had to leave early in the morning. So there would be no time before he left to set things right. But as soon as he returned, she would sit him down for a nice friendly con-versation and hope for the best. Or she was thinking as fatigue pulled her into sleep.

The ache in her back woke her a while later and she shifted again. It nagged off and on until the pain itself seemed to shift and she woke hours later with what felt like the worst period of her life.

* * *

Four days had felt like forty.

Greg dropped his travel bag on the entry floor and glanced at the note Jenny had taped to the entry mirror.

She was at Bess's. She also asked that he call her there when he got home.

Figuring she was involved in yet another project, he told himself he'd call from the clinic after he grabbed something to eat. It was afternoon and all he'd had was the hotel's complimentary coffee and the apple he'd grabbed from the basket on the reception counter when he'd checked out.

He hadn't left the closing dinner for the symposium last night until well after midnight. Dr. Cochran, the physician who would be taking his place in Maple Mountain, had attended also, and the two of them had shared war stories long after the formal functions had ended. Ed, as his colleague had asked to be called, had mentioned an article on a children's respiratory virus in *The New England Journal of Medicine* that Greg hadn't yet read. Since the publication was in his office at the clinic, he'd figured he would get it and read it that afternoon.

He'd downed a peanut butter and jelly sandwich and was on his way back to the door when he again caught sight of Jenny's note.

He wasn't sure what made him decide to call now rather than wait. But he turned into his study, picked up the phone on his desk, dialed Bess's number and started flipping through the bills and mailers Jenny had stacked for him.

"Hey, Bess. It's me. Is Jenny there?"

A moment's silence preceded his nurse practitioner's quiet, "She is."

"She asked me to call when I got back." Picking up a catalog for hiking equipment, he absently flipped through it. "Tell her I'm going to the clinic for a few minutes, then I'll be home. Okay?"

"Actually—" he heard her reply, her tone oddly hesitant

"—rather than go to the clinic, why don't you come over here. I'll tell her you're on your way."

He'd just started to throw the catalog into the wastebasket. It landed, forgotten, on the desk instead. Something didn't feel right.

"Is Jenny okay?"

"Physically she's fine," she assured him. "Just come over. This isn't a conversation we should have on the phone."

It wasn't that something wasn't right, he thought. Something was flat wrong. He could feel that certainty sink into his chest as he left the house, heading out the back door rather than the front because cutting through the woods in back took a block off the distance to Bess's house, and it was faster to walk than to drive.

He'd barely emerged from the shade of the dense trees and started up the gravel road when he looked toward Bess's yellow cottage with its huge, thriving garden. Bess, impossible to miss in her cherry-red sweats, was already on the porch. Seeing him head toward her, she moved to the gate of her white fence.

"She's inside helping me make applesauce," she said, meeting him there. In the quiet of the beautiful fall day, the latch clanked as she lifted it to pull the gate open. "There's something you should know before you see her, though. Physically she really is fine. But she miscarried."

Suddenly rooted to where he stood, his glance jerked to the house. He jerked it right back to the woman closely watching him. "When?"

"Wednesday morning."

That had been when he'd left. "Why didn't she call me?"

"That's something you'll have to ask her."

Taking in the obvious concern behind his quick demand, her low tone dropped even farther. "She just asked me to tell you about the miscarriage because she knew you'd have questions. You know how difficult this sort of thing can sometimes be," she reminded him, empathy heavy in her tone. "She really doesn't want to talk about it herself right now."

Speaking professional to colleague, she hurried on to tell him that there had been no complications and that Jenny was recovering physically as quickly as anyone she'd ever seen. Speaking as a friend, she told him how frightened Jenny had been when she'd realized what was happening and how, after she'd tended her at the clinic before the day's appointments had began and taken her home, Jenny had started crying and hadn't stopped until she'd exhausted herself.

"I made her stay with me the first night," she admitted, "but she was afraid she was imposing, so she went back home. There was really no need for her to stay after that, anyway. I've been keeping an eye on her and she really does appear to be doing better. I haven't seen any more tears."

Greg opened his mouth, closed it again. He usually had no trouble processing information on several levels at once. All that registered at the moment was that Jenny had lost her child, but she hadn't called him. He didn't know if that was because she hadn't felt she could, or if she simply hadn't needed him. Either way had its own crushing impact.

"You should also know that people have been asking about her since she took the end of the week off. I've just told everyone she had a bug. There's no reason for anyone to think otherwise."

Through his oddly paralyzed thought processes, Greg began to realize what Bess was doing. She was sharing what he would need to know when people inevitably commented on Jenny's health. She was also assuring him that what she knew would go no further.

The assurance wasn't necessary. The woman who had tended Jenny's medical needs often seemed to possess all the warmth of a drill sergeant, but she was fiercely loyal to those she cared about. She would also stop speaking forever before she would betray a professional or personal confidence.

With as much experience as Bess had, she would have known how far along Jenny had been—and that the baby couldn't possible have been his. Considering that, it also seemed pretty apparent that Jenny had confided the nature of their relationship to her.

Her graying eyebrows knitted together, concern for him deepening the crow's feet at the corners of her eyes. "Is there anything you want to know about what happened?"

The physician in him had no trouble understanding why Jenny had asked Bess to give him the details. No woman wanted to relive the loss of her child no matter what its stage of development. Having to answer questions about when she first realized something was wrong, and the myriad details that had led her to exhausting herself with tears wasn't anything he wanted to put her through.

He didn't need the details, anyway. "Not as long as she's all right."

Bess's manner became oddly offhand. "Good, then. And by the way," she mentioned, heading for the porch, "I don't think she'll have any trouble getting pregnant again. Just in case you got to wondering."

She pulled the door open then, calling for Jenny as she walked inside the house that sported more lace and feminine do-dads than the tea section at the gift shop and smelled pleasantly of apples and cinnamon.

Not totally sure what to make of the knowing look he'd seen in the older woman's expression, he remained by her front door and watched her disappear into her kitchen.

"Leave that," he heard her admonish. "I can wash those up later. And don't forget to take these with you."

The murmur of Jenny's voice drifted toward him, her tone too low for him to catch what she was saying. But he heard her say, "Thank you," to the woman before she appeared in the doorway. Hugging a grocery sack against the teal fleece pullover she wore with her jeans, she called back a quiet, "For everything," on her way to where he stood.

Reaching him, she took a deep breath, looked up and said, "Hi."

His glance swept her face. "Hi, yourself," he replied. Her eyes were dark and huge against her pale skin, her smile of welcome far weaker than he was accustomed to seeing.

He reached for the bag. "Let me take that."

"It's not heavy." As if needing something, anything, to hang on to, she hugged the sack tighter. "It's just a couple quarts of applesauce. We've been canning all morning," she said, and slipped past the door he held open.

They'd reached the walkway when he fell into step beside her.

"How was your symposium?" she asked quietly, her focus on the grass growing between the cracks.

"Long."

He got the gate, latched it behind them. With gravel crunching beneath their feet, they started along the shoulder of the sparsely populated road.

"Did you have time to stop for lunch?"

He wasn't going to do this. It was just like her to try to mask or bury whatever bothered her most. And if she didn't want to talk about losing the baby that had come to mean so much to her, then he wouldn't test her almost unnatural calm by asking about it. But there was something he had to know.

"Why didn't you call me?"

Jenny didn't know if it was accusation or disappointment she heard in Greg's voice. She was having a difficult enough time trying to figure out everything she was feeling herself without wondering why he even questioned what she hadn't done. She couldn't believe how conflicted she felt over losing the child that had gone from being a source of panic to the focus of her future. By day she lived with a gaping emptiness that rivaled anything she'd experienced before. At night, curled in her bed where the dreams she'd once had for her baby haunted her restless sleep, she battled guilt, which Bess had told her she didn't need to feel because there was nothing she could have done to prevent what had happened, along with a huge and escalating sense of loss.

That loss grew even greater when she thought of the man

waiting for her to respond. She had fallen hopelessly in love with Greg. But she would lose him, too. The reason for living with him, the reason he'd married her, no longer existed.

"I didn't call because I didn't want to take you from what you were doing," she finally admitted, wishing for the numbness that had once served her so well. "I've invaded your life enough as it is."

Paper crackled as she tightened her grip on the bag. It seemed foolish to continue ignoring what was so obvious to them both. "I know I'm the reason you stay away from the house as much as you do. You're not comfortable with me there, and I hate that I've practically driven you from your home. I just didn't want to impose on your support any more than I already have."

The crisp autumn breeze ruffled her hair, lifting the short strands of her bangs around her forehead. The day was beautiful, brilliant with fall color and a sky as clear and blue as her eyes. But it seemed to Greg that she noticed nothing of what he knew would have once enthralled her.

As she kept walking, kept avoiding his glance, he didn't know if he wanted to stop her and make her look at him or simply appreciate that she was sparing him the desolation he'd glimpsed in her eyes.

It was his own fault that she hadn't called him. The distance he'd put between them had made it impossible for her to turn to him when she might have needed him most. But he'd put that distance there because it had seemed to be the only way to keep their relationship from growing more complicated.

Outside her door the other night, he'd finally admitted how much he wanted her caring and concern. Walking with her now, he didn't even question that he wanted her to call when she needed him.

What hit him in the next breath was how unavoidable his feelings were for her, and how much more complicated things had already become.

"You're not imposing on me, Jenny. I told you before, I want you in the house."

"You wanted me there because you were trying to help," she reminded him. And so he wouldn't have to worry about her, she remembered him saying. He said nothing now, though, to deny that her presence was why he avoided coming home. Or that his life would be easier with her gone.

"I appreciate what you did more than you'll ever know, Greg. But the reasons I needed your help no longer exist." She was no longer pregnant. She no longer needed to worry about putting a decent roof over her child's head or about protecting her own reputation. "The way things have been lately, it has to relieve you to know you don't have to worry about me or the baby anymore." She turned ahead of him onto the dirt path, filtered light replacing sunshine. "You can have your privacy back now."

There was no longer any need for them to be together or for her to go with him when he left. As that reality sunk in, Greg drew to a halt.

"You know, Greg," she said, turning to him when she realized he'd stopped. "I'm not sure how I'll do it, but I'm going to learn to protect myself the way you do. I understand why you want to make your own way, but I still used to think you were cheating yourself by letting your past dictate so much of your future."

She quietly studied his face, her own expression utterly earnest. "I can see now there's a real advantage to making it solely on your own. If you don't let yourself get all that attached to someone or someplace, it doesn't hurt so much when you lose them or when it's time to move on."

He had the distinct feeling just then that there was more going on with her than what she was saying. But her wish to emulate him jarred him almost as much as the understanding in the haunted depths of her eyes. The idea that his past had that strong a hold on him threw him completely. He also dismissed it, along with the idea that she just might be right. He was more concerned that she thought he wanted his privacy back, and with how willing she seemed to give it to him.

"If you think I'm relieved about the baby, Jenny, you're wrong."

Her glance fell as she turned away.

"Don't." He caught her arm, turned her back. "You're not thinking of moving out are you?"

"I thought it might be easier if I went back to my grandma's house."

"Easier for which one of us?"

One shoulder lifted in a halfhearted shrug. "Both."

"It won't be easier on me," he insisted. "You're in no shape to go back there and haul wood for heat or start working on it again. Your body isn't through adjusting to the changes it's gone through."

She was being driven by emotion. He felt dead certain of that. He'd counseled enough women who'd gone through what she had to know it was textbook classic for her to push away those around her, to feel sadness, anger and guilt over the loss, no matter what the circumstances.

He'd just never felt those twinges of sadness himself. All the time he'd spent reassuring her and answering her questions about her pregnancy had made him start looking forward to the child almost as if it had been his own.

"You shouldn't do anything heavy or tiring for ten days, Jenny. Give yourself at least that long to think things through, will you?"

Sensing that she might be even more fragile than she appeared, he let her go when she eased herself from his grip. Disturbed by the loss he felt when she withdrew from him, he brought up the only other thing he could think of to buy them both some time.

"It'll be better for you in a lot of ways if you stay." He didn't bother to ask how she would explain to her—their—friends why she wasn't moving with him when the time came. He doubted she'd thought that far ahead. He doubted she'd thought of anything beyond what she'd lost. "We're married," he reminded her. "I know how you hate gossip, and people are going to talk if we separate."

She looked back at him with a faint frown. She clearly hadn't thought of that. That breakdown in her logic only confirmed what he'd just concluded.

"I guess moving right now wouldn't be a good idea."

"It really wouldn't," he agreed.

She said nothing to indicate how she felt about continuing the illusion of being husband and wife as they continued along the shaded path. He said nothing else about it, either. All he cared about just then was that she wouldn't be going back out to that dilapidated old house—and that he'd just bought himself a reprieve.

Chapter Thirteen

Greg sat at his desk, listening to Jenny say goodnight to Bess. She had seemed a little subdued to him when she'd come downstairs that morning, but at the clinic everything about her had seemed normal. For the most part. There was a sadness beneath her smile that was impossible for him to miss. Others simply assumed that the subtle quietness about her was just the low energy that sometimes followed a virus. Bertie Buell had even called wanting to know if Jenny was feeling better and if she should get her flu shot early.

He heard the back door close a moment before Jenny poked her head around the doorway. "Is there anything you need me to do before I go?" she asked.

Even now she sounded fine. But then, she'd been busy all day, distracted by work from the latest change to shake her life.

"I can't think of anything," he replied, feeling as if the ground had somehow shifted beneath his own feet. "Are you working on costumes tonight?"

"Mine are finished."

"Are you going to Claire's?"

"She has a meeting with the high-school band director."

"No plans, then?"

She lifted one shoulder, the motion more dejected than dismissing. "There's nothing to do tonight. You'll be a few hours yet?" she asked, because that was now long he had been staying.

"Less than that."

She gave a little nod, lifted her hand. "Then, I'll see you later," she murmured, and turned from the door.

Had he not been waiting for a phone call from Ed Cochran, he might have taken his files home to work on just so she wouldn't be rattling around the house alone. He had the feeling, though, that being left alone was what she wanted right now. That, and something to do.

If there was anything he'd learned about Jenny it was that she could handle just about anything as long as she stayed busy. He knew she relied on work and projects to distract her from what she didn't want to think about. And heaven knew she'd had more than her share of unwanted thoughts to escape. But she didn't have any distractions now. And she needed escape more than ever.

"Jenny. Wait."

He pushed back his chair, rose from his desk.

He had spent hours last night trying to concentrate on his reading. He'd also spent most of that time with his mind weighed by matters he once would never have considered. For the past ten years, he had called the shots in his career and in his personal life. He had lived free of his past, made his own way and lived as he chose, all on his own terms.

Or so he'd thought until Jenny had looked up at him with her lovely, wounded blue eyes and in all sincerity told him she wanted to learn to detach herself the way he did. He hadn't believed for a minute of those ten years that the past had any sort of hold on him. He'd escaped. He was free. But the very fact that he continued to avoid dealing with the responsibility of his father's estate told him he hadn't yet been able to break that past's hold.

The same feelings that disturbed him every time he thought of his father rushed back to knot his gut in the moments before she reappeared in the doorway. But whether or not he was somehow failing or relinquishing control by not handling the matter entirely alone didn't matter just then. What did was that Jenny needed something to occupy her mind, something to help her escape the sadness she so bravely tried to hide.

"There is something I need," he told her.

Thinking he needed her to copy or track down something for him, Jenny watched Greg lean down and open his bottom desk drawer. The realization of what he was after struck her even before she saw him straighten with a foot-high pile of manila envelopes in his hands.

Looking as if the things might explode, he set the pile on the edge of his desk.

"If you're feeling up to it, you could get started on these. That fund you mentioned really is good idea."

Jenny glanced from the tense line of his jaw to the stack of envelopes he'd been avoiding like the proverbial plague. She didn't know if he'd finally decided to allow her assistance because she wouldn't be around to help after he left, or if he'd simply decided it was time. Either way, she couldn't help feeling relieved for him that he was finally getting on with it, and enormously grateful for the task. She didn't mind being alone at the house. She just didn't want to be alone there with nothing to do but try not to think.

"I'll carry those over for you."

"I can get them."

"I said I'll do it," he insisted, shrugging off his lab coat. "I need to come back here for a while. But I'll bring dinner from the diner."

"I can make something."

"I know you can. You just don't need to do it, tonight. Okay?" Something like exasperation had entered his tone. Or maybe it was just the tension that was always there whenever the estate was on his mind. Whichever it was, the edge was impossible to miss.

She didn't argue with him. Partly because his bringing dinner was really quite thoughtful. Mostly because she suddenly had the feeling the frustration he felt had to do with her, himself or some combination thereof and she simply didn't have the energy to deal with why that frustration was there.

They had two months to go before he left. Somewhere in there she needed to figure out what she was going to do when he did. Right now, she just wanted to get through one day at a time and hope that something would occur to her along the way. Greg's plans were certainly moving along. He'd been trading phone calls all day with the Rural Medical Corps and the doctor who was coming to replace him.

He had his plans, his future. But she felt as if she were living in limbo. For the first time in her life she had no sense of direction, not even a vague idea of what she wanted beyond what Greg would never offer. Even when she'd left behind the mess in Boston, she'd at least had a plan to start over. Now she felt as if she were in an odd sort of freefall and had no idea when or how she would land.

If there were just some way she could turn off her mind, she thought, she would be fine. As worries about her child had popped up at the most unexpected times, as the days passed, thoughts of that loss and Greg's move seemed to hit out of nowhere. They were inescapable when she was alone. And alone she couldn't seem to avoid what she'd always been afraid to allow before the dam had finally broken last week and the tears would fall.

It helped that the assaults didn't seem quite so painful outside her bedroom. While she went over the documents she'd sorted for Greg, focused on how his agitation with them seemed to lessen a little each evening, or when she worked on preparations for the festival—which moved into his living room toward the end of that week—she could bury most of what she felt by throwing herself deeper into whatever required her attention.

For the most part the technique worked fairly well. Claire and her cohorts all remarked on how quickly her energy had returned after her bout of the flu. Even Bess took her aside to tell her how pleased she was to see that she was doing so well.

The only person she couldn't seem to fool was Greg. But then, the man always had been far too observant as far as Jenny was concerned.

"Are you feeling too tired to go to the parade?"

Caught with her inescapable thoughts, Jenny turned from the living room window.

On the street beyond, Claire was running around like a windup toy making sure the little marching pumpkins were in a straight line ahead of the twelve-member community highschool band. The pumpkin queen and her attendants were seated on hay bales on a chrysanthemum-covered flatbed truck across the street in the neighbor's driveway. Farther up the road that had been blocked off earlier that morning, kids on their decorated bikes and makeshift floats were lined up for the start of the sixblock march to the community center where the bunting-draped food and craft booths waited.

"I'm fine," she told him, desperately wanting to be. "I was just thinking how cute the little pumpkins look."

"Is that all?"

"And about how nice it was of you to help hang the bunting last night." With a game little smile, she turned back to the sheer curtains filtering the view. "This town is going to miss you when you're gone."

Greg watched her from where he stood near the front entry. He'd thought to ask if she wanted to watch the parade from the front porch or join the locals and the tourists lined up along the road. He knew she'd planned to go. He knew too that she'd found the escape she'd sought in the preparations and in the time she'd spent wading through the documents he'd finally signed to start probate. She'd mailed them yesterday. Oddly enough, he hadn't felt at all as if he'd somehow relinquished responsibility by allowing her help. What he'd felt had been gratitude for not having to begin the task alone.

He'd also discovered for himself how much lighter a burden felt when the weight was shared.

Watching her now, wishing she could feel that relief, too, he wondered if she hadn't pushed herself too hard. And if maybe he had left her alone long enough.

The muffled sounds of excited voices filtered in from the street as he walked into the room. He knew she wasn't doing nearly as well as she pretended. A couple of times, late at night when he'd finally gone to bed himself, he'd thought he'd heard her weeping. The sounds had been so hushed he hadn't been totally sure. But both times when he'd gone to her door and asked if she was all right and if he could come in, she'd said she was fine and that she'd rather he didn't. Short of ignoring her wishes, the only thing he could think to do was give her the space she seemed to need.

He'd never truly understood how helpless husbands felt when their hurting wives shut them out. What he understood now was that the husbands were hurting, too.

Coming up behind her, hoping she wouldn't pull away, he did what he'd wanted to do a dozen times in the past week and curved his hand over her shoulder. Beneath the soft knit of her autumn-gold sweater, she remained blessedly still.

"Are you okay, Jenny?"

Her felt her slender shoulder rise with her deeply drawn breath. The fact that she nodded rather than answered told him what he'd already suspected. That the brightness he'd seen in her eyes was tears.

"I know you haven't wanted to talk about it," he said, feeling oddly out of his depth. He should know what to say to a woman who'd gone through what she had. And he did. But all the textbook explanations about emotional impact and what her body was still going through seemed as inadequate as he felt at being unable to comfort her. "And I know it's been harder on you than you've let on. I just want to know if that's what's bothering you now."

From the street came a young child's shouted greeting, the sound exuberant and cheerful.

"That's part of it." She offered the admission quietly, her voice steady, her tone subdued. "But I know it'll just take time."

He didn't know what he could offer beyond that. "It will," he said, anyway, remembering how she'd looked that day in the woods. "There really will come a time when it won't hurt so much."

"Promise?"

"I promise."

He felt her shoulder rise again, the deep breath as telling as her nod had been. "You said that was part of what's on your mind. What else is bothering you?"

This time she shook her head.

"Come on, Jenny," he coaxed, and turned her to her face him.

The tears pooled in her eyes hit him like a physical blow.

Lowering her head, she wiped away what she hadn't intended for him to see. But just as she started to turn, he caught her face between his hands.

"Talk to me," he begged, catching another tear with his thumb. "What else is wrong?"

Rather than answer, she tried a wobbly smile. "I thought I was doing better, but I can't seem to stop this."

The smile nearly undid him.

Her lower lashes were spiky from the two tears that spilled over them, her eyes shining with those she held back.

The need to soothe, to console, became a living thing inside him.

The need for her was tangled up in there somewhere, too.

With his thumbs he brushed moisture from where it silently trailed down her cheek. Even as he smoothed those tears away, he lowered his head to catch the one spilling from the corner of her eye.

He wasn't helping.

The thought hit Jenny as his lips caught what she hadn't been able to stop. His tenderness only made her ache even more. And want. There was so much he made her yearn for. So much she needed to let go.

She felt the warmth of his mouth move to the corner of hers, then gently over it, his kiss so gentle she might have wept had she not already been precariously close to doing just that. As it was, a small sob snagged at the back of her throat when he slowly gathered her in his arms.

She didn't know if she loved him or hated him for what he was doing just then. She knew only that he was making it impossible to accomplish what she'd been trying to do when he'd walked in, and deny how much she was going to miss him. How much she already did. She couldn't always tell which she was mourning, her child or him, but she was having a hard enough time trying to figure it out without him reminding her of how badly she didn't want the divorce they would eventually have to discuss.

There never seemed to be an end to the unwelcome thoughts that haunted her nights.

Lowering her head, she leaned it against his chest.

"Are you going to talk to me?" he asked. Cupping his hand to the back of her head, he stroked her hair.

She didn't want to bring up the legal termination of their arrangement. Not now. For that moment, she just wanted to...be.

"I'm going to miss you when you leave."

The motion of his hand stilled. So did the rest of his body.

"I don't necessarily have to go anywhere, Jenny."

It was her turn to hesitate—which she did a moment before she lifted her head.

"I can stay if you want me to."

She couldn't have imagined anything he could have said just then that would have caught her more off guard. Or left her feeling more confused.

Greg saw that confusion join the brightness remaining in her eyes, along with something that looked an awful lot like disbelief. And hope.

It was the hope that had him breathing again.

"I've been talking with Ed Cochran and he's willing to go to Brayborough if I want to stay here. He and his wife just want to raise their kids away from the city, so he said he'd be happy with any place like Maple Mountain. We'd have some details to hammer out with the community there, but it's all workable. If you're interested."

"You want to stay?" she asked, hope still struggling with disbelief.

Encouraged by what he saw in her pretty face, he said, "I really do."

"When did you decide that?"

That was tougher to answer. The decision, he supposed, reaching into the front pocket of his jeans, had come in stages. But the beginning had been the night he'd first admitted how much he wanted her concern and her caring.

"I guess I started thinking about it about the time I bought this."

Pulling out his hand, he held up the wide gold band he'd carried with him ever since he'd returned from the symposium.

"There was a jewelry shop in the hotel in Montpelier. When I saw the rings, I thought you should have one to wear." Especially once your pregnancy started showing, he thought. But when he'd come back, the need for that symbol of marriage had no longer existed. A different need, however, had taken its place. The need to keep her in his life.

With everything she'd been going through, he just hadn't known when to tell her that. Considering the distance he'd put between them before he'd left, he didn't know if she'd even want to hear it.

Jenny blinked from the simple gold ring he held between his thumb and index finger to the quiet certainty carved in his handsome face.

"You were right when you said I was letting my past dictate my future," he told her, palming the ring to trace her jaw with his knuckles. "I just hadn't realized how blind I'd been to that until you made me face why I kept putting off dealing with the estate."

He couldn't believe how much she'd helped lift that burden. Or how good it felt to see some of the sadness fade from her pretty face.

"As for what you said about how I detach myself," he told her, because he'd thought about that, too, "I know I've done it in some ways. A lot of ways," he amended, needing to be honest. "But I was never able to do it with you. I started falling in love with you the night we met. That's not necessarily a bad thing," he hurried to confide, because there had been a time when the word *love* had held only negative connotations for him. "And I know you've taken a pretty heavy hit in that department, so if you don't think you can feel the same way, I understand. I just want a chance to do things right with you."

It had never occurred to Jenny that she would actually be able to feel emptiness dissolve. But she did. With every word Greg said, she'd felt a tiny bubble of hope in her heart expanding, pushing out the edges until there was nothing left but a fullness in her chest that made it feel as if her heart might burst right through. Inside her heart, a little knot of sadness remained, but the warmth Greg caused to surround it, made it so much easier to bear.

With his knuckles still slowly skimming her jaw, she tipped her head. "I already do love you," she confessed. "I thought you probably suspected that."

His touch drew to a halt below her chin. He'd known she felt gratitude. He'd known she'd felt obligated. Friendship had been in there, too. And the physical heat they'd shared had been unquestionable. But when he'd thought her heart might be getting involved, he hadn't understood what loving someone was really all about. When he finally realized what it meant, it never occurred to him that she felt anything like he did when he thought of loving her.

He wanted to be there when she needed him. He wanted to share her life, her bed, to belong with her, *to* her.

He had the feeling that was why he'd never called his lawyer about the prenuptial agreement. Somewhere in his subconscious he'd known even then that his sense of trust in her was absolute.

The ring felt as if it were burning his palm, when he slipped his fist under her jaw and brushed her cheek with his thumb. He never would have imagined how much it would mean to hear those three little words.

"Say it," he asked, as if he wouldn't let himself believe it otherwise.

"I love you," she said, searching his face. She curved her hand at the side of his neck. He had entered her life as a confidant, become her friend, her protector. He was her knight in shining armor.

His eyes darkened as his head descended. "Again."

A faint smile touched her mouth. "I love you," she repeated, but her last word was muffled against his lips.

With one hand at the small of her back, he pulled her closer. She went willingly, looping her arms around his neck, loving the possessiveness she felt in his kiss. There was desire there, too, and hunger, need and unspoken promises. As she kissed him back, her heart beating against his, she let him know she felt all that and more in the long moments before he lifted his head.

She let out a sigh. "I don't mind repeating that."

"Which? The words or the kiss?"

"Either. But you said you want to do this right with me." A light of teasing slipped into her smile as she savored the protective feel of his arms. "What do you suggest we do?"

Easing them apart, he opened his hand, the ring gleaming in his palm. "For starters, we forget about going anywhere. I do feel a sense of belonging in this place," he admitted, having faced that, too. "And I'd really like to raise a family with you here. When we're ready," he amended, making it clear there was no rush.

He picked up her left hand, held the band to the tip of her third finger. "I'd ask you to marry me," he murmured, slipping the ring into place, "but we're already married."

He folded her hand in his, drew her arms back around his neck.

Drawing herself closer, she could practically feel her future falling into place. "You could ask me, anyway."

He grinned. "Do I have to get down on one knee?"

"Not necessarily."

"Good. I kind of like it where I am." He tightened his hold. "So, Jenny Baker Reid, will you marry me?"

"Oh, yes," she whispered.

Greg's heart felt amazingly full as he met his wife's sweet smile. "Thank you," he whispered back, and drew the woman who had healed him into a soul-deep kiss as the boom of a drum and the crash of cymbals started a parade on the street beyond their window.

* * * * *

Don't miss
THE SUGAR HOUSE,
the next book in Christine Flynn's
compelling mew miniseries
GOING HOME

On sale June 2005
Available wherever Silhouette Books are sold.

HARLEQUIN®
Presents

Seduction and Passion Guaranteed!

GR€€K TYCOONS

They're the men who have everything—
except brides…

Wealth, power, charm—what else could a
heart-stoppingly handsome tycoon need?
In the GREEK TYCOONS miniseries you have
already been introduced to some gorgeous Greek
multimillionaires who arc in need of wives.

**Now it's the turn of favorite Presents
author Lucy Monroe,
with her attention-grabbing romance**

THE GREEK'S INNOCENT VIRGIN
Coming in May
#2464

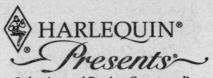

If you enjoyed what you just read,
then we've got an offer you can't resist!

Take 2 bestselling
love stories FREE!

Plus get a FREE surprise gift!

▬▬▬▬▬▬▬▬▬▬▬▬▬▬▬

Clip this page and mail it to Silhouette Reader Service™

IN U.S.A.	IN CANADA
3010 Walden Ave.	P.O. Box 609
P.O. Box 1867	Fort Erie, Ontario
Buffalo, N.Y. 14240-1867	L2A 5X3

YES! Please send me 2 free Silhouette Special Edition® novels and my free surprise gift. After receiving them, if I don't wish to receive anymore, I can return the shipping statement marked cancel. If I don't cancel, I will receive 6 brand-new novels every month, before they're available in stores! In the U.S.A., bill me at the bargain price of $4.24 plus 25¢ shipping and handling per book and applicable sales tax, if any*. In Canada, bill me at the bargain price of $4.99 plus 25¢ shipping and handling per book and applicable taxes**. That's the complete price and a savings of at least 10% off the cover prices—what a great deal! I understand that accepting the 2 free books and gift places me under no obligation ever to buy any books. I can always return a shipment and cancel at any time. Even if I never buy another book from Silhouette, the 2 free books and gift are mine to keep forever.

235 SDN DZ9D
335 SDN DZ9E

Name		(PLEASE PRINT)	
Address		Apt.#	
City		State/Prov.	Zip/Postal Code

Not valid to current Silhouette Special Edition® subscribers.

Want to try two free books from another series?
Call 1-800-873-8635 or visit www.morefreebooks.com.

* Terms and prices subject to change without notice. Sales tax applicable in N.Y.
** Canadian residents will be charged applicable provincial taxes and GST.
All orders subject to approval. Offer limited to one per household.
® are registered trademarks owned and used by the trademark owner and or its licensee.

SPED04R   ©2004 Harlequin Enterprises Limited

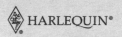

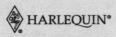